NOW & AGAIN

By E. A. Fournier

For Hugh Everett III:

A man with many failings of both heart and mind,
but a crackling genius, nevertheless. Here's to the
hope that his theory is right.

Mary,

Enjoy the read & thanks for the interest & the willingness to give it a shot. I would be so pleased to hear what you think when you're done.

GJ

TABLE OF CONTENTS:

ACKNOWLEDGEMENT:

I WOULD LIKE TO THANK my patient wife and editor. She was my never-ending source of encouragement and criticism. She kept my story honest and my grammar as close to proper as I could tolerate. Any remaining comma splices, fragments, run-on sentences, typos and awkward phrases are mine, and mine alone.

CHAPTER 1:

THE SMELL OF CLEAN damp earth floated lightly on the breeze that moved through a tidy graveyard in Ohio. Early leaves had started turning color two weeks before; now, high in the boughs, a golden fluttering canopy arched above the stone crosses and white markers. The fat sun gleamed through black branches, and pieces of it rippled across a small pond. Nearby, a few birds called to each other, scolding the mourners around a raised casket.

This wasn't Mike Aldon's first committal service, by any stretch. Still, it was a particularly tough one. The slender minister in his dark suit made brief eye contact with familiar faces. Everyone clustered near the edge of the plastic grass that hid the rich black dirt pulled from the hole. As such ceremonies go, the graveside was lightly attended, mainly adult couples and grown children. A few women held handkerchiefs to their noses, and some dabbed their eyes. The deceased, Leah McCaslin, had been as sweet and straight a woman as Mike had ever met. Her excruciating death from cancer was extended, and demeaning, and even frightening at the end. Pastor Mike had thought long and hard about what was left to say, and he still wasn't done thinking, but he simply had no more time.

"We don't grieve like people without hope. For those of us with faith, like our sister Leah, death is not an end but a beginning." Well, here we go, Mike thought. I hope I'm loud enough. Everything sounds so thin out here. He looked at Leah's sturdy husband, Kendall, and her lean twenty-year-old son, Josh. They stood tight up against the coffin, just as they had stayed beside her at the hospital, and later, close to her in the ICU, and at the end, right next to her hospice bed. Kendall seemed stiff in his suit. His large hand rested on his son's shoulder. Josh's tired eyes stared at something far away while his fingers wrapped tightly around a brass coffin handle. Tucked in beside Josh, Hannah Teel, a young Asian woman, held his other hand with both of hers.

Plowing resolutely on, Mike hoped he could make his thoughts clear. "Death cannot kill us. That's the paradox at the heart of the good news – in death there is life. Paul wrote in a letter to the Corinthians, 'When the perishable has been clothed with the imperishable, and the mortal with immortality, then the saying will come true: Death has been swallowed up forever.' "

The minister paused to glance at the gold and red leaves above him. "I know, standing here beside this grave, these words are hard to listen to; but that doesn't make them any less true. In the letter, Paul went on to quote from Hosea, 'Where, O death is your sting? Where, O grave is your victory?' Don't misunderstand, Paul never meant that death doesn't hurt, or that we shouldn't grieve. No, Paul knew better than that. He was hounded by death his whole life. By the time he wrote these words, he had been shipwrecked, starved, stoned, left for dead, and imprisoned. He knew death inside and out, and death knew him."

Josh pulled Hannah tighter. She tilted her head against him as her eyes darted briefly up to his, and then back at Aldon.

"Death *does* hurt and we *do* grieve, and we should; but we look forward to a time when God himself 'will wipe away every tear from our eyes.' "

The minister looked directly at Kendall, hoping to offer some measure of comfort. "That's Paul's point. That's the key. Death doesn't win. Death doesn't get the last say. Not for Leah. Not for us. And no matter what our eyes see; no matter how our hearts feel, the truth is that death is without power over us."

Kendall watched Josh. The boy's face tightened. It was hard to know what was washing through him. His eyes had returned to the present but they were now glistening black buttons, revealing nothing.

"Leah is more alive right now than she's ever been at any time before. That's what Paul held onto, so long ago, and all those before us who died in Christ, and that's what we need to hold onto, all of us here, at our moment in time. Our bright and present hope is the same as theirs: that one day, in that place of eternal life, we will find Leah alive again."

Mike bowed his head and ever so briefly let himself feel proud about the way his words had rolled out. Clearly, they weren't what he had set out to say, but he was satisfied they were, somehow, what he was meant to say. At least, that was his fervent hope, since they were, after all, what he'd said, and he couldn't have them back. Catching himself, he flashed a guilty prayer skyward as he stepped over to Kendall with his arms open.

* * *

"Hate these stupid things!" Kendall angrily unknotted his tie and it hissed as he yanked it from his collar. He tossed it through the open back window of his black crew-cab pickup and hurled his suit coat after it. Suddenly, his anger fled and he stood with hands braced against the truck, and his head down.

The afternoon was warm and sunny, despite the telltale signs of fall. The air had a taste of fullness to it that spoke of a long languid summer, and winter still held at bay. It was one of those rare Midwestern days that deserved to be cherished.

* * *

3

After the minister left, Josh had stood quietly beside his father and shook hands and hugged friends and relations. They both endured the awkward after-service smiles and pats and small talk. And then, at the end, they stood there alone, unsure what to do. Abruptly, Kendall had walked away, shrugging off his coat. Josh and Hannah trailed after him, but then Josh stopped. He looked again at the coffin, perched above the open grave, circled by all the glory of an autumn day, and grieved.

Hannah carefully wrapped an arm about him. "I'm so sorry, Josh."

He struggled with his emotions. "It's just one of those things. I...I can't talk about it the way pastor does."

"You don't have to," Hannah replied softly. "There's no right way, and no one's keeping score. If you want to be by yourself, I'm okay with that; that's not a problem. But afterwards, I mean later tonight, I'd stop by the house, if you want."

Josh looked down at her. "We'd both like a...a woman in the house, again." He gave her a soft hug and a half smile. "Besides, he likes you almost as much as I do."

Hannah kissed him on the cheek. "Oh Josh, this is so hard."

A shadow from a cloud ambled across the nearby pond. Josh noted its passing. "I guess I need a little more time here. Just me and Mom. Okay?"

She nodded, trying not to tear up.

"Go give Dad a hug. He needs one, too."

* * *

Kendall turned from his truck as Hannah stepped up to him. She squeezed his arm and looked into his eyes. "I'm sorry for your loss, Mr. McCaslin. I don't know what else to say. That sounds so empty...so...I just wish I could..." Deep sobs suddenly captured her. Hannah's carefully constructed wall against grief let

4

loose and the held back tears flowed unchecked down her face. "It's just not fair!"

Kendall enveloped her in his big arms and tenderly rocked her back and forth until she regained some control. The fresh scent of her perfume reminded him of his wife. He gently straightened her up and patted her shoulders. Hannah took a shuddering breath and let him gently lift her chin until they were eye-to-eye.

"They help, dearie. The words help. I never understood how much they meant, until now. And I don't know why they help, either, but they do."

Hannah dug out Kleenex from her purse and wiped her nose. "Sorry for this. I just...it just all came over me." She shook her head. "And I'm supposed to be the one comforting you."

"You are." He brushed her hair affectionately with his fingers. "You're kind. That's what Leah said about you." He caught her pleased look. "You didn't know that, did you?" Hannah toyed with his hand as he continued, "And it would comfort me a lot if you could be there for Josh. Promise?"

She nodded and managed a sad smile before walking off across the grass to her car. Kendall wiped at his nose with a quick hand, and then moved quietly toward his son.

"Josh, we need to go."

"I know."

Kendall waited. "Mom's better off now. She's not..."

"Yeah, I know."

Kendall stood still. Josh didn't move. "Josh?"

"I said, I know."

"You have to walk away. I know it feels wrong, but we have to leave her here. It's part of the deal."

* * *

Josh's head rocked softly against the passenger seat cushion. He was far away again. The V6 grumbled in a low gear as Kendall guided the pickup around the asphalt curves of the cemetery road. The sheer beauty of the sun-filled day was ironic.

Kendall glanced over at his son. "Where'd you leave your car?"

"Huh?"

"Your Mustang? At the church or home?"

"Um," Josh slid up and shook his head like a diver coming up from the water. "I left it at church...near the side door."

Kendall checked the intersection and then pulled out onto a feeder highway and rapidly accelerated toward the freeway. "Yeah, okay."

Josh continued to stare out the side window with empty eyes. "Dad, what're we gonna do?"

Kendall glanced over his left shoulder as a gap opened in the line of cars entering the on ramp. He wedged into line and was rewarded with a timid honk. "I'm droppin' you off at your car, that's what." Kendall scowled into his side mirror at the compact red sedan behind him.

Josh found himself suddenly angry – angry about the truck, the traffic, the sunny day, the season, the horrible normalcy of it all. Pain rolled over him in a sudden swell that caught him unprepared and pulled him under.

"No!" he said with a strain to his voice. "Stop it! Stop acting like it's all fine." He drilled his father with a look. "You know what I'm talkin' about! How can you pretend it's okay? I mean after everything? It's just not...it's not..." He choked up and couldn't continue. Furious with himself, he turned away and viciously punched his door.

Their black pickup shot up the freeway ramp and merged into the fast moving traffic.

Kendall drove silently for a time and then responded. "Look, we go on. We just go on. It's not pretending; it's just what it is. It's what you do." He glanced at the back of Josh's head. "None of us is okay. We just let it hurt, and we go on anyway."

Josh snapped back, "Well, I'm done hurting. I don't have anything left. It's all gone, okay? It's just one big, empty hole. I don't feel anything and I don't care about anything. I'm just..."

"Yeah, yeah, you're just angry. I know. Kick the chairs, bang the windows, pound the doors; I know." He held out a clenched fist for inspection. "Check *my* knuckles sometime. Don't you think I've been there, too?" Kendall sighed. "We're blood, Josh. We're built the same way. Be pissed. It's okay. We'll get through this; you *will* get through this. Hear me?"

Staring straight ahead at traffic, Josh said nothing.

Kendall changed lanes and sped around a slow car. "Look, would you stay at the house tonight? There's beer. I got food. I...I just don't want you to be alone...pissed or otherwise." A sweet expression crossed Kendall's face. "Okay, I guess I don't want to be alone, either. You know what I mean?"

Josh kept staring ahead but his voice was softer. "Yeah."

A sea of brake lights suddenly glowed red ahead. Josh blinked and then shot up straight. He braced a hand on the dash. "Hey! Look out!"

Kendall jerked up. "Shit!"

He jammed the brakes and swerved to avoid the green car in front of him. His extended screeching of tires was swallowed by the solid impacts of nearby metal bodies. The green car slammed another vehicle and spun. Kendall skidded and fought the chattering wheel to avoid a pileup. Behind him, the red sedan he'd earlier cut off slapped his rear end and sent them both into sudden fishtails.

Kendall struck his head hard against the door frame and bounced back, trailing bright blood. A sudden impact wrenched the truck. Josh smacked into his side window and it exploded around his face in a thick halo of glass shards. Still sliding helplessly, their pickup clipped a bumper. Air bags erupted as they blindly climbed up the back of another car.

Around them, the freeway descended into a chain reaction chaos. Horns blared. Vehicles swerved and crashed. In a deadly mathematical progression, response times kept decreasing as the collisions kept piling up.

A pricey convertible slammed the center divider and its air bags deployed with sharp bangs. Behind it, a late model jeep with a trailer rolled up the hapless convertible and spun its knobby off-road tires on top of the screaming driver. Finally catching some traction, the jeep tossed itself and its trailer over the divider barricade and onto the opposite lanes. Horns, brakes and heavy collisions erupted from the other side of the freeway.

Blood streamed into Kendall's eyes as he tried to focus. He felt disconnected from what he was seeing. Everything was slowed and he experienced an unexpected calmness; he was an observer in the carnage, no longer a participant. Sounds echoed hollow and strangely remote. His truck shook violently, but to Kendall it seemed gentle, like a boat riding a heavy sea of oil.

On the passenger side, Josh swatted at the deflating air bag and brushed safety glass out of his hair. He smelled the sharp stink of scorched rubber and the heavy sweetness of gas. The truck shuddered from late collisions. Josh watched his father shake his head and was momentarily distracted by the blood flying from his hair.

Looking forward, both men stared through the web of cracks in their windshield, attracted by large falling shadows. They realized that airborne vehicles were tumbling from the other side of the freeway and smashing down upon trapped cars on this side. Awareness flickered into tardy action as they struggled with their seatbelts. A huge flipping Chevy 4x4 suddenly swallowed their windshield view. They screamed as it struck down with an overwhelming crunch.

Kendall and Josh were back in their truck speeding down the busy freeway. They jerked their hands up in defense but there was no accident. They gasped and stared up but no overbuilt Chevy tumbled through their windshield. They were okay. *How was that possible?* There was no transition, no warning. They went from death to life in less than the blink of an eye. A lot less. No blink. It was nothing. They had passed in a seamless move from being crushed, to driving freely down the expressway again.

"What the hell!" Kendall grabbed the steering wheel in a residual panic and accidentally swerved. Horns honked. He swerved quickly back and shot a strangled look at Josh.

Josh's eyes frantically darted around. "I don't get it!"

"Didn't you hit the window?"

"Yeah..." Josh stared at his unblemished side window and touched his hair. "I thought we were killed." He looked back at Kendall. "You were bleeding."

Kendall rubbed at his forehead and checked his clean fingers. "Yeah..."

Brake lights suddenly flared red just in front of them. "Look out! It's starting again!"

"What?" Kendall swerved and hit the breaks. "Shit!"

The small white van ahead of him struck a car and spun. Kendall fought the wheel. "Behind! Josh, we're gonna get hit from behind! Remember?"

Josh caught a flash of gold in his side mirror and braced himself just as their pickup was rear-ended.

Forewarned, Kendall kept better control. His head still struck the door frame, but not as hard. "Ouch! Air bags, Josh! Watch out!"

"What's goin'on?" Their truck hit something. Kendall's face was propelled toward the steering column as an air bag flashed open to meet it. Josh slapped the side window, but this time it didn't break. Air bags belatedly exploded around him as their pickup tore off another car's bumper and climbed the center divider.

Outside, the freeway descended into chaos. Horns blared. Vehicles spun and crashed. Mayhem ruled.

A Mercedes sideswiped a van and slammed into the center divider. Behind it, a Suburban, towing a boat, rode up the Mercedes and flipped itself over the barricade and onto traffic speeding the other way. Horns blared from beyond the divider. Collisions started. The mathematical progression of chaos spread on the other side of the freeway.

Kendall slumped in his seat. Blood welled from a cut above his eye. His face was coated in the pale dust from the deployed air bag. The steering wheel throbbed to the vibration of their laboring engine. Kendall shook his head and tried to make sense of things. He slowly realized that they were wedged against the center divider with their nose in the air.

"Back it up!" Josh shouted in panic. "You know it ain't over yet!"

Fumbling into action, Kendall struggled clumsily with the clutch. He pumped the pedal and jerked at the shift lever, but it wouldn't drop in. His words came out thick. "Whaddya talkin' about?" Then he looked up in horror at the windshield, and it all came back to him. "Oh, yeah!"

"Get us outta here!" Josh fought to free his tangled seatbelt.

From outside, they heard trapped people start screaming. Both men caught the deadly shadows of airborne vehicles tumbling their way.

"Oh, my God!" Kendall got it into reverse and tromped the gas. The pickup shuddered in protest and scraped hard against the concrete as it jerked backwards.

That was when the deep throated call of a semi's air horn cut through the noise. On the other side of the freeway, a massive, gleaming gas truck jack-knifed and started its slide toward the divider.

Josh screamed. Kendall looked up just as a flipping Lexus SUV swallowed their view. He threw a useless arm up as it hit with an overwhelming crunch.

Kendall and Josh were speeding down a wet freeway. They were okay again: no accident, no cuts, no air bags, nothing. A light rain pattered the windshield as wipers slapped methodically back and forth to clear it.

Kendall gripped the wheel with white knuckles and glared. "Dammit! What is this?"

"You have to do somethin' sooner!"

"What're you talkin' about?"

"Something different. Right now!"

"How is this happening?"

"I don't know."

"Hey, wait..." He looked up, confused. "It's rain-ing?" He touched the windshield with a hesitant finger. "Josh, it's raining!"

"Huh?"

Josh looked strangely at the streaming windshield. He listened to the wet drops drumming against the cab. *How can it be raining? What in the world? No time for this!* "Forget the rain! Change lanes! Now! Hurry up!"

Kendall slashed left and clipped a black Taurus. The raging driver honked his horn over and over again. Kendall cranked right. A panel truck swerved and laid on his horn.

"Make 'em move!" Josh desperately looked around. "I don't care what you have to do! Get us off this free-way!"

Ahead, a sea of brake lights suddenly flared red. Josh screamed, "Too late!"

"The hell with it!" Kendall spun the wheel and floored the engine. Tires smoked on the slick road. Other drivers dodged around him, or bounced off. The pickup did a 180 and narrowly evaded a sliding black Camry that would have rear-ended them.

A sudden passenger side impact whipped Kendall into the dashboard. Caught off guard, Josh slapped his head against the side window and glass exploded in a halo of shards.

The soaked freeway was filled with sliding and crashing cars. A van towing a trailer catapulted over the center barricade and vanished onto the opposite freeway. A furious blare of horns and a flurry of heavy crashes ensued from the other side.

Inside the pickup, Kendall rubbed his bleeding forehead. Josh brushed at the pieces of safety glass stuck in his wet hair. Rain streamed across his face through the shattered window. In the distance, falling vehicles began to crush trapped ones. From some-where, a semi's air-horn blared. Josh stuck his face out into the downpour and squinted to see more clear-ly. Without warning, a black dump truck careened out of the rain heading straight for him. Josh fought his seatbelt. The massive truck swiftly filled the window. Josh yelled in terror as it ripped through the door with a sickening crunch.

Instantly, Kendall and Josh sped down a sun-filled freeway in heavy traffic. The sun visors were down and the radio was playing country music. No death. No rain.

Josh gasped for air and looked at his chest, surprised to be whole. "We gotta try something else!"

Kendall grimly swerved back and forth, looking for a way out of his lane. "I am, I am."

Josh's body shook as he looked around, clearly in shock. His voice stuttered. "Where's the rain?"

Kendall was angry. "I don't care!"

Behind them a blue van braked and honked. Kendall glanced in the mirror and did a double-take. "What the hell? Wasn't it...red behind us last time?"

"No, black or..." Josh was losing it. "Screw that! Just cut across the lanes!"

Kendall swerved right but got a horn. Josh stabbed a look back. "Wait! Wait for the taxi..."

"Taxi? Where's that panel truck?"

"Panel truck?" Josh did a quick check. "Now! It's clear! Go! Go!"

Kendall brutally veered right and swooped behind an airport taxi. Determined to continue right, he bulled his pickup through the traffic and brushed the nose of a shocked Ford in the slow lane. Ahead, a sudden sea of brake lights surfaced; all glowing red.

"Dad!"

"I see it."

Kendall madly snaked the truck through braking vehicles trying to escape the roadway. "Almost there. Hold on!"

He jerked the wheel to get onto the shoulder, but he'd cut it too close. His truck's tail caught the merest edge of the back bumper of a braking Honda, but the effect was cataclysmic. Their truck abruptly twisted left, went out of control, and flipped.

Kendall was thrown up and down against his seat-belt as his world rotated: wheel, window, wheel, window. Josh's head shattered the glass next to him and then struck it again and again, on each roll. Loose debris in the cab rotated with them as they tumbled over and over.

Behind them, the freeway was chaos. Horns blared. Vehicles spun and crashed.

A Cadillac glanced off a shuttle bus and then slammed into the divider. Behind it, an RV, towing a trailer with dirt bikes, rode up the Caddy and then ponderously tipped over the center barricade and fell onto the on-coming traffic. Horns blared from beyond the barricade as the havoc spread.

Kendall opened his eyes to an upside down world. He was hanging in his seatbelt. His forehead was bleeding but gravity kept his eyes clear. Josh's face was crisscrossed in lacerations. He grimly fought a twisted belt with one hand. His other arm hung limp and he was suspended above a caved-in roof and piles of safety glass.

From outside, they heard the distant sounds of trapped people and falling cars. Kendall released his seatbelt and dropped in a painful heap onto the roof. He rolled to all fours and began to awkwardly crawl towards Josh when he heard the loud blast of an air horn.

On the other side of the freeway, a massive gas tanker truck jack-knifed to avoid the growing pile-up. As the cab rolled over, the doomed driver pulled his air-horn, and the gleaming trailer slapped onto the roadway in a cascade of sparks. Broken cars were tossed aside or flattened as the trailer slid toward the center divider. Embedded steel supports inside the barricade sliced open the skin of the tanker when it slammed home. Gas spilled over the sparks and erupted into an immense concussion of vaporized fuel and fire.

Kendall and Josh ducked, throwing their arms over their heads. A flashing avalanche of flame and truck parts swallowed their view.

And now they were back in the quiet pickup, humming down the freeway in traffic. They screamed! They thrashed at their clothes! They were on fire! *But they weren't. They were fine. The truck was untouched.*

Josh cried and huddled in his seat, arms around himself, rocking against his seatbelt. "Please stop it! Please God! Stop it! Please!"

"I was on fire!" Kendall looked wildly at his clothes and his hands. "I was – Josh? You okay?"

"Make it stop! Please make it stop!"

"How can I make...? Listen to me!" Kendall reached out and grabbed at him.

His son pulled away. "No more. I can't do it."

"We gotta beat this somehow."

"We can't. We're in hell."

"This is not hell. It's somethin' else."

"We'll never beat it."

"If we don't, it's gonna keep happening." Josh's eyes grew wider. Kendall tapped the brakes and swerved looking for openings. "Josh? Answer me!""

"What?"

"Don't freak out on me. At least now we know."

"Know what?"

"How it all ends!"

A yellow Jetta Sportwagen braked behind them and honked. Kendall whipped a look in the mirror. "Now it's yellow? Weird!"

"What?"

"Guy behind us. Stop saying 'what.' Tell me if I'm clear."

"I can't do this."

"Yes, you can! Can I go yet? C'mon!"

"This is crazy. It's not happening!" Josh was frantic and weepy.

"Get in the game!" Kendall shouted harshly. "Either you help me, or this'll never stop! We can beat this."

"You don't know that!"

"It's better than crying!"

Josh flinched, as if rocked by a blow. Shame and anger leaped across his face.

14

Kendall was stone cold. "Now? Can I go? Check for me!"

Josh clenched his teeth and flashed a look back and to the right. "A-Almost! Wait for...where's that taxi?"

"Can I go? C'mon, c'mon, c'mon!"

"Yeah! Now! Go!"

Kendall muscled the truck to the right. He ducked momentarily behind an orange Toyota and then, heedless of the dangers, slashed right again, clipping the nose of an older pickup. The surprised driver cramped his wheel to avoid a collision and rolled, tossing used furniture across the lanes. Cars behind him swerved and hit each other.

Kendall glanced in his mirror. "Sorry."

Josh looked ahead and saw the brake lights flaring red. "Dad!"

"I know. I know!"

Kendall recklessly swerved around a braking car, barely missing his bumper. "Brace yourself."

He gunned the pickup off the freeway and leaped onto the shoulder. Gravel rooster-tails spouted behind him as the bucking truck howled up the steep embankment. Just below, the freeway chaos had begun.

"Get your belt off now! You know it's gonna twist!"

The pickup smashed through shrubs and small trees. A mirror ripped off as they powered up the steepening hill toward a guard rail at the top.

Josh struggled with his seatbelt as he was tossed about the seat. "Tryin'! Damn thing won't work!"

Kendall yanked off his own seatbelt. Unexpectedly, the bouncing truck scraped a boulder and skipped sideways in the gravel. Kendall tried to recover but it bucked a deep hole and suddenly ground out. The motor shrieked and seized. Kendall's body flew from his seat and slapped the windshield. Everything crunched to a stop. The smoking truck groaned as it slowly tipped sideways, towards the driver's side, and back down the embankment.

Josh freed his belt. "Dad?"

E. A. FOURNIER

The truck tipped more steeply. Josh kicked his twisted door open and jammed his feet against its armrest to keep it ajar while he extended a hand back down to his groggy father.

"Dad! Move it! You know what happens next!"

Kendall heard a remote voice but couldn't make sense. He knew he needed to move but he couldn't remember why. From below him, an air-horn blasted a warning. Kendall jerked awake. He grabbed at Josh's hand like a drowning man. "Get out! Out! I'm comin'! Out!"

Kendall transferred his hold onto the center console in the nearly vertical world of the crew cab and let go of Josh's hand. "Hurry!" He yelled as much to himself as to Josh.

Kendall pulled himself up far enough to grasp the now dangling seatbelt in a death grip. The truck continued its slow motion roll over.

Josh was poised at the door, waiting. Kendall furiously yanked himself up the belt with both hands and tackled Josh. They were both catapulted out the open door as the truck rolled away and tumbled downhill.

Below, vehicles were smashing onto trapped cars and the jack-knifed gas truck slid inevitably toward the center divider.

Kendall jerked Josh to his feet and shoved him ahead. "Up the hill! Now!"

Josh didn't hesitate. He raced off in a mad dash with Kendall right behind him. Both of them clawed and scrabbled up through the underbrush. Reaching the top, they felt the concussive whump of the tanker's detonation and heard the roar rising behind. They leaped the guard rail together. A torrent of flame and truck parts howled by just above their heads and continued on into the air.

The two men rolled wildly down the opposite side, with their arms swishing through the tall grass, to arrive at the bottom in a tangled heap. For a time, neither man did anything but gasp for breath and stare at the blue sky above them.

16

Josh slowly propped himself up on his elbows and swallowed enough spit to lubricate his voice. "Is that it?"

Kendall coughed and rolled onto his side. "Just wait."

Josh sat up. He checked his hands, front and back. "Wait for what?"

"Hopefully nothing."

"You mean it's over?"

Kendall gently probed his bruised forehead and shrugged.

Josh looked at him. "So, you were right?"

Kendall painfully sat up and cocked his head to the side. "Always a first time."

Josh staggered back up the berm and carefully gazed over the guard rail, shielding his eyes.

Kendall gingerly rose to his feet to follow but stopped. He grabbed wonderingly at his suit coat, holding out the sides. "Hey Josh, what the hell?" He swayed a bit on uncertain feet and looked at himself. "When did I put this on?"

"What?" Josh looked curiously down the hill at him.

"My suit coat! I took it off first thing before I got in the truck." He shook his head and laboriously crawled up the hill after Josh, muttering, "That's just nuts."

Together they peered down at the horrific devastation below them. The massive tanker fire raged across both sides of the freeway, its unrelenting flames roiling from the wreck in bloated orange waves. Thick black smoke swelled into a solid column high in the air. At the edges of the accident, injured people wandered aimlessly. Bodies and twisted cars were strewn everywhere. Faint sirens wailed a promise of help while the distant stutter of helicopters grew louder.

"What just happened to us?" Josh asked, still staring downhill.

Kendall tipped his head back following the column of smoke up into the air. "We survived."

"Did we?"

"I think so." Kendall puzzled at something he saw below him. He stretched higher on the brow of the hill and unconsciously moved his head forward as he looked more intently down the embankment. "Josh?"

"Yeah."

"What color's my truck?"

"What? Why?"

"C'mon. What color?" Kendall's voice had become hard. This was no idle question.

Josh moved nervously. "Black..."

"Yeah. Right. So, what color is...*that* truck?"

Josh stared down the hill at their flipped and abandoned *red* truck. He blinked a few times and then his face went empty. "That's not your truck."

CHAPTER 2:

THE REIVERS CORPORATION headquarters building in Pasadena, Maryland presented a striking edifice; as well it should, since it was the expensive result of a spirited architectural competition. Seated on a forested plot of high ground within a manicured twenty acre campus, the unusual three-story, reflective skinned building commanded a pleasant view of Beards Creek to the west and Glebe Bay to the northeast. It was positioned perfectly to take advantage of its unique woodland views, and yet close enough to Chesapeake Bay for visitors to smell the sea. Perhaps that was why the owners of the large homes that used to grace the very private Burgh Lane fought so hard to keep their property. Still, with the high-level government contacts and deep pockets that Reivers' founder controlled, it was only a matter of time before the fears of eminent domain convinced them to settle for the generous cash offer that was already on the table. Two years later, after the winning architect had executed his startling vision, there was not one shred of evidence that those unique homes had ever existed; even quaint Burgh Lane itself was gone.

Only twelve miles southeast from Baltimore, Reivers' corporate executives and their distinguished guests had easy access to major airports as well as the largest seaport in the Mid-Atlantic States. In fact, Baltimore's Inner Harbor was once the second leading port of entry for immigrants to the United States, a fact not lost on many of the world's most prominent citizens as they made their own journeys to visit the powerful brain trust at *the Reive*.

Unknown to many outsiders, and unappreciated, even by those who worked inside, *the Reive* had far more building beneath its grandiose surface façade than above. Indeed, there were other, equally expansive subterranean areas under all the other surface structures that dotted the acreage. Some of these lower floors, principally those in the main building, were relatively accessible to visitors and divided into the surprisingly diverse endeavors of the corporation, including medicine, process industries, energy, agriculture, literature and the arts, computer science, physics, archeology, general science, to name a few. These divisions were staffed by a panoply of highly paid, bright minds that efficiently churned out the many breakthroughs, insights, advances, and inventions that fueled *the Reive's* staggering fortunes, and kept its New York financial firms supplied with fresh meat.

The levels beneath these public floors, however, were accessible to only a select few. In fact, these deeper rooms were rarely mentioned, and certainly did not appear on any unsecured schematics or architectural renderings. Still, these protected catacombs were the very heart that pumped the oxygenated blood of Reivers Corporation. Without them, far more than a single company stood at risk, although no one fully comprehended how fragile the muscle had become or how uneven the heartbeat.

* * *

Deep inside a secure section of the main building, in a multi-storied open space nicknamed *the arena*, a series of low-toned computer alarms beeped insistently. Concerned technicians in white coats moved quickly among tall banks of semi-transparent, flat screen monitors. Each bright rectangle was mounted flush beside others, with the lowest one set at a height just under eye level, and the highest at about ten feet. These colorful walls of moving images faced each other across narrow corridors that marched, rank upon rank, until they completely filled the shiny tile floor of the arena. From one of the many second and third level balconies, the constantly changing walls of color and light below took on the appearance of a sparkling maze within which the technicians scurried like lost people searching for an escape. Though imprecise, the image bore a certain semblance of truth.

The live-action points-of-view presented on the screens had ethereal, almost floating qualities to them. Some views bobbed along and followed people walking, others hovered above school classrooms or beside scientists working in complex labs, still others glided behind children running on playgrounds or next to people preparing food. There were office workers busy in cubicles, commuters racing by on freeways, passengers boarding flights, and angles into corner offices in high rise buildings. Everything was in high definition sharpness and in full spectrum color and yet, the overall impact was disturbing; the arena felt so public and the images displayed, so private.

Taken as a whole, the screens represented the immediate, ongoing slices of the branching multiverse. The images were captured in-real-time by less-than-bacteria sized nanorobots and retained within the massive underground memories of the Reivers Corporation archive. The archive itself was the single biggest product *the Reive* produced, as well as its most irreplaceable resource. The ultimate relational database, everything that happened at *the Reive* connected in some inescapable way to the archive.

Within the hierarchy of *the Reive*, the arena floor technicians held a critical but undervalued place. Perceived more as brawn than brains, each floor tech, or often more than one, was aligned with unique teams inside the corporation. A floor tech's investigative work was driven by the needs and projects set by specialists above him, who were committed to one of the many endeavors currently competing for archive search time. Similar to the highly charged buyers and sellers in the pit at the New York exchange, *the Reive's* floor techs skillfully traded for time and space on the powerful workstations in the arena.

Alarms in the archive meant a serious degradation of one of the bundled signals initiated by the nanos and propagated through the membrane that enclosed one of the myriad of timelines. At least, that was what they traditionally meant, and why the techs dubbed them *branestorms*. Formerly, alarms were exceedingly rare and typically of short duration, with full event capture smoothly resumed. In fact, many older techs, now senior techs or section supervisors, could recall years with no alarms at all. In recent days, however, the warbling of a branestorm was progressing from a weekly to a nearly daily occurrence, and the end results were troubling.

This time the alarm was focused on a medium height screen whose images were rapidly distorting and losing coherence. The first responders quickly paired off, each with different diagnostic equipment. One tech probed the connections while the other waved a handheld sensor device and noted the readings. More techs raced up just as the screen suddenly devolved into digital snow and, just as abruptly, the alarm switched to a prolonged, single tone – which indicated a total loss of signal.

All the techs stared in shock at the hissing screen. Sweating and out-of-breath, a senior tech in a tie bustled up to the group and paused dumbfounded before the disrupted screen. He dug out a palm-sized device, manipulated it for a moment, and then watched as the screen went black. Discouraged, he continued tapping on his tiny screen until the tone cut off. The small group assembled beside a nearby workstation to debrief when the sudden warbling cry of a new alarm scattered them again.

Two levels above the arena, Quyron Shur, a slender Asian woman, hurried down a transparent hallway overlooking the arena. Glancing below, she scanned the walls of screens to locate the display that had triggered the second alarm, but couldn't see it. She stopped beside a door and pressed her palm against a subtle rectangle in the wall. The door opened with a soft pop and she quickly entered one of the balconied offices. Inside, there were transparent walls all around, although a few sections of glass had been tinted to provide a sense of privacy. Except for a wide, multi-function workstation near an inner wall, the office layout was stark in its simplicity. Quyron smoothly crossed the room, waved the computer awake, and activated multiple, razor-thin screens as she swiveled her mesh chair beneath her.

Hurriedly fluttering a hand near the central display as an ID sign-in, she scowled. "Hello? Faster would be nice."

Complex icons and data swiftly populated the interface. Using deft finger and hand motions she paused, enhanced, cut, and saved pieces of the colorful gibberish. Gathering her selections of data with a quick hand, she tossed them onto one of the side screens. Next she typed a flash of code and then watched as her recently cleared middle screen repopulated with dense columns of numbers and symbols, all changing as they scrolled up. Quyron rolled close to the display and began to methodically scan the lines for incongruities. "Echo," she said out loud. "I'm going to need a hand with this."

* * *

One of the turning points in the establishment and exploitation of the multiverse, and part of what made Reivers Corporation possible, was the rapid development of practical quantum computers. The core of a classical computer obeyed the well understood laws of classical physics, a quantum computer harnessed the unique properties of quantum mechanics to create a new mode of information processing.

The idea surfaced when scientists were confronted by the *atomic divide*. They knew that at some point in their technological battle to pack ever higher processing power into ever smaller packages, they would arrive at sizes that were no larger than a few atoms. When that happened, problems would arise, because at the atomic scale, physical laws switched to quantum mechanical laws. Why, no one knew, but the prospect of these problems raised a fundamental question. Could an entirely new kind of computer be devised based on the principles of quantum physics?

A classical computer was binary and had a memory made up of *bits*, where each bit represented either a zero or a one. The fundamental unit of information in a quantum computer was a quantum bit, or *qubit*. A qubit could exist not only as a zero or a one, but also as a blend, or superposition, of those states. In other words, a qubit could exist as a zero, a one, or simultaneously as both a zero and a one. This ability allowed for far greater flexibility than the binary system and held out the enticing promise of elevated speed, since multiple computations could be performed simultaneously.

As it turned out, in practice, when the qubits were in a state of decoherence, much to the scientists' surprise, they performed simultaneous calculations not only in our own universe, but also in *other universes*. In essence, qubits were smears of probability that not only opened the windows to the reality of other timelines, but also offered a tenuous path towards simulated sentience.

* * *

Quyron found nothing suspicious in the data so far. Her hand unconsciously stroked her chin as she talked to herself. "What the hell is going on? The propagation curves are solid all the way to cutoff."

Outside her office wall, she heard the warbling alarm change to the single sustained tone again. Distracted, Quyron went to the transparent wall and stood quietly staring down. Below, a covey of techs gathered in front of a hissing, static-filled screen. As she

24

watched, the monitor was disrupted by a senior tech and it snapped to black. Shortly after that, the tone was silenced.

Quyron returned to her workstation wearing a troubled expression. No longer interested in the columns of data still scrolling on her screen, she waved them away and brought up 3-D schematics of the arena. She had just rotated the view and zoomed in to an area deep beneath one of the buildings when a soft chime tinkled.

Quyron double-tapped a small titanium barbell that she wore in a rim piercing of her right ear and softly said, "This is Quyron."

She noticeably stiffened at the familiar voice and then looked puzzled. *How could he know about this already? Isn't he out of the country? What time zone is he in?*

"No sir, I wouldn't say that. It seems to be growing in severity though and I..."

She stopped as the other voice cut in. She let him talk but obviously disagreed with what he said. When she sensed an opening, she jumped back in. "Maybe, but how can we know until we're able to isolate the root cause of..."

Her comment was stepped on again. She flared her nostrils as he talked. Finally, unable to be silent, she forced a question into the conversation. "And what if I'm convinced it's not a transmission problem?"

She listened briefly and interrupted. "I'm well aware of that, but you have to face the other possibilities... Look, if all you wanted was a rubber stamp, then why did you send for me?"

Forced again to listen, she drummed her fingers and then swiveled her chair to glance at the arena. Additional techs were flooding onto the floor. She perked up. Something new was happening.

She suddenly realized the other voice had paused, so she quickly filled the space. "I know it's just a handful of lines so far. The trick is to find out what's really happening, and I'm worried we're underestimating...yes, you, you're underestimating. I'm saying there's something else behind this."

Below her, the walls of displays were rapidly changing. Similar images began to crowd onto more and more of the monitors. Various views of a terrible freeway pileup started to populate across the rows of screens. Quyron rose from her chair and stared. Some of the images showed aerial views, others hovered beside the drivers, and a few views were actually inside the damaged vehicles. A set of deep, sonorous tones began to ring through the arena.

"I'm sorry. We have an acquisition overload alarm. Some large group event...an accident – yes, car accident, and – just a moment..."

Quyron had quickly opened chains of windows on her screens while she talked. As fast as she could open them, all began overflowing with data

"The nexus is overwhelming the nanos and the archive and..." She grimly opened more engineering modules and watched the crashing trends as the multiplied lines continued to multiply.

"...I have to deal with this now...right, sometimes there's no choice...I'm sure you do. Thank you, sir."

She disconnected with a tap to her ear and harshly called out. "Echo? I need an assessment right now and your best case scenario!"

CHAPTER 3:

HAMILTON TERRACE CURVED through an older neighborhood in Turpin Hills. Stately trees on the boulevard nearly touched their upper branches across the patched asphalt. As in many areas in Cincinnati, young families had refurbished the vintage homes over the years, and refilled the quiet blocks with children and noise. Today, however, was beyond anything that had ever happened before.

Anxious homeowners filled the yards and side-walks, all drawn by the distant sirens and the ominous tower of smoke from the freeway. Some teens tapped their iPhone screens checking for news. All eyes tracked the flashing lights of emergency vehicles wailing by on Beacon Street, a block away. Flocks of boys on bikes swirled about, gathering speed, then joyfully flew off to gawk at whatever there was to see.

Kendall and Josh staggered along the uneven sidewalk, moving against the current of the loose crowd. Josh limped and Kendall pressed a bloody handkerchief against his forehead. A few women cast questioning looks their way, but no one asked anything.

Kendall glanced around, momentarily confused. "We almost there?"

Josh motioned up the road. "Yeah, we cut through that playground ahead and we're at the back of the church. You need to stop?"

"No. I don't know." He twisted his head and squinted as if something inside was hurting. "I don't know what I need. I just want to get home."

The road ended in a cul-de-sac right in front of a small park with playground equipment. Josh paused and turned in a slow half circle, taking everything in. "Does this all look right to you?"

"What?"

"This." He waved his arm at the neighborhood.

"Not sure. Like what?"

"The road, the houses... I don't know. Things feel... off."

"Since when did you spend much time here?"

"It's not...I used to cut through here a lot from church and..."

"From church?"

Josh tossed a wry smile at his Dad. "Yeah, Jimmy and me...Okay? So maybe we didn't spend as much time in youth group as you and Mom thought...you know?"

Kendall stopped. He rolled his eyes. "Oh, that's great. Your Mom woulda been so pleased."

"Yeah, so, anyway... I know this road pretty well and..." He scrunched his face and squeezed one eye shut and then another. He looked left and did it again, then right. "It's doing this weird thing – stuff around me feels odd and then it feels okay, and then odd again; like, back and forth."

Kendall sobered. "Anything you can put your finger on?"

"Yeah, those trees," Josh waved a hand toward a pair of large trees across the street. The breeze through their leaves rustled like old paper. "Somehow, I'm positive they're in the wrong places."

* * *

28

There were only three cars in the Central Christian Church parking lot, and since one of them sat smugly in the slot marked *Pastor*, that left only two that could possibly belong to Josh. None were Mustangs.

Kendall scowled, "I thought you said you parked it by the side door?"

"The Mustang?"

"Yeah, the Mustang!" Kendall shot back. "Whaddya think I'm talkin' about?" His irritation turned into doubt. "Your car. Your..." He massaged his temples and grimaced. "God, what's with us?"

Josh stubbornly stared at the parked cars. "Hang on – I was at a meeting here and..." He tried to pull his jumbled memories into order but he kept finding things left over. "After the service, you wanted both of us to ride together to the cemetery."

"Yeah, in my truck, that's right." Kendall tried to hold that thought. "You...I remember..." He looked tentatively over at a blank section of the lot and pointed. "You parked it right over there, didn't you?"

Josh vigorously rubbed his head as if trying to scratch something inside. "I don't think I have it anymore."

Kendall was disgusted. "Don't tell me you left the keys in it again?"

"Not hardly." Josh patted his pants and felt the comforting bulge of keys on a ring. "They're right here."

He pulled out a ring of keys. Dominant among the small, nondescript silver keys was a fat, black one with a shiny "H" on the back. Looking perplexed, Josh rolled it over in his hand. "So, why should this one look familiar?"

Father and son stared at each other. Josh thumbed the *open lock* icon on the key. The bright red Honda, next to the Pastor's car, cheerfully clicked its locks up and winked its running lights.

Josh hesitantly walked to the driver's door and delicately pulled it open. "Is your brain feeling itchy?"

"Somethin' like that."

Josh pulled the car door wide and looked inside. "I got things in my head that I don't remember... remembering before."

Kendall blinked his eyes rapidly and looked startled. Something had just happened inside his head. "What kind of things?"

"Like this red car. I do remember buying it. But I didn't. And I know I parked the Mustang over there before Mom's funeral, but I remember I parked this one right here before the young adults' meeting."

"We gotta get outta here!" The older man was suddenly frantic. He wrenched open the Honda's other door and jumped in. "Right now! Hurry up! We really need to get home!"

* * *

The Honda raced down a tree-lined street and swiftly climbed a short driveway to a comfortable brick-faced suburban home. As soon as the car braked to a stop, both doors clicked open and father and son sprung out. They moved quickly toward the front door, Josh in the lead, and then awkwardly stopped.

Josh shoved his hands in his pockets and stepped back from the three steps leading to the front door. "You first."

* * *

Most large Midwestern homes have roomy foyers that double as mudrooms for the inevitable wet and freezing seasons. The McCaslin family home was no exception. The area inside their front door was spacious, the floor was stone, to welcome wet boots and shoes, while the paneled walls were furnished with ample hooks and cubbies to accommodate gloves and hats and the multiplicity of coats.

As Kendall entered his home he was halted by the unsettling sight of a woman's coat and strap purse. Behind him, Josh stood poised between the doors, distressed by the warm aroma of cooking.

30

From another room, a sunny female voice carried easily into the foyer. "Kendall? Is that you?"

Leah McCaslin calmly walked into the front room carrying a dish towel. She was slender, smiling, and dressed in jeans and a soft sweater. "Dinner's gonna be a few minutes yet – Oh, Josh, I didn't expect you to be here."

As she got nearer to her silent husband, a growing concern filled her face. "What? You look like you've seen a – what's wrong? Kendall, your head's bleeding!" She rushed up to him, anxiously checking his forehead.

Kendall suddenly wrapped his arms around her and his tears flowed. "Leah! My God! Leah..."

Leah didn't understand but responded warmly to the embrace. "Hey, it's okay. Honey, it's gonna be okay. Take it easy. What's going on?"

Confused, and a little self-conscious, Leah looked over at Josh, only to see that he too was falling apart. Leah automatically reached out to comfort him. "Oh Josh, sweetie, come here."

She circled her free arm around her son and drew him in. "I don't know what's happened to you two but I'm sure everything's gonna be all right."

CHAPTER 4:

EACH OF THE MANY meeting rooms at Reivers Corporation was named after a type of bird. This aided in identifying the rooms and indicated a sensitivity to nature, which was deemed important to the overall public relations of the company. In keeping with this custom, the largest conference room, located in the executive wing, was named the Marabou Stork room and had a tasteful plaque outside the double doors with an artist's rendering of the huge bird in flight. This impressive African fowl boasted one of the widest wingspans of any land bird – more than 12 feet – and seemed appropriate for the largest conference room it designated. Overlooked, perhaps, were its diet preferences for carrion and human garbage, along with its disturbing outward appearance. It had a naked, pink head and long pink neck, devoid of feathers, with a white ruff at its collar and black and white plumage below. Starkly white, extremely long legs completed the picture. The white legs were not white by nature but by its practice of defecating on itself with a kind of whitewash. This collision of imagery and habit went a long way to explaining its unfortunate, but more common name, the Undertaker Bird.

The mid-morning team review, held in the Marabou Stork Conference room, was a standing bi-weekly update to Reive senior management. Heavily attended by teams and their staff, its stated purpose was to highlight progress from the many active projects raiding the archives. In practice, this was the opportunity for ambitious managers to shine, along with their teams, and to make their case for additional access or people. It was also the moment for waning projects to be defended and for new proposals to be touted for their potential.

The flip side to all this professional sharing, however, was the darker reality of a battle for dominance waged by gifted partisans with extremely capable staffs. The blood flow in this well-appointed room was virtual, but the combatants played for keeps: slashed projects freed up time and personnel, expanded projects amplified power and spread influence. Few things presented here were surprises, and fewer still held the interest of more than a narrow slice of the assembled specialists. Today's meeting was about to be an exception.

Jonathan Newbauer, the Senior Vice President of Operations, was chairing the meeting only because the founder and Chief Executive was out of the country. Newbauer gulped iced water from a cut crystal glass and counted the minutes until he could escape back to his office. Balding and heavy, Jonathan consoled himself by noting that herding these particular cats was not what he was hired to do. He stole a quick look at Quyron, who sat next to him, with her hands calmly folded, and cursed her roundly inside his head. *God save us from snooping women!* He knew he was sweating but he couldn't stop.

The remarkable U-shaped conference table was handmade from African ribbon mahogany, no doubt an attempt at continuity with the avian namesake of the room. The hardwood was hand rubbed with a natural clear finish and complemented by the unique chairs gathered around it. To gain a seat at the table was considered a badge of achievement, and it set one apart from those consigned to the outer chairs, forced to share space with the lower staff and support personnel.

Presenters generally stood at the open end of the table where bright, wall-sized screens were suspended from the ceiling behind them. However, in practice, they were free to roam wherever they wished, since subsidiary screens dominated two other walls, and convenient eye-level interfaces were clamped along the entire inside lips of the table.

Currently, all the screens were filled with sets of captivating 3-D graphics and enhanced photos. Neville Vandermark, a vibrant middle-aged man in a stylish tie and a crisp lab jacket, was delivering a lively presentation. Neville, a physicist, was an early hire of the foundational group that created *the Reive*, and as such, enjoyed a great deal of power and autonomy; both of which he exercised freely.

Flanking Vandermark were two longtime members of his team, and both hired due to his lobbying efforts. Song Lee Hahn was a short, coldly introspective biophysicist from South Korea. Her lifelong struggle for professional recognition was as much a fight against her own culture as it was against the male dominated scientific community. Behind, and frankly towering over Song Lee, stood Taylor Nsamba, a quantum physicist from Africa. Always impeccably attired, Taylor spoke with the slightly European flavor to his language that was typical of his native Uganda.

Vandermark was clearly enjoying himself. "It's been a long hunt, and I won't deny it. However, we're confident that we've finally tagged the right wave function, at the right time. And here he is."

A series of photos flashed across the screens showing a pleasant-faced scientist with brown hair. To an outsider the images might have felt invasive, like covert surveillance shots: here he was in a lab with research assistants; there in his office; at a hotel conference podium delivering a paper; at home with his wife and child; in the morning in his car; late at night working at his desk.

"This is Dr. Joseph Severson, a research scientist at the Center for Applied Genomics in Canada. He works hard, and he works his people hard." Neville smiled. "We can verify that."

The screens transitioned to images of a multi-storied research facility next to a huge brick and glass hospital complex.

"And this particular center is connected to a hospital called The Hospital for Sick Children, so the good doctor's motivation is always just outside his window."

The screens showed layered images of sick children being treated in hospital rooms, their families interacting with staff members, and finally, a series of interior shots of Severson working beside gowned medical techs in a crowded, equipment strewn lab.

"We think our bright boy is right on the edge of a breakthrough to identify the disease genes for Autism Spectrum Disorder. Well, to be more accurate, one of his alternate versions will. So far, we've tracked him through seventy-three major splits and sifted the numerous subset branches and, if the good doctor will just make up his mind, we'll have it."

An animated build-slide illustrated the linear flow of numerous parent and child lines, along with their associated branches, spreading left to right from Severson's initial timeline.

Vandermark nodded to Song Lee and, in a practiced handoff, she continued the story without a hitch.

"About 1 in 88 children in the United States has autism, or a related disorder. Among boys, the rate of autism spectrum disorder is 1 in 54."

As the petite Korean talked, the images dissolved into a variety of animated bar charts and line charts. Her voice grew more confident as she warmed to her topic. "Around the world, the rates are growing at 14% per year, and as yet, there is no consistent medical way to identify the disease except by behavioral observation. We discovered that Dr. Severson had isolated potential glitches in a DNA region, namely chromosome 16, and in particular, a range of bands at positions 16q12 through 21."

Complex chromosomal ideograms with their characteristic multi-colored banding patterns appeared on some of the screens. Other images grew the bands to a larger size and identified the actual cytogenetic locations of the range of genes Hahn was talking about.

"We've copied his work into our own labs and are now ahead of him. He's definitely on to something. We think that if we can understand the gene encoding mutations in the..."

"Please, Dr. Hahn," Vandermark interrupted with a smile, "there's no 'if' here. And let's not get bogged down. The takeaway for this group is that we got it. And we will understand it very soon, one way or another. We always do."

Beside him, Hahn wore a pleasant porcelain face for the audience but inside, a familiar furnace glowed red hot.

"And it was such a fluke we tracked this guy anyway." Vandermark grinned at the faces around him. "Honestly. Our own Joey Severson, I mean the version of Dr. Severson that we have in our own line, is a Canuck corner druggist – and not a very good one either, from what I hear. Really!"

Only a few scattered laughs responded to his joke. Neville sniffed to cover his misstep and made a small, hurried hand signal in the air. All the screens immediately reverted to the Reivers company logo.

"Okay, that's our last update, for now. I just want you to know that my team appreciates your efforts to help us." His look went first to those around the table and then to the employees in the galleries. "We couldn't do the important work we do without you."

Wearing his well rehearsed warm and serious look, he waited a beat and then nodded at the large African standing quietly beside him. "Anything to add, Dr. Nsamba?"

Taylor carefully shook his head. "Not at this time, except, of course, to add my gratitude to yours."

"Then, unless there are questions?" Neville paused briefly, checked the room for hands, and then caught Newbauer's eye. "Thank you for the time, Jonathan. Echo, no further slides."

There was polite applause as the presenters sat. All the screens went to black, leaving only three small white dots and a blinking square in the lower right corners.

Newbauer nodded to Quyron and she rose to walk toward the open end of the table. A sudden low buzz of confused comments spread around the room. Obviously, this speaker was unexpected.

Newbauer raised his hands defensively, "I know this is not on the agenda and I apologize in advance for whatever inconvenience this causes. However, I have been...instructed to give some time to Quyron Shur, one of our archive specialists. She will update us on the recent," he consulted some scribbled notes, "flux event and those other transmission troubles we keep having." He looked at Quyron, puzzled. "Is that right?"

"Close enough, Mr. Newbauer. Thank you."

She stood relaxed, facing sets of guarded eyes. "And I regret the disruption from your important work here, but I believe something irregular is happening in the multiverse."

Quyron took a few steps to the center of the presentation area. She had everyone's attention now. "The truth is we're not quite sure what we're facing, and yet my team and myself feel a growing sense of...urgency." She paused for effect. "We have never seen transmission problems like these before, and their numbers and severity are increasing. We can't explain it. In addition, our initial investigation into the recent overload event exposed something that disturbs us even more. Frankly, we'd like your reaction to what we found."

Quyron quietly watched the faces around her, waiting. Baffled, Newbauer muttered, "Well, okay. You've sufficiently baited the hook. Carry on then. We're waiting."

Quyron launched into her presentation, her voice clipped and businesslike. "Initially, post event, nanos were sent to tag all familial segments. We chose a standard .15 decisional radiance from the parent, and filtered for temporal proximity."

Quyron spoke to the ceiling, "Echo, please run the parent event."

All screens immediately displayed a high resolution, aerial view of a crowded freeway. A lone dog dashed across the lanes and a single car braked. A surprised van smashed into that car's back bumper. The minor mishap quickly escalated into chains of more serious accidents behind them. Rising chaos spread across all the lanes and eventually reached over the centerline barrier to involve vehicles on both sides of the roadway. The freeway disaster culminated in a massive detonation of a gas truck.

"Pause, please."

The view froze on all the screens. A bloated wave of orange flames, tinged with blue, was held still in the act of engulfing a swath of defenseless cars.

"This is the parent event TL-1708-NAOH-RT1, a major vehicle accident near Cincinnati two days ago, in real-time. Echo logged it as a D5-level nexus due to the number of splits and branches and sub-alternate lines spiraling out of it. Nothing unusual there, except for its magnitude, but it, surprisingly, pushed an atypical temporal spike right up through our entire system. Since then, as I said, we've dispersed fleets of fresh nanos into the new archives to hunt for branch deviations."

Quyron put her hands behind her back and demurely tipped her head. "For completeness, let me say, our investigation actually returned eighty-eight potential deviants, but Echo disqualified eighty-four of those. The remaining four have been edited in lag-time order, along with enhanced views. I've included ID slates in between each line for clarity."

Quyron glanced up again. "Echo, isolate the target vehicle."

The scene quickly rewound to somewhere in mid-accident and zoomed in on a clump of entangled vehicles. A cross line target reticle appeared and settled over a black pickup truck.

"Pay attention to this vehicle. Echo, replay the parent event and then add the edits, one after another."

The earlier scene rewound to the beginning and re-played. The reticle smoothly tracked the truck through the event to its final destruction by a tumbling Chevy 4X4.

The next shot was a digital slate with an ID tag indicating a different timeline. Like the parent, this child line began just before the accident. This time the truck reacted more quickly but ended up pinned against the center barricade where flipping cars still crushed it.

A slate appeared with a new ID tag. The next sequence began from the same place again, but this time it was raining. Suddenly, the pickup swerved across the lanes even before the first collision had happened.

Newbauer and Vandermark blinked their eyes in sudden alertness. Vandermark leaned forward in closely guarded interest.

On the screens, the desperate pickup spun around, rammed into other cars, and became stuck. An out-of-control dump truck plowed through the side of the trapped pickup in a horrifying T-bone collision.

Some staff members winced at the distressing violence. Song Lee Hahn remained stoic, her mouth held in a tight line.

A new slate appeared. This time the pre-accident weather was sunny. The actions of the pickup were immediate and clear. It swerved recklessly trying to get off the freeway, well before any braking or collisions had begun. Its efforts were frustrated at the edge of the freeway when it caught a bumper and flipped over numerous times.

Some of the division managers shifted nervously. A few researchers whispered stunned comments. Hahn jotted a hurried note into her binder.

On the screens behind Quyron, the gas truck erupted again and engulfed the cars in roiling waves of flame. A new slate appeared with a new ID tag. This time the red pickup under the reticle expertly threaded through the traffic, fought across all the lanes, and was already headed off the freeway before the initial collision had even started.

Vandermark was spellbound. Newbauer sat mesmerized, watching the final actions on the screen in front of him.

The truck bounced up the steep incline and struck a rock. It slid dangerously sideways and stalled out in a hole. Slowly, it tipped over sideways. Two men crawled out from the passenger side door as the truck tumbled back down the hill. On foot now, the injured men raced frantically up the hill as the chain-reaction-accident progressed below them.

"Echo, freeze."

Around the room, a striking image of the two anxious men in mid-flight was held suspended on all the displays. Quyron moved to stand in front of one of the large screens behind her.

"During each of these four child lines, the men in this truck behaved as if they knew what was about to happen. As if they were testing alternate solutions to avoid a death they had *already* experienced."

The room was hushed. Everyone soberly chewed on the unimaginable implications contained in those remarks.

Vandermark spoke quietly but it penetrated the room. "Oh what a tangled web we weave..."

Quyron turned to him. "Excuse me?"

"Quyron, I'm sorry, but it seems to me that you've gone to a great deal of trouble to make a case for what is clearly not possible. I'm not saying you set out to deceive us. I'm sure you meant well, but your efforts are misguided."

Quyron fought to keep her face neutral. "Continue."

Vandermark looked around the room, seeking agreement. "For those of us used to the complexities of the archive, we ignore nexus points. They're nothing but knots of confusion. In practice, they're irrelevant to our real work, and we skip over them; but not you."

Enjoying himself, he got up and began to play to the audience. "No, you jumped right into the middle of one and came out with...confusion. So you can manipulate data and slap together clips and trucks and people; so what?" He noted the brief wince in Quyron's eyes. "Oh, I'm not saying you don't believe what you've presented here. No, I'm just saying, I'm not persuaded. And it seems to me that none of us here should be surprised that your findings are so illogical."

Quyron looked steadily at the smug scientist. "Did I say they were illogical?"

The satisfied look vanished as Vandermark sharpened his voice. "Please! You're testing our patience. Timelines are unaware of each other, by definition. You know that. It's a demand of the wave function itself."

The scientist modulated his voice to add some artificial warmth. "You know I'm right. None of us are aware of the splits happening right now, in this very room. Right now, I'm sure you're agreeing with me, somewhere. And somewhere else...you're fleeing the room in tears."

Quyron smiled darkly but her eyes betrayed nothing of her feelings.

"Okay, fine, sorry about that, but *the point* is that neither of us is aware of the splits, and neither are our copies. It's a law of quantum mechanics. Everything depends on it. There are no exceptions."

Quyron coldly indicated the men behind her, still caught in their freeze frame. "Tell that to them."

Vandermark shook his head, feigning exasperation. "Oh yes, your amazing truck drivers! Let me count the impossibilities. They were aware of their own branching. And not only that, but they were actually interacting across those branches. Oh, and not just interacting, let me be clear, they were *jumping* between segments. Wait! And not just jumping but keeping their memories intact so they could use that knowledge in the next line. Does that about cover it?"

Quyron breathed in through her nose. "That's only the most obvious implications but my..."

He pounced on her words with an icy tone. "Well then, maybe you're right, that's not *illogical*. It's laughable!"

Quyron grimly replied. "How would you explain it then, Dr. Vandermark?"

He waved his arms dismissively at the room. "There's nothing to explain. I've told you. You're lost in a nexus! You've cut together nano errors, or random data, I don't know. Maybe you're tracking the wrong truck. Clearly, there has to be a rational answer. Or is this some – some twisted joke you or your team prepared? Or Echo?"

A clear, young, confident female voice came from the speakers in the ceiling. "There are no mechanical or technical errors indicated, Dr. Vandermark. It is not random. It is the right truck. And I cannot joke."

Quyron folded her hands in a forced calming technique, but her words still carried an edge. "You saw the same timeline segments we all saw, Dr. Vandermark. Despite your comments, this is no trick. I have no agenda. You can parade around the room and wiggle all you want, but these men reacted before they should have...four indisputable times! Help me explain it."

Vandermark ignored her challenge, acting as if she hadn't spoken at all, and turned to Newbauer. "Jonathan, we obviously need to assign someone more...*familiar* to look into all this."

Quyron bristled, "I'm sorry, but the truth is, that's not your choice."

Vandermark looked harshly at Newbauer and the VP squirmed as he replied. "Quyron and her team were brought in and financed by the President himself."

"And why wasn't I informed?"

"But I assumed you were."

"I see." Vandermark took a quick breath, held it, and let it out slowly. "My apologies, then, Ms. Shur, for my...intemperate remarks."

Quyron nodded slightly.

Vandermark returned to his seat. "It's just hard for those of us at the front of the battle to be patient with those who are counting noses from the back – so to speak."

Quyron briefly locked eyes with him and wondered again why she had chosen a field that tolerated such arrogant asses. "I can see how you'd feel that way. In my work, facts are facts, and you deal with them honestly, wherever they're found."

Newbauer noisily cleared his throat. "If we could get back to your...your update, please? Is this, whatever it is, connected in some way to the other problems you were hired to check on?"

Quyron cocked her head. "The transmission issue? I don't know yet. This event seems different but I'm becoming convinced that something we're doing may be at the root of both."

Vandermark reacted, "Something we're doing? What does that mean? And who's we?"

"Unknown."

"I see, another hunch. I'm almost afraid to ask if you have any evidence to back it up?

"Not enough."

Vandermark took a quick drink from his glass of water. "Ms. Shur, what if I were willing to accept your earlier analyses regarding your...truckers?"

"I wouldn't believe you."

Some surprised laughs erupted from the gallery and then quickly choked themselves off in embarrassment. Vandermark took it in stride.

"Of course, I can appreciate that, and I wouldn't blame you. But for the sake of the moment, and ignoring everything I've said to the contrary, how would *you* explain what they did? What are they?"

Quyron gazed at the attentive faces around the room. Many of the eyes were fixed on the still image of Kendall and Josh. Everyone was definitely caught up in the moment.

"How they do what they do is unclear," she answered in a steady voice. "But I think they are something we've never seen before, never imagined."

Quyron stepped back from the screen and she too stared at the freeze-frame of the men. "I believe these two are natural-born jumpers. I don't know how else to explain it. My guess is they are a kind of mutation within the multiverse – a failsafe, if you will.

She held Vandermark's eyes ever so briefly as she paused. "I don't know how many there may be, or if these are the only ones, but their sudden appearance now is not an accident – it's a response."

She gave a nod toward Echo, and the frozen scene played on. Everyone silently watched as the men re-animated to continue their race for the ridge top. They leaped the guard rail just before flame and debris roared through behind them.

CHAPTER 5:

IN THE TREES OUTSIDE the brick-faced McCaslin home in suburban Cincinnati, it was after midnight. The fall air was cool and still, and the stars in the black sky were bright. An adult barred owl, with wide facial discs around dark eyes, sat her silent watch in an oak tree near the red Honda. Pale brown body with white mottling above and brown streaking below, the silent killer was nearly invisible on her perch. Her head rotated smoothly through half its impressive arc while her compact body remained motionless. Her large eyes settled on a repetitive movement below.

An anxious mouse was transporting seeds from summer storage to winter larder. His grey back hunched and stilled as he carefully crossed the grass to the rain gutter's down spout next to the driveway.

Hidden under feathers on either side of the head, an owl has openings, called apertures, in place of ears. Typically, the holes are asymmetrical, which helps to triangulate on the location of very subtle but specific sounds – such as seeds scraping on dirt or fur rubbing against grass blades. Owls have four black talons on each feathered foot – three curve forward and one backwards, creating an exceptionally effective snare.

The barred owl released her talons' mechanical hold on the branch and fell forward into a deadly silent descent. Her primary flight feathers had leading edges that were fimbriate; that is they had comb-like extensions to muffle the whisper of air passing over them.

The mouse moved unaware, other instinctual business cluttering his mind, until talons closed upon him like a multifaceted trap. A single swallowed "cheep" and the tinny tumblings of seeds upon the metal spout were all that escaped.

And multiple universes tumbled away undetected around the moment. In one, the owl missed. In another, the mouse fought back. In countless other variations, the mouse abandoned his seeds and made it to the gutter; the owl was distracted and looked the other way; the grass was not mowed and so the mouse passed unseen; the owl perched in the elm instead of the oak; the mouse waited for a better night to move his food; a car passed by and spoiled the hunt; and on and on in a myriad of possibilities, all realized and superpositioned upon each other, without a whit of trouble or observation.

The owl flared her sound-dampened wings as she reclaimed her perch with the prize, oblivious to the universes that had spiraled off her every wing beat. Pleased with the fat, warm meal ahead, she considered the night with her merciless eyes before turning to her repast in earnest.

* * *

In an upper bedroom of the house, Kendall's eyes were wide open and troubled. He had a butterfly bandage on his forehead and a nasal attachment in his nose. The nose probes were strapped to his head and connected to a coiled hose, which in turn was coupled to a CPAP (Continuous Positive Airway Pressure) unit sitting on his bedside table. The cumbersome apparatus hissed rhythmically, keeping time with his breathing. Apparently, he snored, which was new information to parts of him when Leah chided his forgetfulness. He minimized the lapse as he relied on his other memories to guide him through the filling of the water reservoir, the positioning of headgear and hose and bed covers, be-

fore the lights went out. His newly familiar fingers rediscovered the soft switch that turned it on. The whole
experience was reminiscent of the rest of his strange
day, a marriage of opposites: death, life; pain, joy; confusion, clarity; and now strange and familiar. He
opened his mouth and, surprisingly, air streamed out
as long as he left it open. Sealing his lips again, he felt
no internal sensation of the elevated air pressure at all.
How that prevented snoring, he hadn't a clue.

He gazed over at Leah – his precious, lost and re-
found love – safely asleep beside him, and silently marveled to himself. He shuffled through his memories and
wondered again where he was, what he was, and what
he knew or didn't know. He knew, for example, that he
didn't snore but he knew he did now. A moment's
thought took him back to the sleep apnea test and the
net of leads they attached to his scalp, his face, his
chest, his arms, and his feet. He could see again the
friendly face of the matronly technician clucking,
"There you go. All wired up and snug as a bug. Your
job is to go to sleep now and we'll all be watching you.
Okay?"

And he knew he never took a snoring test.

What had happened on that freeway? His one clear
notion was that sleep was no longer on his agenda for
tonight. He fumbled in his alien memories until he saw
again an image of the soft off/on switch behind the
heating dial, and then reached out in the dark to deftly
shut it off.

* * *

Josh sat at the head of the dining room table wrapped
in a blanket and working a laptop. A nearly empty
glass of milk and a cell phone crowded his elbow as he
typed and moused with an easy efficiency.

The McCaslin dining room was large and carried a
cheery but relaxed country feel. The sturdy mission
hills style oak table with matching slat back chairs sat
on a cream and rose colored rug which Leah claimed
made her think of her home. Against the wall, an oak

47

china cabinet displayed off-white pottery, Grandma McCaslin's Havilland china and a small collection of pale pink Depression glass. Four sets of windows were hidden behind closed wooden shutters and an oak sideboard completed the wall. Above, a curvy wrought iron chandelier cast a soft illumination over the table.

Josh noted the sound of Kendall coming down the stairs and barely looked up. "Couldn't sleep either, huh?"

"Not a chance. You?"

"Afraid to go to sleep."

Kendall acknowledged the comment with a grunt and disappeared into the kitchen. Josh heard sets of cabinet doors being opened and shut, one after the other, along with the rattle of china and numerous thumps and mutterings. Josh shook his head. Finally, he heard the refrigerator door open and then milk filling a glass.

Josh moused the computer and talked without turning his head. "So, I found this Dell laptop in my room, okay? And a part of me knew the password, even though it's one I never thought of before. And another part remembered that I only use Macs."

Kendall appeared beside the table holding his glass of milk. "Yeah, and since when did Mom move the glasses to the wrong cabinet?"

"Left cabinet? Right cabinet? Try finding chips." Josh was tense. "Get used to it! Everything's shifted. Oh, and by the way, I don't live at home anymore – right?"

Kendall slid into a chair and took a swig of milk. "Right. I know – well, some part of me knows."

"And yet, here I am."

"Yeah, here we are."

"You wanna know somethin' else? I called Hannah's number on my weird cell phone, but it's somebody else's now."

"Her phone number?"

"Yeah. Some guy...said it's always been his number for years."

"You sure you dialed right?"

"Oh yeah. I talked to the dude twice, and it's late, okay? So I checked online. Guess what? No facebook."

"Whaddya mean? She's not on facebook? You mean her...page?"

"No, not her face page. Not her profile. Not her anything. There's no *facebook*."

Kendall stared at him blankly. "No facebook?"

"Yeah. No facebook. It doesn't exist. I even Googled *Zuckerberg*, and he's nowhere either."

They sat and stared at each other across the table. Kendall finally said what they both were thinking. "Where in the world are we?"

Josh shrugged. "I checked my e-mail. Nothing from Hannah – ever. I searched all over the place. Her family never adopted her, she never lived at her apartment, she never went to her college, and she never worked at her work. Huh? Where is she?"

Kendall softly set his glass down. "I don't know, Josh."

"We got Mom back but I lost Hannah. This is seriously messed up! Is that mom upstairs – really Mom?" Josh was getting louder. "I mean she's not the one I held hands with when she was dying, is she? So, if she's not that one, than who is she?" He looked away, trying not to break down. "If I go to sleep here tonight, what am I gonna wake up to tomorrow?"

Kendall was shook up but tried to calm Josh. "Look, I don't know about Hannah but I know Mom is as real as we are. Okay? All of this is real – it's just not...*our* real."

"How do we get back?"

"Back?" Kendall flared, "Back to where Mom's dead? Is that where you'd rather be?"

Josh reacted as if he was stung. "No...not that, but..."

"But what? What do you want me to say?"

"Nothin'. It's not that." Josh seemed lost for words. "Look, I've been down here a long time and I think I may have found an idea about this."

Kendall looked at the laptop and then at Josh. "What? Don't tell me you Googled it? I don't even want to hear it. You know what I think of that stuff."

"Can I just show you somethin'?"

Kendall shrugged his agreement. He was concerned about Josh but he couldn't believe anything on the internet would explain what they'd been through.

Josh worked the laptop and it flickered back into its search history, flipping through earlier pages.

"I tried a lot of stuff that went nowhere – things like *out-of-body experiences* and *near death* and *head trauma.*'"

Kendall rolled his eyes. Josh nodded. "I know, I know. I had to start somewhere, okay? For awhile, nothing went anywhere helpful until I stumbled on this link here."

Kendall leaned forward to see clearer. The display showed a complex search list with a single item highlighted in blue: *Many lives in many worlds: Article: Nature. Max Tegmark. In this universe, Max Tegmark is a physicist at MIT, Cambridge, Mass.*

Following this entry was a space and a linked address: *www.nature.com/nature/journal/v448/n7149/full/448023a.html.*

Josh had his finger poised over the *Enter* key. "Okay? So then I clicked it."

"Wait. Who's Max Tegmark?"

"Forget him. He's not what matters."

Josh pushed the key and a new image popped up. It was the landing page for a weekly journal. The red banner at the top had prominent white letters across it that read, *Nature – International weekly journal of science.* A smaller font indicated the date it was first published online, *4 July, 2007.* Directly beneath the banner, it read: *Access – To read this story in full you will need to login or make a payment (see right).*

Kendall shook his head in disgust. "You gotta pay just to read the damn article? Typical! And it's five years old anyway. What a rip-off!"

"Yeah, so what else is new?" Josh agreed. "But the teaser here down below was all I needed."

Kendall squinted over his shoulder as Josh read from the screen. "Accepting quantum physics to be universally true, argues Max Tegmark, means that you should also believe in parallel universes."

Kendall leaned back in his chair, newly uninterested. "Oh great, what are we now, Dr. Who?"

"Just listen to me, will ya? I'm tryin' to explain how I found this stuff. Gimme a minute and I'm tellin' you, it's gonna sound like what happened to us. You'll see."

Kendall was completely unimpressed. "Yeah, yeah, I'm listening, but it also occurs to me that I'm gonna need a new truck in the morning."

Josh gave him a dirty look and then resumed his reading. "Almost all of my colleagues have an opinion about it, but none of them have ever read the original document about it. The first draft of Hugh Everett III's Ph.D. thesis, which celebrates its 50th birthday this year, is buried in the out-of-print book, *The Many-Worlds Interpretation of Quantum Mechanics*."

Kendall finished his milk and waited until he was sure Josh was done. "And? Is this Hugh guy somebody who matters?"

"He does now. He didn't used to be important but, as far as I can tell, today's science big wigs are in love with his ideas."

"What's that mean?"

"Just what I said. I don't know what changed. Hugh Everett III was 27 when he wrote his paper. Nobody took him or his theory seriously then, so he walked away, took his PhD with him, said the hell with them, and did somethin' else."

"So what? Maybe mathematicians don't like people with numbers in their names. Where's that leave us?"

"Well, here we are, all these years later, and suddenly old Hugh's lousy theory is the hottest girl at the dance. How about that?" Josh watched his Dad carefully, hoping for a spark of real interest.

Kendall fixed him with a vacant look. "Good for him. How does that help us?"

51

"I'm not sure yet." Josh was uncomfortable. "But maybe – and I'm being serious now – maybe we oughta *talk* to him."

"What?" Kendall shot up out of his chair. "Are you kiddin' me? Things aren't strange enough already, now we're supposed to go talk to a dead guy?"

"He might not be dead," Josh shot back, defensively. "You don't know everything."

"That's crazy! He must be what, in his 80's? And even if we find him alive, what the hell do we ask him? What's he supposed to know anyhow?"

Josh looked up at Kendall with a cold, sober expression. "I'm not sure. All I can say is, I've been sitting here readin' and re-readin' his paper, and while there's lots of stuff I don't get at all, the parts I do understand, scare the hell out of me."

CHAPTER 6:

THE CARVED WOOD and glass doors of the Marabou Conference room opened wide as attendees flowed out of the adjourned meeting and into a sun-filled foyer. Running the length of the conference room, a large balcony overlooked a foliage-filled atrium where pairs of whimsical birdcages were suspended above reflecting pools. The open space echoed with the cheerful songs of mockingbirds, finches and wood thrushes.

Neville Vandermark pushed through the talkative crowd. He had his eyes fixed ahead as he rapidly moved toward the executive offices at the other end of the building. Hahn and Nsamba had to rush to keep up with him. Behind them, archive managers and their staffs were gathering into ad-hoc clumps of agitated discussions.

Vandermark glanced darkly in Nsamba's direction as they kept walking. "Taylor, I want to know everything there is to know about these jumpers – the ones in the presentation and the ones in our own line."

"Yes, of course. I can get the teams assigned to search the archives and work out the protocols with Echo – but the ones in our timeline? What do you want with them?"

"You don't get it, do you? If what we saw is actually true, the only way it could possibly work is if Quyron's jumpers were jumping into themselves in other lines – lines that lagged their own. Are you following me?"

"I am starting to, but...why are you so concerned about our line?"

"Well, we sure as hell don't want them jumping here, do we?" *Am I the only one who sees this threat for what it could be?*

"I didn't think of..."

"No, you didn't. Lucky for you, I did. So, once you find out where our local boys live and who they know and all that, I want you to take a security team and escort them to the warehouse at *the Point*, and keep them there."

Nsamba was shocked and almost stumbled. "What? You – you mean kidnap them?" Shocked by his own words, he furtively checked about to make sure no one had overheard.

"I didn't say those words," Vandermark replied, still walking. "But I will say that I don't care how you get it done."

"Neville, this is not Kampala." He hurried to pull even with Vandermark. "We cannot grab people off the street here. I know you are upset about Quyron but..."

Vandermark stopped and drilled him with an ugly stare. "I'm not upset. I'm being pro-active. Something you should consider doing more of." He lowered his voice. "Why do you think we built those warehouse cells, if not for something like this?" *Just because you lie to yourself doesn't mean that I do.*

Nsamba looked around to make sure no one except Hahn was nearby. "I never understood why you built them." Song Lee, standing silently nearby, felt just as uncomfortable as he did.

"Well, now you know." Vandermark said smugly.

The tall Ugandan was cowed but persistent. "I will gather a team but, seriously, I will still need some kind of paper to justify us in case we..."

"Fine, I'm sure I can get some official looking authorization signed off by some flunky, if it will make you feel better, but your best bet's still gonna be to stay under the wire."

Nsamba was offended. "I know how this works better than you do, I'm just saying that without some cover we..."

Vandermark snapped at him. "And I'm saying if I said you'll get it, you'll get it!"

Nsamba nodded, his reaction carefully shielded, and moved off toward the elevators. Vandermark tapped a tiny phone clip on his lab coat. "Echo, get me Cap over at Liaison...okay, track him then. I'll be right here."

While he waited, he gazed out the wall of windows in front of him. His eyes traced the horizon where rows of windswept clouds sailed the lower third of the sky. "Song Lee, you need to move up the final trials."

Behind him, Hahn was startled to be addressed. Her face betrayed her anxiety. "But I've told you, we can't be ready any sooner than next week. We're moving too fast already. I still have more testing I need..."

Vandermark glared at her over his shoulder. "You seriously think I don't know about your *secret* test jumps over the past weeks? What do you take me for?"

Hahn reached a hand out to steady herself and suddenly looked ill.

Vandermark gave her a crooked smile. "It's not even that I hold it against you - I'd probably do the same thing in your shoes – but no more whining, okay? Let's be a big girl."

Hahn steadied herself and urgently visualized sun dappled rocks in a quiet stream and languid koi floating serenely in the current. She refused to defer to him or reply to him.

His voice turned harsh. "You will be operational by tomorrow – and *my* people will be in the seats."

"Your people?" Caught off guard, she lost her struggle to stay calm. Her carefully structured internal picture shattered. "The – the cradles are experimental. Don't you understand that? We're still working things out." She folded her arms and stiffened. "I'm not comfortable with the idea of..."

He immediately cut her off. "My people can handle the risks. That's the point. That's what they do – it's

55

their job." Vandermark's phone clip emitted a tiny note. He instantly tapped it and turned away from Hahn.

"Cap? Vandermark. Heads up, I need a sign-off to detain a few people, ASAP." He listened briefly. "Yeah, the highest possible. It just needs to look official – right, whatever. We'll be crossing state lines though...so... Okay. Call me back on the other number later – yeah, that number. I'll dictate something and your guys can convert it into the legalese crap, okay? Right. Bye."

He disconnected and, without a beat, focused back on Hahn. "And I don't give a damn about your comfort."

"But you heard Quyron; we need to make sure we're not causing something. I've told you we're moving into areas no one has..."

Vandermark suddenly leaned down and got face-to-face with her. His dark eyes bored into hers. "Stop babbling nonsense and listen carefully, *Doctor*. I didn't fast-track you and buy you every toy you ever dreamed of just so you could balk when I needed you, now did I? Or do you miss that drafty apartment in Seoul where I found you, and those ignorant grad students and the stink of cold kimchee in the dark?"

Hahn bowed her head slightly and lost her way. "No. I – I understand. But I..."

"Do you?" Vandermark recognized the moment. If he believed in anything, it was his faith in his gift to know how to bend people to his needs. "We're at the tipping point of an era. No more dead ends. No more groveling for scraps in the timelines. We get to make the future we want. And no one, not you, and not some glorified analyst, is going to deny me that. Not even some overactive timelines. Is that clear enough for you?"

The rebuke left Hahn speechless. Vandermark straightened back to his full height. His voice was all business again, but it was clear there would be no further discussion permitted.

"You'll provide a revised timetable by tomorrow morning. Is that understood?"

"Yes."

Vandermark abruptly turned on his heels and ascended the gracefully curved glass stairs nearby as he headed for third floor. Oblivious to his beautiful surroundings, he was already tapping his phone as he climbed. "Echo, get Walters in personnel. Yes."

Song Lee Hahn's fingers had curled into tight balls, the nails making sharp dents in her palms. She had promised herself never to return to the petty male world of South Korean academia. Still, at the moment, this felt far worse. Yes, she had her labs and her experiments, and little oversight – he was right about that – yet it didn't seem enough anymore. She couldn't help but admire Vandermark's mind but she was repelled by almost everything else about him, and she was beginning to detest herself for being so caught. Could Quyron be right?

Hahn watched until Vandermark disappeared at the top of the stairs. She was overwhelmed by the work she had ahead of her. Revised timetable! He didn't seem to realize she had to revise an already overly aggressive timetable. It was one thing to alter lines on a schedule but quite another to make the revisions actually happen. This would necessitate equipment reworks, revamped target formulae, adjusted engineering workloads, added computer time, adjusted man-hours, not to mention the obligatory excuses and, her favorite, the telling of lies. She felt dishonored. The speed the new schedule demanded would increase errors, as she well knew, and there were no solutions for those. After all, who had time to check anything anymore?

Hahn hurried back down the hall, flexing the feeling back into her cramped fingers. She audaciously promised herself brighter days ahead and stuffed her qualms into a stone box in the corner of her mind, and sealed the lid. From now on, as far as she was concerned, the multiverse would just have to fend for itself.

CHAPTER 7:

KENDALL'S EYES OPENED slowly. The morning light filled the soft white curtains with a fresh glow. The first thing he noticed was his irritated throat. He coughed to clear it but stayed warm under the covers as he woke up. For a moment, he felt disoriented. His eyes struggled to synchronize reality with his mind but he was unsure which way he was facing in the bed – toward the outside or toward Leah? A blink and a wider stare revealed a second pillow nearby and an empty place in the bed. *Empty place?* Startled, he sucked in air, sat up and stared at the vacant half of the mattress. His mind whirled with fear and regret. "Leah?"

He scanned the bedroom trying not to panic. "Leah?"

The bedroom door opened quietly and Leah breezed in wearing a bathrobe. She smiled at him. "Didn't know you were awake."

Kendall drank in the sight of her and tried to swallow his emotional turmoil. "Where...ah, where were you?"

"I slept in the guest room." She came and sat beside him on the edge of the bed. "You started really snoring when you came back to bed. I guess *somebody* decided not to wear his mask." She looked at Kendall with concern. He was holding tight to her hand. "Hey, you okay?"

"Just a bad dream and...my throat is sore."

Leah grinned at him. "I shouldn't wonder!" She suddenly closed her eyes and made huge comical snorting noises through her nose and throat.

"Oh c'mon!" He poked her in the side and she jumped with a squeal. "It can't be that bad!" He laughed and put on a glum look. "Besides, it's not like I do it on purpose."

"I know, dear. So, want to tell me about the nightmare?"

"It wasn't a nightmare, exactly, it was just...I thought I'd lost you and then, when I woke up, I wasn't sure it was a dream." He wrapped a protective arm around her and pulled her close.

Leah touched his cheek. "Did you find me again?"

Kendall nodded. "When you came through the door just now."

"That's sweet."

He nuzzled her neck. "A nightmare with a happy ending."

Leah daintily unwrapped his arm as she got to her feet. "Oh no you don't! I know how this story goes. I don't have time for your *happy endings* – I've got things to do today."

She quickly dug through a few drawers in her dresser and grabbed clothes on her way to the bathroom. "I get the shower first, okay?"

Kendall smiled. "Do I have a choice?"

Her cheery voice came from behind the closed door. "No. I'm just being polite. I'm always first because you always like to go downstairs and make your coffee, right?"

"What if I wanted to change things this morning?"

The bathroom door clicked into a locked position. "Not this morning! Go make your coffee, dear."

But he didn't leave the room. He sat motionless and enjoyed the simple sounds of his wife getting ready for the day. Was this one of the advantages of multiple memories? Did the part that so hungered for a return to these lost, everyday things, instruct the other parts to shut-up and revel in what they had? He didn't care

59

about the explanation. He just knew that he enjoyed all the small sounds this morning: her brushing her teeth, the shower coming on, her feet splashing, the water going off, the tiny squeal of the squeegee that she used to keep the doors from streaking, the towel in her hair, the slither of cloth over skin, the hair dryer and the brushes, and all the little precious noises of a shared life.

He got up and slid into his bathrobe, and quietly went downstairs, lest she discovered him listening and wondered what was wrong.

* * *

He was sitting at the kitchen table sipping his first cup of freshly brewed coffee when she came in.

"Well, don't you look all relaxed?"

He smiled at her. "What's wrong with that?"

"There's nothing wrong with that. I'm just surprised is all." Leah measured water into a small pan and pulled together the fixings for oatmeal. "I figured you'd already be calling the insurance company about your truck and talking to the police and letting work know what happened and – I don't know, things like that."

"What're you doin' today?"

Leah set the pan on the burner and measured out the dry oats. "I want to get things ready for winter. I have to clean out the flower beds, take out the annuals, store the pots, cover the bushes, finish raking – the usual craziness, why?"

Kendall took another sip of his coffee and tried to sound casual. "Need some help?"

Leah was pulling out a bag of raisins when what he had said sank in. She slowly turned around and put a hand on her hip. "Kendall McCaslin, what has gotten into you?"

"What? I just thought you could use some help."

"What about your truck and the police?"

"That can wait another day."

"What about work? You're always saying they won't know what to work on without you."

"Maybe it's time they learned."

Leah looked at Kendall and smiled uncertainly. "Yardwork? Really?"

His eyes caught the steaming pan behind her. "Your water's boiling."

Flustered, Leah jumped around and pulled the pan back from the burner. She grabbed a wooden spoon and put the pan back on the burner as she stirred in the oats and added a little nutmeg and cinnamon. She glanced at him and then turned back to the stove. "It's that accident isn't it?"

Kendall finished his coffee and brought the cup over to the sink beside her. "Maybe I'm startin' to see things differently now. What if we just say that?"

Leah turned down the burner to let the oatmeal simmer and got out a bowl. She looked at him a long time before answering. "Okay," was all she said.

Kendall headed back upstairs for his shower, calling over his shoulder. "By the way, I made enough coffee for two. And after I convince Josh to help us, I bet we'll get done in time to go out for lunch."

Leah shook her head as she poured the hot oatmeal into her bowl and added raisins and brown sugar. She smiled to herself and dumped in an extra pinch of sugar.

CHAPTER 8:

TAYLOR NSAMBA PERCHED on the edge of his desk toying with a set of small nesting baskets, a gift from his sister in Kampala. Woven from dyed raffia, they were shaped like miniature huts, each with its own detachable conical top. They were graduated in size and designed so that each one could fit snugly inside another. Nsamba's long fingers danced as they manipulated the tiny huts in and out, spreading them in a straight line, gathering them back into a single hut, and then repeating the process.

"I understand your priorities, Tobias, you can stop repeating them." Nsamba kept moving the little baskets as he talked. He was on a speaker phone with two senior arena floor techs, and the conversation wasn't going well.

"I get it. I do. But here is what you don't seem to get. Dr. Vandermark has changed all of our priorities. Okay? Quyron's jumpers are the only things he wants tracked now. Got it?"

A confident male voice replied quickly. "Yes, but the new fuel experiments on E75Q2 are at a critical point and so close to a solution – couldn't we split time between that and...?

Nsamba nearly fumbled one of his baskets. His voice lashed out. "Phillip? Are you still on the call?"

A careful, younger voice answered. "Yes."

"Was there any confusion about what I said to Tobias a few moments ago?"

"No sir."

"Do you think you can carry out these instructions without alerting Quyron or her techs?"

"Absolutely."

"Then you do it. Congratulations on your promotion. It is your group now. Am I making myself clear?"

There was a slight pause and then Phillip's voice again. "I believe so."

"What?" Tobias sounded agitated. "Taylor, you can't just shuffle seniority on a whim. I won't stand for it. You don't have..."

Nsamba curtly chopped his comment off. "Take a few days and relax, Tobias. In fact, it would be best if you just tabled all your research. Phillip is going to need total access to our computer time allocations to handle this. Thank you, gentlemen."

"But..."

"Tobias! Unless you want a longer vacation, I would stop talking now. Go home and check back with me in three days."

There was silence on the line. Nsamba let it go on. He continued stacking and unstacking his little huts.

"Okay then." Nsamba's tone was back to warm but firm. "Phillip, I expect updates as soon as feasible – that's all for now."

Phillip's voice sounded cautious. "Thank you."

Nsamba ever so slightly shook his head. "Echo? Disconnect."

The young female voice responded clearly and immediately. "Of course, Dr. Nsamba. And Joanna has Mr. Benton waiting in your outer office."

Nsamba methodically stacked the nesting huts one last time into a single unit and placed it precisely on the corner of his desktop. He breathed in quickly and exhaled. Stepping away from the desk, he stretched and waved his arms in a boxer's warm-up – alternating to the left and then to the right, to get the blood flowing. He marveled at himself, so many years from the ring and still he warmed up the same way. How predictable, he thought.

"I will see him now, Echo."

The door clicked open and a broad shouldered man wearing tailored slacks and shirt walked in with a calm familiarity. "As promised, we got some info and an address."

Aaron Benton's eyes were never completely still and his body remained coiled even when at rest. Benton was a senior internal security professional – one of Vandermark's additional people, brought in when the special research group was set up two years before.

Nsamba crossed around and sat at his desk. Framed African folk art decorated the walls behind him, interspersed with handsome landscape photographs of the austere bush country of Northern Uganda. He folded his hands on the desk pad. "You are quick. I am sure Dr. Vandermark will be pleased."

"Glad to hear it, but it's not like these people were hiding, huh?" He smiled, knowingly. "Here's what we got so far. Kendall McCaslin and Josh McCaslin – father and son. Father's co-owner of a residential heating company, has a nice little house in the suburbs of Cincinnati. Son's in the army but, for the moment, he's home on leave. Those are the high points. We'll confirm all this, per usual, but it looks to be solid. I think we're good to go."

Nsamba looked at Benton silently. Benton calmly looked back – both comfortable in the empty moment. Nsamba broke first. "You understand what you're being asked to do?"

Benton rolled his shoulders nonchalantly. "Think so. We're workin' out the *how we do it* but we sure don't get the *why we're doin' it*. So, why?"

"An unusual question for you, isn't it?"

Benton considered for a moment, and then conceded the point. "Yeah. Sorry. Must be gettin' old."

He turned to leave. "Besides, I can tell you don't know why either, and it's buggin' the hell outta you."

"How can you tell that?"

"I ain't that old."

64

Benton quietly left the office, closing the door behind him. Nsamba swiveled slowly in his chair until he was facing one of the photographs of the bush country. He sat and stared.

CHAPTER 9:

LEAH TOPPED OFF Kendall's coffee and sat back down to an open newspaper. The kitchen was bright and cheery, with light oak cupboards and white table and chairs. The remains of breakfast were on the table and Kendall pondered the coffee mug in his hands.

Josh grabbed for the serving plate, his mouth still chewing. "Anybody else want the French toast?"

Leah didn't even look up from her reading. "You go ahead, dear."

Kendall smirked at him. "It'll help you come out even, since you took the last of the bacon, too."

"Yeah, yeah."

Leah looked serious as she studied the text of an article about the recent traffic disaster. "The death toll's risen to 25 now and it says that there are 10 still listed as critical and 43 as serious or stable. They estimate another 50 were treated and released. Says they're investigating the cause and still trying to identify victims and vehicles."

She patted Kendall's hand. "Thank God you two made it out with barely a scratch. It's amazing, really."

Kendall gingerly touched his healing forehead. "Well, maybe a little more than *barely*, but close enough." Josh shot a murky look at his father and was treated to a silent *shut-up* in return.

Neither look was noted by Leah. "You better call the police today, before they call you. You should have done that yesterday, you know."

Kendall huffed an exasperated breath. "I need to talk to George first and then look at trucks and then I'll get around to the police. What do they care anyway? I'm just another victim."

Leah got up and started collecting plates and silverware. "Do the police first, honey. I'm sure they're wondering what happened to you." She carried a stack over to the sink and looked back. "And who's George?"

"C'mon, we've had the same insurance agent since we bought the house. You know, good old George, George, ah...whatever his last name is, over at...Cornerstone."

Leah returned for the rest of the dishes and paused with an empty juice glass in her hand. "You're the one that switched us to Allstate four years ago because of all those ads you liked, and there's no *good-old-George*, or any other kind of George over there that I'm aware of." She tipped her head slightly. "I think there's maybe a Vince that helped us last time you got in a scrape." She leaned over him with some concern. "Maybe that bonk on the head did more damage than you think."

"Wait just a minute now, that's..." Kendall was automatically getting up on his high horse, determined to defend himself. "That's ridiculous, I remember..."

Josh kicked him carefully under the table and Kendall swallowed whatever he was about to say next. "Ah! Well, I do have a headache this morning – didn't sleep worth a damn again. Hate that CPAP thing! What'd I just say, *George*? Stupid. I meant *Vince*. Yeah, Vince at Allstate, that's right. George?" He glanced in Josh's direction. "Who in the world's George? I must be losing my mind."

Leah gathered the last of the plates and rinsed them and started to load the dishwasher. "Kendall, don't forget the police?"

Kendall was getting up and putting on a baseball cap. "I told you, I won't forget."

"*First.* Do the police *first.*"

"Fine, I'll buy the truck *after* I talk to the insurance company, to Vince, and *after* I talk to the police."

Kendall walked by Leah and gave her a peck on the cheek. "Happy now? Let's go, Josh. You're driving."

Josh stuffed a last bite of dripping toast and handed the dish to his Mom before he followed Kendall out the door.

* * *

The District 2 Cincinnati police department parking lot, off Erie Avenue, was overflowing. An unhappy uniformed officer, wearing a day-glo orange striped vest, straddled the curb at the lot entrance and tried to direct cars in and out. Tempers were short and the right lane blockage on Erie was starting to impede the morning's traffic flow.

Inside the single story brick building, Kendall and Josh were crammed into plastic chairs in a corner of the waiting area. The room was noisy and moist with humanity. Kendall idly flipped a paper tab with the number *73* printed on it as a colorful cross-section of irritated citizenry milled around him. Josh sat relaxed and seemed to enjoy watching some of the more interesting characters nearby.

An unflappable, black female police officer with a clipboard scanned the crowd with experienced eyes before she settled on them. She walked directly up to Kendall, ignoring everyone else, and spoke with an inner city attitude. "You part of the freeway crash?"

Kendall came out of his trance and looked up. "Number 73?"

"Forget that. You told intake you were the red Crewcab?"

"The what? Oh...yeah..."

"The one on the shoulder? Flipped and burned?"

He smiled tiredly. "Sounds like mine."

"We been lookin' fer you." She waved him to his feet with the clipboard. "C'mon."

Both Kendall and Josh nervously got up. The officer stopped, cocked a head and stared hard at Josh. "You in the truck, too?"

Josh nodded with a timid grin. "But just ridin'."

She looked him over and mentally added his face to her list of future perps. "Come on then."

She pushed through the disheveled room like an icebreaker through soft sea ice. Kendall and Josh were tucked in behind her and hoped the crowd didn't pinch back together before they squeezed by. The policewoman never gave a look back as she flowed by the mobbed intake desk and into the station bowels.

Their little flotilla moved down a busy hallway, bearing toward the right side. They passed many people heading the other way: uniformed cops and men in ties, mostly, but none of them made eye contact.

The police woman paused briefly before they turned a corner. "Since you're the red truck, you're goin' to the big room." She smiled grimly and then led them off again.

* * *

The female police officer opened a heavy door with a frosted glass pane labeled *CR-2*. She waved Kendall and Josh into the long, harshly lit conference room and against a wall beside the door. She smiled widely at the room, waiting for everyone to note her entrance, aware that this moment would be jabbered about for days, and more than pleased to be at the center of the cause. "Figured you'd be interested in these guys. Moved 'em to the front of the line. They were in *big red*."

The weary people in the room stopped what they were doing and stared. Some were seated, others were standing in groups, all paused in mid-talk. There were uniformed police, middle-aged men in shirtsleeves, and a few women with beat-up laptops. A cheap metal and laminate conference table held stacks of grisly accident photos, forensics reports, point-of-impact analyses, skid charts, marked up transcripts, and a grubby army of coffee cups.

Unit Leader, Lieutenant Vic Chadek, stood next to a large whiteboard that was literally covered with colored lines and extended notations. Wearing a conservative tie with rolled up shirt sleeves, he held a dry erase marker poised in his hand, and contemplated the interruption with an edgy glare. "No shit?"

The police woman nodded in smug satisfaction, "No shit." She glanced at the other people in the room, winked, and then exited, closing the door solidly behind her.

Vic capped his marker and dropped it onto the metal lip of the whiteboard with a loud clack. He tossed a half-hearted smile towards Kendall and Josh. "You're in a Crash Investigation Unit, gentlemen, and my name's Chadek – Senior Investigator, Lieutenant Vic Chadek. Do I need to tell you two what a hell of a crash we had here?"

They both silently shook their heads.

"I wouldn't think so." Chadek leaned over the table and glowered at them for a few seconds, just because he felt like it. "We're all happy as hell you finally decided to check in, 'cause we weren't havin' a lotta joy readin' VIN numbers off your...remains. You know what I mean?"

They continued to stand quietly against the wall – deer in the headlights.

Chadek pursed his lips as if tasting something sour. " Oh, yeah, why don't you go ahead and take a seat, guys. Sorry."

Kendall and Josh hurriedly grabbed the nearest heavy grey metal chairs available and dropped into them. They placed their hands on the table but their fingers kept vainly searching for something to do.

Vic didn't sit. Instead, he pulled out a chair, angled it and placed a foot on the seat so he could lean over and rest his elbows on his knee. "You got some ID's on ya?"

They quickly dug out drivers' licenses and placed them on the table. Chadek nodded at a nearby officer

70

and the man gathered the cards and left the room. Josh nervously followed the man with his eyes until the door clicked shut behind him.

Chadek motioned at the debris across the table. "Let me tell you about this CIU. We analyze impact speeds, skid marks, point of impact placement, time distance, friction, flammables, roadway factors, lighting – stupidity – you name it. And when we're done, I do a reconstruction. You know what I find, every time?"

He stopped and watched them. His nostrils flared. "I find there's no such thing as an accident. Get it? Things don't just happen – they happen for a reason. There's always a cause, and in a mess like this, there's lotsa causes, but there's always a first cause."

The officer reappeared with their licenses and handed Vic a couple of enlarged printouts. He studied the sheets intensely for a moment and then nodded to the officer. The man snapped the plastic licenses back down on the laminate and returned to his place at the table.

"So...Kendall and Josh..." He looked at each one in turn as he said their name. "Just so you know, I haven't had a lotta sleep and I'm gettin' a lotta heat. It's comin' all the way from the mayor's office, and from Captain Broxterman's office..." His voice was rising. "And all the way down to that Geico lizard, all screamin' at me to finish my damn reconstruction! But I can't! Why?" His words dropped back to a conversational level. "Because I'm a professional."

He leaned even further forward on the table, supporting himself with a hand, and fixed them with a menacing look. "Know what's holdin' me up?"

Kendall and Josh wore empty expressions. They hadn't a single clue what the right answer was but they knew they were in deep trouble.

Chadek didn't blink. "Your truck."

"Our truck?" Kendall spoke louder than he meant to. He quickly lowered his voice. "We were just part of the accident, like everybody else."

"Yeah," Josh chimed in. "What'd we do?"

71

Chadek made a show of arranging his chair and sitting down, but he never broke eye contact. "It's more like what you didn't do." His focus snapped to Kendall's eyes. "And, just for the record, Kendall, you and your truck were not like everybody else."

He cocked his head, first one way and then the other, like a robin listening for worms. "That, boys, is the end of my cheerful little intro to the conversation we're about to have. Comfy?"

Kendall and Josh didn't move a muscle.

"Good. Now, talk to me. Take your time. Take all the time in the world. Tell me exactly why you did what you did and – especially – *when* you did it!"

CHAPTER 10:

QUYRON RUSHED INTO Jonathan Newbauer's outer office and smiled briefly at Sophia, his administrative assistant. "Sorry, I only found out a few minutes ago. Has it already started?"

The solidly built blonde looked up from her wide screen activities and shrugged at Quyron. "Don't worry about it. It was a last minute deal anyway. And they're having problems with the connection – always something." She smirked. "They're probably still working through the what's-up-guy-greeting thing. You know how they are."

"Yes, I do."

Sophia walked briskly over to the inner office door and tapped firmly as she opened it.

Quyron paused in the doorway to comment softly, "I don't know how you stand this every day."

Sophia smiled innocently, "The pay, dear, how else?"

The well-appointed inner office was airy and bright, with sunlight streaming through a bank of windows. Newbauer waved Quyron to come in. He motioned her to take a seat facing one of the triad of screens that formed the centerpiece of his lavish meeting table. Jonathan vainly struggled with a complex remote device trying to improve the severe picture interference washing across the displays. Nothing he did was helping.

The voice audio snarled and popped in some strange signal-to-noise synchronization with the visual distortion. "I...I don't understand but there's...very troubling in the..." Unmistakably, the screen image was the head and shoulders of a man, but it was hard to identify much beyond that.

Quyron seated herself across from Newbauer and close to the image of the man on the screen as he continued, "...need time to evaluate these...and to decide on a..."

The interference came in waves, but plainly, the frequency was increasing. Quyron found herself forced to guess at what he was saying.

"Sorry about all the...Singapore's still tweaking... grid...Did...see Quyron?"

Newbauer made a puzzled face at Quyron. Looking back at the screen, he stabbed at what he hoped was an appropriate response. "Yes, Quyron Shur has just joined us." He spoke loudly and in a slow cadence, as if he was talking to the near deaf.

"Hello, Quyron..." Noise swallowed the rest of the comment and then the voice squawked back, "Wish I could say...nice to...you but...can't...I can't see you, I mean."

"I understand," she replied. Quyron gazed helplessly over at Jonathan. He rolled his shoulders and set the remote down. The man on the screen was talking again.

"They're saying...give up for now...so try audio-only...kay with you?"

Newbauer slowly and loudly replied, "That's Okay with us."

The screens abruptly cut to the Reivers' corporate logo and, thankfully, the audio immediately cleared up. A strong male voice resonated in pristine clarity. "I hope that's – is that better?"

Both Quyron and Newbauer quickly nodded, relieved. Newbauer answered, "Much better. Clear as a bell."

The voice replied, "Good. Okay then. Sorry about all the hassle – they wanted to do a beta test on their paired particle grid – I guess entanglement communication still has a few bugs. Anyway, I just wanted to report that I made the required speeches, I cut the silly ribbons, did the happy handshake routine and put up with all that fuss here, like a good CEO. They take all that so seriously over here. The bottom line is, our Asian Archive is now public, blessed, and official."

"Congratulations! That's great!" Newbauer gushed. "That'll open things up there – the nanos, the searches in other languages, the cash flow, our market penetration, everything."

"Fine, fine," the voice replied flatly.

Newbauer leaned forward. "What about the, ah," he furtively glanced at Quyron. "You know, the rest of the trip?"

"Yeah, yeah, I'm getting to that. Just so you know what's up, Quyron, the other reason for the timing of the trip was a series of hush-hush Beijing meetings. But now with what's happening in the multiverse, I'm thinking of cancelling them to head back immediately. My pilots say if we did that, the turnaround should be able to..."

Newbauer jumped in his chair, as if shot. "What!? You must be joking! That would be a disaster! Do you have any idea the hoops we went through just to get the right officials to even consent to..."

"Shut-up, Jonathan." The rasp of irritated authority vibrated from the speakers. "I know exactly what this could cost us and I'm weighing the options. If you can't remain calm and rational, I don't want you to speak at all. Do you hear me?"

Cowed, Newbauer slumped back a bit in his chair. "Yes sir."

"Quyron?"

"Yes, I'm listening."

"Okay, here's the issue. These Chinese meetings are key to our Asian expansion plans. They could easily double our reach and open whole new timelines, but I'm torn. I'm really worried about the rash of alarms in the archives; in hindsight, I probably should never have left. Echo forwarded your findings but...I still can't quite connect all the dots."

Quyron furrowed her brow. "Neither can I. The apparent loss of access to certain timelines is increasing but I still haven't any idea what's causing it, or how to stop it."

Newbauer watched Quyron and felt his distaste for the woman fester with every word she spoke.

"*Apparent* loss? I wish I had your hope." The voice sounded plaintive, almost resigned.

"It's not hope, sir. I'm just trying to stick to the facts as we know them. The nanos and Echo simply can't locate the missing lines anymore. Once the transmission cuts off, we can't reinstate the links or locate the nanos. That is, technically, all we really know for sure."

"How about the new development – your jumpers? Could they be part of the cause?"

"At this point, I don't know." Quyron was mildly surprised at how current his knowledge was. "I'm working under the assumption that they're a result of something else. But until I have more data, they're a side issue."

"Understood. These timeline transmission troubles are very distressing to me. There's a lot at stake."

"I know that."

"What does Echo say? Any suspicions? Predictions? Does she offer any...suggestions?"

Quyron paused. *What does Echo say? He's in daily contact; he could ask her himself. Or is he concerned about something Echo knows that I'm not asking about?* She replied, "Nothing much. She simultaneously tracks and analyzes everything – but as far as causes go? No. Nothing. Predictions? I'm not sure what you mean. What should I ask her?"

There was an awkward break in the conversation, followed by other, muffled voices. "Sorry, I'm getting an up or down request from our hosts in Beijing. I'm on the fence here – do the meetings, or head back? Any thoughts? Quyron?"

Quyron felt out of her depth. "Sir, I don't know what to advise. You have my reports – I don't know how immediate the threat is, or how serious. I'm feeling my way and I'm very concerned. I'm not sure how much more your presence here will add. You can pretty much follow everything from there. I can't offer much more than that."

"Jonathan?"

Newbauer stared at the logo on the screen and frowned. "From a financial viewpoint, it's a no-brainer. You have to do the meetings. The future of the company depends on our pushing into Asia, and the dollar potential that this represents for us is..."

The voice interrupted with a caustic laugh. "Not to mention your potential bonus, and yaddi-yaddi – got it Jonathan. You can stop with the rah-rah." Jonathan wore a sour look. "Okay. I feel like I have to do the meetings then. But if I get concerned with something I hear, I'll be hightailing it out of here as fast as this jet can go, no matter how that affects the bottom line."

There was another interruption at the other end with hushed voices and some laughter. "Gotta go. There's a meet-and-greet starting here. I'm depending on you, Quyron. Give it your best."

Quyron remained a bit baffled by the conversation. "Thank you, I will. Have a good trip." She turned to Jonathan, wondering if he had anything more to say. Jonathan ignored her and pouted.

"Oh, and Jonathan?" The voice sounded almost jovial now.

After a moment, Jonathan begrudgingly answered, "Yes?"

"Even though I can't see you, I'm sure you're wearing your hurt look. Am I right?" Jonathan's face immediately switched to a neutral expression. The voice continued, "Sorry, I couldn't resist. I'm depending on you, too. Okay? Bye for now."

CHAPTER 11:

DR. HAHN SLID between two man-sized carbon ceramic cradles and ran an affectionate hand across one of the smooth surfaces. Contrived from the marriage of silicon carbide fibers with the high temperature resistant properties of ceramics, the glasslike composite material glistened in a deceptive display of beauty that belied its toughness. The advanced technologies that Hahn had gleaned from the timelines provided her materials engineering team with a polymer route to near stoichiometric silicon carbides and resulted in a matrix composite shell that made her scientific heart glow.

The lower sides and bases of both cradles sprouted thick cables and multi-colored connectors that snaked toward packed equipment racks standing in the aisles between them. Tired teams of technicians moved erratically through the ordered chaos, troubleshooting routers and verifying readouts. While there seemed to be an overall logic to the arrangement of the complex gear and the movements of the staff, the scene was clearly a *work in progress.*

Fargo, a tough looking young female, settled into the fitted seat inside one of the cradles and reached for a sleek pair of virtual reality glasses. Her body glistened in form-fitting cyber fabric and her head was encased in a wire-laden, flexible helmet. In the other cradle, a lean and scarred male slid gracefully into his own cockpit. Salazar pulled on cyber-gloves and adjusted his VR shades with an icy efficiency and then peeked over at Fargo and, unexpectedly, winked.

Large transparent covers, crowned with antennae, hung on cables waiting to seal the riders inside. A senior technician signaled for the lid above Fargo to begin its descent and hopped up the rungs of a small step-stool in preparation for snapping the cockpit locks. He tapped his ear bud communicator as he watched the smooth downward motion of the cover. "Radio check. Go"

Fargo heard the call, glanced up at the tech, and then touched a point next to her ear. "Point net, this is Fargo. Reading you five-by-five."

The cockpit cover settled easily into place and the tech snapped the locks to secure it. "Affirmative. Point net confirms Cradle Alpha is live and wide."

Fargo made a funny face at him, "...and ready to ride!"

On a level above the cradle floor, Hahn entered her glass-walled control room flanked by technicians. At Fargo's quip she twisted to glare back through the windows toward the lower level. She swiftly stepped to one of the consoles and punched a lit button. "This is Point net master control – cut it, Fargo!" Her harsh voice dripped with bitterness. "This is not one of your *ops*, is that clear? This test will remain professional from beginning to end. You hear me?"

Over the speakers came the unfazed, breezy reply. "Yes, Ma'am, clear as clear. Outsy-daisy."

* * *

Vandermark walked quickly down a secure hallway in one of the key buildings of *the Point*, a covert research facility hidden beneath the Reivers corporate umbrella. He was talking rapidly into the phone clip on his lapel. "I'm sorry for that but it's the best we can do. Call me when you're groundside. And don't use that paperwork unless you absolutely have to."

The small, highly secure campus of buildings that made up *the Point* was only five miles north of the Reivers headquarters, on the other side of the South River Bridge in Anne Arundel County, but virtually unknown to the employees of the mother company. A recent addition to *the Reive's* holdings through a third party proxy, *the Point* had been quietly carved from the heavy woods just east of the town of Parole, Maryland, and a few hundred yards below the Harry S. Truman Parkway. The nearby sleepy town had earned its name from its history as the Civil War site where Union and Confederate POWs were exchanged.

Vandermark turned a corner in the windowless hall and approached a security guard blocking access to a metal door. He spoke quietly into his phone, "Taylor, hold on. I'm at a checkpoint."

The young guard looked up as Vandermark irritably waved a lanyard with his photo ID at him. The officer smiled in nervous recognition, "Good morning, Dr. Vandermark."

Vandermark ignored the greeting and simply stepped up to slots in the wall beside the door. He slipped a hand into the fingerprint reader and stared into the eye level retinal scanner as he clearly vocalized the words, "Neville Vandermark."

The door buzzed as the lock released. The guard started to wish him a good day but Vandermark had already rushed through. In fact, he was already talking into his communicator again. "Okay, back. I'm about to view the trials now but the truck's already in final phase. If everything checks out, we'll be mobile by the time you get back."

He listened for a brief moment and then spat back, "Deal with it! Just make sure you get both of them. Call me when it's done."

He tapped the phone clip, cutting the connection, and entered a small elevator.

* * *

Hahn sat at the center of her master console and studied multiple screens that showed two bored security guards standing outside a door: one was tall and thin, the other overweight and short. Hahn spoke to Fargo and Salazar using a nearly invisible, fiber-thin headset. "These are Echo's suggested targets within our range. They stand just outside the wall to this building, but fifteen timelines away."

Behind her, exiting the elevator, Vandermark moved into her line of sight and nodded. Hahn gave him the slightest of reactions, and continued her briefing. "You will test targeting and jump entry; you will execute the full set of control parameters we talked about, and finally jump exit and jump re-entry."

Inside Cradle Alpha, Fargo studied the two guards in her VR glasses. She blinked through multiple screens and settled on the heads-up-display, swinging her cross-haired targeting reticle from one guard's head to the other. "Damn! I know these guys. And here I thought Echo was gonna find me a girl for this test. I know I'm gonna hate jumpin' into guys."

Hahn scowled at the comment over the open mike but plowed on with a little heightened intensity. "Of course you know them, what did you expect? Pay attention. In this test, the start of the jump is triggered by you, but the end of the jump..."

Salazar's voice on the line interrupted her. "Admit it Fargo, it's not the guys you hate, it's their male organized minds."

Fargo shot back, "Oh yeah? Let's just see who gets mind control first then, smart guy."

Hahn erupted with a blistering voice. "Enough! Both of you!" She slashed a quick, menacing look at Vandermark and continued in a harsh tone. "Listen to me! I said the start of the jump is yours, but I can stop it at any time. Understand? *Any time!*"

Fargo smiled to herself as she watched the targeted guards slouching around their door. She ignored Hahn's comments and goaded Salazar. "Tell you what, Mr. Organized. I'll let you pick your target first and I'll still beat ya."

Leaping up from her chair, Hahn's face flushed with splotches of anger. Her English language suddenly defaulted to a more basic form. "You not listening! This is test, not stupid game!"

Hahn was ready to pull the plug on the whole process. She stared defiantly at Vandermark, ready to do battle, when Salazar's unruffled voice floated out of the speakers.

"Look Doc, don't get your undies in a twist, okay? We got ya covered. You do your thing up there in the fancy lab, and let us do ours down here in the...*multicaves*. No worries."

Hahn swallowed hard and took a sharp breath. She stiffly sat back down in her control chair and tightened her jaw. "I am not in twist, you...shit. I am trying to give instructions to imbeciles." Her console techs turned, surprised at her language.

In her cradle, Fargo grinned, knowing they'd gotten Hahn's goat. "We're cool, doc. Been called worse. You go ahead."

Hahn ignored the looks around her and steeled herself. "Okay. Remember, after you jump, we can see and hear you in the archive monitors, but we're five seconds behind. And once you're riding, you can't hear us."

Salazar gave a thumbs-up to Fargo. "We got it, doc. We did read the material. Let's get it on." Fargo smiled back in his direction and flipped him off.

Hahn was unrelenting. "And don't expect to read their minds. That is not possible. Don't even try. Your job is just to take control."

Fargo's exasperated voice came back over the speaker. "Doc, throw the switch, will ya?"

Vandermark reached over Hahn's shoulder and depressed the talkback button. "This is Vandermark. Cut the bullshit. Focus on the goal. This needs to go well. Don't disappoint me."

Hahn flipped a switch and pushed a couple of buttons. Beside her, the techs monitored their individual readouts and nodded assent. Hahn looked down at the sealed-in jumpers, a level below her. "Echo, activate the cradles."

"Initiated, Dr. Hahn," the familiar female voice immediately replied over the speakers.

A low pitched tone thrummed from the walls and rose in strength as the console readouts went active.

"Power nominal," Echo continued. "Targeting active. Transfer potential online."

In the jumper lab, the technicians stepped back from the sealed cradles as the thrumming climbed the scale. Inside the cockpits, Fargo and Salazar tensed as they waited for the go-ahead. Around them, the composite skin of their cradles glowed and began to change hue.

* * *

Two tired guards stood watch near a closed exterior door. The thin one swirled dirt with his foot. "What time is it?"

The heavier guard leaned against a wall, rocking his torso back and forth in a repetitive motion, and scowled. "What difference does it make?"

"Just wonderin'."

"Well stop wonderin'. You already asked me that anyway."

"I know." He kept working the dirt with the toe of his shoe. "I was just wonderin' how much time passed since the last time I asked."

"Shut-up. It won't make it go any faster."

"Yeah, but..."

"Hey?"

"What?"

"Cover for me, will ya? I'm dyin' here." The fat guard hoisted his bulk from the wall and took a step away. "I gotta go see a man about a horse."

"A horse?" The thin guard looked queerly at his partner.

The heavy guard turned back. "That's what my Dad used to say whenever – aw, forget it. Look, I gotta take a leak, okay? 'Sides, all they can do is fire me."

"You can't. What'll I say if they call?"

The fat guard shook his head as he walked off a short distance. "Tell 'em I'm...takin' a whiz! I don't care." There was the distinctive sound of urinating. "C'mon, they're not gonna call anyway, and besides...WHOAH!"

Both guards abruptly jerked upright into stiff, unnatural poses. They staggered with awkward steps and twisted at the hips. Suddenly, the guard who was urinating, charged his partner.

"Sal! You creep! You knew he was peein' and you forced me to jump him anyway! I'm gonna kill ya!"

Under Fargo's control, the fat guard viciously kicked the legs out from under his still flailing partner. The thin guard fell heavily to the sidewalk and howled, grabbing a knee.

Fargo looked down at the wet stain on the fat guard's pants and made a face. "Disgusting!"

Salazar, inside the skinny guard, finally gained control and forced him painfully back to his feet. "You said it was my pick. What a whiner!"

"Pretty clear who got control first, huh? Loser!" Fargo threw a wild roundhouse punch that should have dropped the skinny guard, except that Salazar ducked, just in time. Unbalanced, the fat guard's follow through almost spun him to the ground.

"Really? I'm not so sure you're in control." Salazar danced around Fargo, taunting and poking her ride. "Hey fat girl, your zipper's down."

Livid, Fargo vainly tried to swiftly rotate the fat guard in opposite directions to catch Salazar, but the skinny guard was always ahead of her.

All of a sudden, Salazar slapped Fargo viciously in the face and then ran off, laughing and leaping. "Catch me if you can, little Miss! Hoo-hoo! Look at me!"

"Dammit! This body's such a tub-a-lard! C'mon! Step on it, fatso!" Fargo pushed the out-of-shape guard to the max but she was helpless to grab Salazar. "Wait'll I get his hands on you!"

"Dream on, lard-butt, all you can do is sweat. You're too late anyway." The thin guard easily dodged the fat guard's feeble attempts to corner him. "Time's up. Remember? Hahn said we gotta practice doin' the old switcheroo. So...see ya around!"

The thin guard abruptly stopped moving. Slack jawed, he shook his head and swayed on his feet.

Awake inside his cradle again, Salazar studied his HUD and swung the cross-hairs off the skinny guard and locked onto the fat guard's head. His finger touched the trigger as he broke into a nasty grin. "Target, lock, and jump!"

Both guards once again jerked and twitched but they were soon back under the control of the jumpers. Unfortunately for Salazar, once again, even with his lead, he wasn't first. Fargo, now inside the thinner, quicker body, immediately seized the heavy guard by the shoulders and jerked him brutally toward her as she head-butted him in the face. "Welcome back, slow poke! Who's in control now? Hoo-hoo yourself, fat boy!"

Salazar, inside the fat guard, shrieked in pain and pawed at his nose and eyes. Fargo pranced in a circle around Salazar, mocking him. "C'mon, test those parameters! Fatty-fatty two-by-four, can't fit through the bathroom door! Let's go! Time's a wastin'!" She pointed at his pants and laughed. "Hey buddy boy, your zipper's *still* down!"

Salazar looked down and made a show of bending over as if to zip up but it was only to cover his sudden reach for the ground. The fat guard came up fast with a handful of dirt and tossed it in Fargo's face. The skinny guard groaned and grabbed for his eyes. Taking advantage, Salazar crushed him to the ground with a bruising tackle. "Who's down now, *girlfriend*?"

Fargo instantly bucked him off with a knee to the groin. Both rolled around on the ground trying to get the upper hand. The struggle abruptly escalated. It was obvious that the mind riders had acclimated themselves to the bodies they controlled. Fierce kicks and raw punches flew back and forth. Attacks and defenses that neither guard had any experience with flashed between the two men as their riders sought to disable each other.

In the control room, Hahn glared at the archive screens showing the intense fighting. She turned to Vandermark with a look of loathing. "What is wrong with your people?"

Vandermark calmly returned her look. "It's what you asked for. They're testing everything you require – they're just doing it their own way."

"Well, I've had enough of them and their own way. This test is over." Hahn stabbed the jump override button on the console and then glowered for the entire five long seconds of waiting until both guards suddenly went slack and the jump ended.

* * *

Outside their door, both guards writhed on the ground and moaned in agony. For them, the injuries were real and some of the damage would be permanent. The skinny guard rolled to a sitting position, keeping his hands on his face while fresh blood coursed between his fingers. "You broke my nose! I'm bleedin' like a stuck pig! What the hell got into you?"

"Me? What's with the Kung Fu crap!" The fat guard rocked back and forth in a fetal position, his hands shoved in his crotch. "Oh God, I think I'm bleeding inside. Hey, I can't feel my feet." His legs made feeble crawling movements. "And you head-butted me!"

* * *

Hoists lifted the unlocked cradle covers. Technicians started the laborious task of unhooking helmet and body connections. Removing their glasses, Salazar and Fargo looked around. They were keyed up and excited – like star players at half time when their team was winning. Sal explored his face with inquisitive fingers and Fargo gingerly touched her nose. They were physically unmarked and completely unhurt. They looked at each other and started laughing.

Salazar tapped his communicator and glanced up toward the control room. "Hey Doc, why so quick? We were just startin' to get a feel for things. Man what a rush!"

At the control room windows, Hahn watched the opened cradles and the riders with open contempt, and didn't bother to answer Sal. She flicked a look up. "Echo, all data on this test is part of *the Point* access protocol."

"Of course, Dr. Hahn."

Vandermark joined her at the glass. Hahn refused to look at him as she asked, "When will I be allowed to use competent help again?"

Vandermark reacted with sudden heat. "When my project is done!" He belatedly realized he had spoken too harshly. *Damn this woman! If I didn't need her...stop that! You're better than this. You catch more flies with honey than vinegar.*

He tried again, softer this time. "Look, Song Lee, I appreciate how you feel, but you know we both want the same outcome; we only disagree on the path. Can't you see that?"

Hahn gave no ground at all. It no longer mattered to her if they agreed on anything. "What other questions do you have for me?"

Vandermark gave up on his clumsy subtlety. "Suit yourself! I consider this test a success. Now get going and make sure everything's ready for the truck."

Hahn stiffened and walked away from him.

The two hapless guards were still visible on the screens as they continued to rock in agony. The skinny guard struggled to get to his feet and failed. Vandermark's eyes passed across them, unmoved.

"Wait! I do have one other question. What about the range issue?"

Hahn stopped. "The range is still the range. Nothing new. All we've learned is that if we're not within a hundred yards...the rider can't ride. That's all."

Vandermark scowled at her. "Still a hundred yards! That's gonna be a bitch."

Hahn rotated her shoulders so she could give him a slight, ironic smile, and then left the room.

87

CHAPTER 12:

LONG STRINGS OF BLUE and white plastic pennants hung listlessly above sparkling rows of new cars and trucks. Jake Sweeney Chevrolet occupied more than half of the block between West Kemper Road and Princeton Pike, and had been in business at that location for more than thirty years. In fact, a third generation of Sweeney's lurked just inside the showroom doors, dressed in ties and shirtsleeves, and ready to sell anything with wheels.

Kendall had decided on the truck he wanted as soon as he was done with his Allstate agent, but it took most of the day, and three dealerships, to find the right flavor.

The wide garage doors on the outside wall of the main building slowly lifted as a new, black Chevy Silverado V8 rolled out and pulled next to the showroom doors to honk its horn.

Inside the waiting area, Josh took a quick look up from his open laptop to spot his dad motioning at him from the truck. He quickly grabbed his jacket, tucked the computer under his arm, and hurried out, muttering to himself, "Finally."

Surrounded by the black and gray interior of the pickup, Josh breathed in the heady scent of new leather and looked at Kendall's smiling face. "Happy now?"

Kendall waved his arm around. "So, whaddya think of her?"

"What can I say? Black is your color."

Kendall put the truck in gear and drove toward the exit from the lot. "I'll take you for a spin before I drop you back at your car."

Josh clicked his seat belt and burrowed into the leather. "Nice! How much more was this than the old one?"

Kendall pulled out onto West Kemper and made a satisfied noise with his mouth. "Well…think about this. My credit's better now than it ever was before."

Josh considered that for a few seconds. "No, that's not right. You mean it's better *here* than it was *there*." Josh flipped open his laptop and propped it beside him on the large center armrest.

"Yeah, however you want to say it – then, now, here, there, whatever." Kendall smirked. "Where's *there* anyway?"

Josh stopped fooling with his laptop long enough to look seriously at his father. "As far as I can understand things, *there* is *here* too."

Kendall checked the traffic and turned left onto Princeton Pike to head toward highway 275, planning to show off his purchase at freeway speeds.

Josh rotated his laptop back and forth. "Ooo! Wait. Wait! Pull over! Now!"

Skittish with his new ride, Kendall suddenly yanked the truck across a lane, swerved up against a curb and braked. He anxiously looked around. "What? I don't see any brake lights. What's wrong?"

Josh watched the lower corner of his laptop screen as he tipped and turned the computer. "Damn, I had three bars. Now I got none."

"Huh?"

"Back it up – maybe twenty feet or so." He hunched over the seat and pointed back at a car battery shop. "Over near that office, I bet."

Kendall scowled darkly but dumped it into reverse and slowly backed up.

Josh kept his eyes on the corner of his screen. "Yeah, better. Yeah...there! Good. Park it right here. Great!" He clicked on his browser and watched it load.

Kendall started tapping his fingers on the black leather-wrapped steering wheel. He twisted his rear-view mirror until he could see Josh's intent face. "Hey Josh?"

"Yeah."

"What are we doin'?"

"Ridin' their connection." He looked up defensively. "Hey, if they didn't want people to ride, they shoulda encrypted it, y'know? It's not that hard." He typed a website address into his browser and hit *enter*.

Kendall rubbed his eyes. "Okay. But...so you're gettin' a free ride to the internet. Why now?"

"Cause we're lookin' for Hugh Everett. The physicist, remember?" Josh keyed a user name and password into a website welcome page.

"Yeah...well, *you're* lookin'."

Josh waited for the website to confirm his account and load the members' home page. "See, here's the deal. The *new me* happens to be a member of *Net Detective*, the number one internet detective site."

"The new you, huh?"

"Yeah. The new guy inside – from here."

"So, you found out this new paranoid Josh of yours joined a private detective site?"

"Uh, just a sec." Josh spelled the letters out loud as he typed. "H-U-G-H, space, E-V-E-R-E-T-T, enter. Okay. Uhh, M-A-R-Y-L-A-N-D, enter. Okay."

Josh looked up at his dad and thought for a moment. "He – I joined a month ago – $9.95 for three months. I mean not *me*, I mean the *me* in this time-line...is what I mean."

Kendall played with his deluxe visor and flipped the vanity mirror lights off and on. "I wonder what happened a month ago in this timeline that would make you join a detective site?"

Josh's face was devoid of any expression for a few seconds. "What happened to me? I mean, what happened to *this me*?" It suddenly all clicked together for him. "Oh, to make me join, you mean? Just a sec, let me think about that."

Josh paused and mentally sorted through his doubled memories and then grinned wickedly. "Which Dad is askin'?"

"Which dad?" Kendall rolled his eyes. "Oh, forget it! Are you done yet, or can you speed it up so we can take our ride?"

Josh checked the Net Detective's results. "Hmm. Lots of Everett's in Maryland. Hey, wait. A couple of these actually look pretty good. As a matter of fact, let me see..."

Kendall was tired from the day. "You know findin' this guy won't help. His theory's crap. I can't even understand it."

Josh busily moved his mouse and selected something new. "Hugh Everett's a place to start, that's all I'm hopin'. If he's alive..."

An impressive array of new results populated the screen and a slow smile lit up Josh's face. "Well, well, well, good old Net Detective. Look at this. There's an 87-year-old Hugh Everett living in the Althea Woodland Nursing Home in Silver Spring, Maryland. There's even a MapQuest link. Cool."

Kendall remained unengaged. "How do you know it's even him? Like you said, there's probably plenty of Everett's."

Josh smugly stuck his face closer to his screen. "Because I know *this* Hugh Everett got a physics Ph.D. from Princeton in 1949. And he worked at the Pentagon – that's a nice salary for the time. Bought and sold houses in Virginia and Maryland – boy, real estate's gone up..."

Kendall swiveled in his seat, shocked. "That stupid site knows all that?"

Josh scoffed, "Oh, that's just the top level." He scanned the offerings on the left side menu. "I could also check his credit history, mortgages, military records, secondary school and college GPA's, passport and visa info, criminal records, longitude...*longitude?* Are they kidding?"

Kendall was hooked. "Does it have his phone number? Maybe we could just call him."

"Sure." Josh hurriedly checked his list of entries and then checked again. He shook his head. "Nothin' listed."

Kendall slapped the steering wheel and blew out a breath of air. "Oh for cryin' out loud! It's got all that other worthless stuff for you to play around with but no phone? Stupid!"

Kendall flipped on his blinker and checked the side mirror. "Your free ride's done. I'm droppin' you back at the car."

Unfazed, Josh continued to study the Everett information. "I dunno. Weird. But at least he's alive, and we found him."

Kendall pulled out. Somebody honked. Kendall growled back in a fury as he accelerated.

"Dad, you know we gotta go there and at least talk to him."

Kendall switched lanes and made a sudden U-turn to head back to the dealership. He refused to answer Josh or even look at him. With a quick punch of a finger on his steering wheel controls, he turned on the radio and let it blast out a piece of music.

"Dad?"

* * *

Leah paid no attention to the usual morning concert of birds chirping in the trees outside the bedroom. She watched as Kendall packed a suitcase opened on the bed. "I still don't understand why you have to go to Maryland, of all places. We don't know anyone there. And why so sudden?"

Kendall went into the bathroom and pulled together a toiletries bag. "It's complicated."

"And Josh too?"

"Josh too."

Kendall zipped up the toiletries bag and dropped it into the suitcase. Leah sighed. "And I suppose the reason is complicated for him too?"

"Trust me." He shoveled underwear, T-shirts and socks from his dresser to the bag.

Leah folded her arms. "What about work?"

"I have sick time. I checked."

"What about Josh? He just started."

Kendall checked the bag for anything he'd forgotten. "He's takin' time off without pay." He tossed in a few handkerchiefs and closed the top, and avoided looking at her. "What is this, a thousand questions?" He pulled the large metal zippers closed around the suitcase until they met at the handle. He hoisted it off the bed and set it on the floor.

Leah watched him check his pockets to confirm his billfold, phone and keys. "I just wish I knew why you two won't tell me what's going on."

Kendall stepped up to Leah and gently touched her shoulders. "'Cause we can't. Just gimme a kiss and stop worryin'."

Leah dutifully kissed him. Kendall held her eyes with his for a beat. "I'll call you. Believe me, I'd explain if I thought I could. I'm sorry. We gotta go if we're gonna catch the plane."

He lifted the suitcase and headed out. Leah walked behind him as far as the bedroom door, and stopped. Her eyes were filled with worry.

Kendall moved quickly down the stairs. "Josh? Let's go."

CHAPTER 13:

THE MCCASLIN FRONT doorbell rang twice. Kendall walked in from the kitchen and passed the staircase on his way to the front door. "Josh," he called upstairs, "we need to leave right away, okay? I'll get the door."

Behind him, Leah stopped in the kitchen doorway to watch. She was finishing a last cup of coffee and already wore a denim jacket with her purse over her shoulder. She was all set to ride along with Josh to the airport; ready to be sad again when she waved him goodbye. She used to think that mothering ended somewhere after high school or college, but that was before she became a mother. Now she knew that moms didn't have expiration dates.

Kendall opened the door to a trio of large men on his porch. Taylor Nsamba stood nearest to the door and smiled warmly at him. "Good day. How are you, Mr. McCaslin?"

The imposing African was impeccably dressed. He had his hands clasped loosely in front of him. A half step back on either side, Aaron Benton and another thick-shouldered security agent nonchalantly looked on.

Kendall was puzzled as he studied the men. "Fine. I'm fine. Have we met?"

Nsamba tried to put him at ease. "No, no, not at all. I'm sorry if I confused you. I'll be brief, I promise. I just need to ask you and your son, Josh, a few questions. Would that be possible?"

Leah drifted in from the kitchen doorway to the foyer to get a better look. "Kendall, who's at the door?"

Kendall sensed something wasn't right. "Sorry, but we're just heading for the airport. My son's been home on leave from the army and...we're kind of in a hurry." He put on a pleasant expression as he reached to shut the door. "Maybe some other time?"

Josh, in military fatigues, appeared at the head of the stairs with a huge duffel bag and started down.

Nsamba briefly noticed Josh in the background and nodded at Kendall, "I understand, but it's important. And it will take but a moment, I assure you. If we could just step inside."

"Not now," Kendall replied firmly. "We really need to leave. Sorry." He started to close the door.

Nsamba put a firm hand against it. "Please?"

Kendall pondered the hand and the two silent men watching him. He thought he saw their bodies tense, and he noticed something metallic glisten in their hands. "Get the hell off my porch! All of you!"

Nsamba stepped back. The two agents promptly closed ranks, and aimed pistol-shaped electroshock stunners.

Benton spoke in a peaceful, everyday voice. "Let's do this the easy way, shall we?"

Kendall tried to slam the door but the men were already moving through it. There was a sudden blue spark accompanied by an electronic snarl. Kendall dropped like a stone and had a massive seizure on the welcome mat. Leah screamed. Her coffee cup shattered on the tile. She reached out to help her husband but was violently shoved aside as the men invaded the front hall.

Benton spotted Josh. "There's the other one, on the stairs!"

Josh saw his father convulsing on the floor and his mother crawling to reach him. *What the hell!* Two men charged up the stairs brandishing weapons and shouting. His eyes narrowed. *Oh no you don't! I'm not that easy!* For Josh, everything suddenly slowed down as he flashed into a serene, adrenaline powered zone, and his combat training took over.

He effortlessly hurled his heavy bag onto the startled men and nimbly vaulted the banister. The agents fell in a painful tangle. Benton tumbled backwards down the stairs, striking his head on a riser, and dropped his stunner.

Josh sprinted for the front door but saw more agents rushing in. Two of them already restrained his Mom. He changed directions and raced for the kitchen, hoping the back door was still clear. Benton, at the bottom of the stairs, grabbed at his legs to slow him. Josh viciously kicked his face and swept up the fallen stunner in two smooth movements as he dashed by.

He bolted through the kitchen. Two more agents burst in the back door. He stabbed at the first one with the stolen gun and pulled the trigger. The stunner snarled and flashed; the agent shuddered in full body spasms, scattering kitchen chairs as he fell. The other lunged at Josh, but he was off balance and narrowly missed. Josh used the man's forward motion to yank him down into his up thrust knee. The man collapsed with a grunt. Josh danced out the open door and rushed headlong into the backyard.

Pausing to pick a direction, Josh darted left across the stone patio. He intended to leap the neighbor's fence. Always a fast runner, his long strides quickly ate up the distance to the barrier. His mind raced with plans to get a phone, steal a car, call out to a neighbor, find some way to get help. Suddenly, a white hot jolt of pain erased it all. He fought the thrashing convulsions with every fiber of his adrenaline saturated body but he finally collapsed face down in the dirt, twitching. A dart with a tiny antenna protruded from a muscle near his shoulder.

Nsamba and a couple of security agents crossed the patio. They looked down at him. Other agents, some limping, joined them. Aaron Benton walked up to the group with a bloody handkerchief pressed tightly against one side of his face.

Nsamba shook his head as he looked around. "That was messy. Okay, clean it up before the neighbors get curious. Pull the van in the garage and load everybody there."

The agents worked smoothly together. One knelt on Josh's spine and zip-tied his hands behind his back. Another jerked a black cloth bag over his head. The agent who was limping zip-tied his ankles and gave Josh a parting kick in the kidneys before he was dragged off.

Benton ran his tongue around the inside of his bleeding mouth, exploring the damage that Josh's foot had made. "We're gonna hafta take the wife too, right?"

Nsamba shrugged irritably. "We are now, yes. We have no choice."

Benton nodded as the two of them headed back into the house. They waited at the outside kitchen door while agents exited with an injured partner slung between them. "Kid put up quite a fight, didn't he? Still, when I was younger and smarter, he would never have had a chance."

Nsamba raised his eyebrows and glanced Benton's way. "Too bad we are neither now."

CHAPTER 14:

IN MIDDAY TRAFFIC on a Maryland freeway, a compact rental car sped by with its blinker on. It crossed a lane and took exit 29-B to the right.

Inside the cramped car, Kendall and Josh leaned forward, straining to see the street sign at the end of the ramp. Josh clutched a crumpled printout and nervously looked back and forth from the paper to the road ahead. Kendall spotted the sign first. "That's Buckingham. Okay, left."

He turned left onto a tree-lined road that passed through an old, stately neighborhood. Each house had its own character and the yards were large. Kendall vainly checked each intersection. "I thought you used to have a street-by-street thingy on your phone."

"Yeah, I did...once," Josh shot back, annoyed. "And I used to have a girlfriend, too."

"Oh, yeah." Kendall's jaw clenched. "Sorry. Never mind." He sniffed, wishing he'd never brought it up. "What's next?"

Josh took a breath. He consulted his printout. "Make a right on Weaver, and then we should see it on the left side."

Kendall made an exasperated sound. Josh looked up. "What now?"

"Nothing...it's stupid. *We're* stupid!"

Josh was upset. "It's not stupid to try to figure out what happened to us."

"It's not that; it's just that the closer I get to this guy, the dumber this feels. According to him we just made a buncha *worlds* everywhere we didn't make those wrong turns. And we made more where we coulda gone straight but didn't – doesn't that sound stupid to you?"

Josh looked out the window. "There's Weaver. Take a right."

The rental car turned right. Soon it passed a thick wooden sign with carved flowers and raised letters that read, *Welcome to Althea Woodland Nursing Home.* Kendall pulled into the small designated parking lot just beyond the sign and stopped. Josh got out first. He slowly looked around.

The nursing home was a well maintained single level structure with large windows and a pleasant rustic feel. A wide and gently curved sidewalk led from the parking lot to the main entrance. There was a relaxed atmosphere about the place that hid the highly efficient and medically astute underpinnings. The main building was split into two wings – one side dedicated to self sufficient seniors, the other to less ambulatory residents. All of the rooms had generous sized windows that faced the gardens and trees that were the hallmark of the facility.

Josh bent over and peered into the car at his father. "You gettin' out?"

Kendall pulled the key and opened his door. "I don't like places like this." He came around the front of the car and doggedly headed up the sidewalk toward the front doors. "I don't wanna end up in one, and I don't wanna visit the inmates who did."

Josh stood by the car watching him walk away. Kendall looked back. "What are you waiting for? This was your idea."

* * *

A husky, middle-aged nurse's aide, with a softened New York dialect, happily guided Kendall and Josh down a wide carpeted hallway in the home. The décor was cheerful and there were numerous residents out and about. Kendall was jumpy and Josh was subdued, but the chatty nurse's aide was in her zone.

"See, nursing homes, they're like their own little towns – friendly, but everybody's nose is stuck right up everybody else's business. I mean, you know how it is, if you sneeze, the other gal wipes her nose, you know?"

She patted the shoulder of a slender woman with wispy hair pushing a walker. "Hey Louise, you're really toolin'. I hear they got snacks in the sun room. First one gets the pick of the litter."

As they moved on she noticed that Kendall was keeping to the center of the hall. "First time?"

Kendall reluctantly raised his eyes. "Been other places. Not here."

"Yeah, it can get to you when you're not used to it. Me? I love it here, I really do, honest, but I'll give you a tip, you can't judge a book by its cover, you know? Some of the best lookin' residents we got here, ain't all here. Take Mr. Montgomery over there."

She waved at a dapper man with an empty look gliding along the wall railing. "Hey Monty, how's it goin'? Nice threads." The good looking man's face brightened briefly at the words. Just as quickly, his eyes slipped back out of focus again.

The aide leaned in to them and lowered her voice as they continued by. "Spiffy, huh? Always in a different suit, cuff links even. He was a buyer for Nordstrom's, got clothes to die for, but nothin' upstairs to match. And he doesn't talk. I only heard him say one word, once; and then it wasn't really a word, word, you know? He was rubbin' the sleeve on his suit and he looks at me and says, '129,' just like that."

She crossed to the other side of the hall to brush the hand of a wheelchair-bound woman rolling herself along using her feet. "Bernice, nice to see you outta that room. What happened? TV on the fritz?"

They made their way across the connecting hallway through large opened doors from the more ambulatory wing to the more disabled side. The number of aides working in the hall and in the rooms markedly increased. Josh noticed that the smells had intensified as well. He heard the unnerving sounds of dementia from behind a few of the closed doors.

"Feels different here, don't it?" The nurse's aide motioned around them. "The residents call it *crossing to the other side*, like *hasta la vista*, you know? We call it *going to the far side* 'cause things can get pretty curious over here."

She pointed forward at a room with the door nearly shut. "That's his room, ahead on the left. Dr. Everett - now he's a special case. He's not a real doctor; he's one of those other kinds, you know, some numbers guy. He was here before I got here, and he's still here. Guys don't usually hang on that long. Anyway, he's a real special case. He don't look like much but he's there. You know?" She tapped stubby fingers against her forehead. "He's really all there. Nothin' typical about him."

She pushed open the door. "Well, here you are." When they hesitated to move, she smirked at them. "Go on. He ain't gonna bite ya. He can't even get outta the bed."

Kendall and Josh timidly entered a narrow, darkened room. A silent TV dangled on an empty wall. The blinds were closed tightly over the huge windows, denying any knowledge of the day outside. A bedside tray held a plastic cup with an articulated straw poking through the lid. Nearby, making a crumpled tent under the sheets, in the center of a high-sided hospital bed, was Hugh Everett III. He was a twisted and wizened old man, and his shallow breathing carried a rattle in it.

Josh realized that he was walking bent over, on tiptoes. Feeling foolish, he stood up straight and cleared his throat. "Excuse me?"

There was no response from the bed.

101

Josh went closer, put his hands on the side rails, and looked down at him. "Mr. Everett? Can you hear me? Are you Hugh Everett?"

Old Everett opened surprisingly bright eyes, blinked wetly, and studied Josh. His voice, when it came, was thin and small. "Heard ya the first time."

Josh just stood there. "...okay."

"I'm Everett. Have we talked before?"

"What? No."

Everett stared at Josh's face. "You from here?"

"Ah, no...not from the nursing home."

"I know that much." Hugh's irritated voice seemed to be warming up. He tried again. "You from here?"

"Okay. I...think so. Why?"

Old Everett grunted. The answer didn't suit him. "No. Not a *why* question. A position question." His tongue studiously explored a cheek. "This isn't a dream, is it?"

"No."

"Good, 'cause I was having this dream that...where did you two come from?"

Kendall stood awkwardly in the center of the room and decided to pitch in. "Ohio? We took a plane from Ohio."

Everett exhaled noisily in annoyance. Gnarled fingers appeared from beneath the sheets to scratch his nose. He blinked repeatedly. He motioned *no* at Kendall with a finger. "Bracket that. Restart everything. My fault. Different question."

Everett took hold of a rail. He pulled himself steadily closer to Josh. "You ever heard about parallel worlds?"

Josh cracked a hopeful smile. "I read your paper."

Hugh's eyebrows went up. "That's a first. Understand it?"

"Not all of it."

"S'okay." Everett coughed and hacked at something in his dry throat. He motioned feebly at the bedside tray table.

Josh looked and then understood. He brought the water glass over and stuck the straw between the old man's dry lips. Everett sucked in some liquid and then waved the glass away.

"Try again. New approach." He caught Kendall's eyes. "Think before you answer, 'kay?"

The two nodded their heads in unison.

Everett made a clicking sound with his teeth. He narrowed his eyes. "Are both of you from this, ah...timeline?"

Josh and Kendall looked at each other with relief. They seemed to relax and get excited all at the same time. Josh spoke first. "We're not sure. We don't think so. That's why we came to find you."

Each grabbed a chair and shoved it close to the bedside of the shriveled old man. Kendall came relatively close to smiling. "We didn't...start here, in this...time deal, whatever you call it. At least I don't think we did. We were born somewhere else but we're here now – but we remember both times – if that's what you mean?"

The old man smiled with growing excitement. His arthritic fingers coiled and uncoiled in pleasure. "I think *that* just might be exactly what I mean." His eyes danced. "Tell me how you got here. Tell me everything – every single thing – exactly."

The words began to flood out of Josh like a river in the spring. "See, we were in these car accidents and they kept happening over and over until, until we survived; but some of the things here are wrong, like the color of Dad's truck and my car, and I have a PC instead of a Mac, and Mom is alive again but Hannah's missing and...I mean, not everything, but...it's messed up, you know?"

Everett drank it in like nectar. "It's not messed up; it's an alternate, a line that follows a new path. Think of it as a child line to your parent timeline. If it wasn't different, it wouldn't work."

Josh stared at the old man, astonished by the implications. He didn't know what he thought; he wasn't sure he could even take in what the old man had said.

Everett abruptly cocked his head. "Wait a minute. You jumped lines, and yet you kept your memory of the former lines? Is that what you meant?"

Josh looked at him blankly, trying to follow. "I don't know about jumping lines, but things just switched without any warning and then both memories were there – all the memories – new ones and old ones, all jumbled up. That's what's so hard; there's new memories that half of you doesn't remember, and then old ones that all of you knows aren't true anymore."

Kendall chimed in. "Yeah, it's tough to keep everything straight. And we're afraid to explain what's goin' on inside because it sounds..." He lowered his voice, "It sounds insane."

Everett's face became suddenly thoughtful. "Jumping and remembering...neither one should happen, but both together? That's absolutely not supposed to be... allowed."

Growing excited, he hooked his other crippled hand around the bedrail. With surprising strength, he yanked himself up into a near sitting position. "And sudden death is the trigger! Strange, but hey, what do I know? That's why it's a theory." He giggled to himself. "Wouldn't Schrodinger's cat have been surprised?"

Josh and Kendall weren't following the old man's comments at all but they kept watching him, confused.

"Whose cat?" Kendall asked.

Everett's eyes glowed in the brightness of an epiphany. "Forget the cat. Schrodinger's dead. It's you that's important. Who would have suspected? Nature's wild card! I'm glad I'm still here. I've been waiting a long time for people like you."

Kendall felt lost. And when that happened, he usually grew cynical. "Like us? People like us? Whaddya mean waitin' for people like us? What the hell are we?"

Everett swayed as he barely held his position against the bed rail, but his face glowed. "Think of yourselves as counterweights. You're what's going to bring everything back into balance."

They looked at him and tried to fathom what he meant. Finally, Kendall pushed back in his chair. The rubber feet squeaked loudly against the floor. "Not us. You can just forget about that. We didn't come all this way to help you out of some balancing act. We just wanna know what happened to us."

"And what's the sudden death thing?" Josh added firmly. "I told you, we didn't die; we just kept re-doin' that same crash and then..."

"No! You don't get it!" Everett interrupted him with a sudden strong voice and then slumped back on the bed, exhausted by his effort. "It's not the same crash. It's decision points. Every crash is a new option, a new timeline, a new choice – that's what happened to you. You died, Josh; you died, again and again."

The old man's eyes darted back and forth in thought. "You were killed in each crash – at least your body was, but you weren't in your body anymore, were you? That's the wrinkle. See?"

"I'm dead?"

"Yes, you're dead; both of you are dead, in that line. But you and your father apparently jumped to *other you's* in *other lines* and got other chances. I think that's how it worked." He looked suddenly pensive. "Why it worked that way is a whole different question."

"And buried?"

Everett closed his eyes, exasperated with slow minds. "Yes, buried. I should expect so, unless they cremated you."

Josh looked horrified. Kendall abruptly stood up and walked away from the bed. He wandered over to the covered windows, and peeked out through the curtains at the pastoral scene outside. Finally, he looked back at the dried up old man huddled under the sheets.

"No. There's no way that makes sense. Your theory's nuts. It's gotta be." He came back to stand behind his chair. "If I spin off whole universes and timelines every damn time I turn around, I'd feel somethin', wouldn't I? I know I would. I'd hafta! And I don't feel a thing."

Everett cracked one eye open. He pursed his lips in glee. "Is the earth spinning? Are we orbiting the sun?"

"What the hell's that got to do with anything?"

Hugh opened his other eye and sighed with sheer intellectual delight. "Do you feel it? Do you feel dizzy? No. But is it true? Yes! The earth rotates 360 degrees every 24 hours! She orbits the sun every 365 days! And you're riding on her, and you don't feel a single thing. Do you? Huh?"

Kendall was momentarily silent but unconvinced. "That's different. There're reasons. They can prove those things. But what about your...many worlds deal, huh? It's all made up. Things can't work that way. It's a bunch of...sci-fi bullshit!"

The old man smiled sadly, "You really think so?"

"Damn straight I do! Normal life ain't like that. It can't be."

Everett nodded, pleased that the argument was won. "Ah! That's true, normal people live their normal lives unaware of the multiverse – but you and your son have never been normal people. You just didn't know it until now." He looked at each of them in turn and then smiled in a slightly predatory fashion. "And the fact that you're both standing here in my room *in the wrong timeline* arguing with me, proves it beyond a shadow of a doubt."

He beamed at them. "Q.E.D."

CHAPTER 15:

A MUSCULAR YOUNG MAN sat at a table in a small windowless room. He was tapping his fingers and moving his shoulders to a musical beat. His light sweater was open at the front and it allowed the glimpse of a harness and the bulge of a shoulder holster. On the table in front of him was a thermos, a silver communicator unit and a slim rectangular remote, like a high tech garage opener. He was listening to music from tiny wireless earphones, the volume cranked high enough so that a thin tune spilled out of his ears and into the room.

The comm in front of him suddenly beeped and flashed. The man couldn't hear it but he noticed the pulsing light. He hurriedly yanked the tiny phones from his ears and guiltily stuffed them in a shirt pocket. He swept up the comm and pushed the talk button. "Yep, I'm here. Go ahead."

He listened briefly and then replied. "Copy that. Walk 'em in. Here you go."

He thumbed the remote. The heavy door near him buzzed loudly and opened outwards. Another armed guard stepped in followed by Vandermark and Nsamba. The exterior guard immediately exited and the door auto-locked behind him.

Vandermark and Nsamba nodded a greeting to the interior guard and then crossed the room to the two metal doors in the opposite wall. They briefly slid open small view ports built into each door face and glanced in, one after the other, and then stepped back.

Vandermark was upset with Nsamba. Keeping his voice low, he was obviously continuing an earlier conversation. "Do you think for a minute I like all these complications? Believe me, I have enough problems."

Nsamba was clearly not happy. "Complications?" He stepped closer to Vandermark and harshly whispered at him. "Assault, kidnapping, false imprisonment – these people haven't done anything."

"Not yet. Don't be naïve."

Nsamba flared black eyes at him. "I'm not being naïve. I'm stating a few *minor* facts that make me extremely uncomfortable."

"I've explained all this. You know what's at stake. You saw the timelines. These people could become a problem for us. Just think of it as...detainment until I'm sure we're safe."

Behind them the comm unit beeped again. The interior guard answered. "Yeah? That time already? Okay." He smiled at something the other guard said. "Copy that."

He buzzed the door open to admit a third guard carrying a set of trays with three covered meals and water bottles. Nsamba watched the food go by and looked darkly at Vandermark. "Spare me your finer points; I already know how stupid I am to listen to you."

* * *

The jumper lab at *the Point* was hopping with activity. An additional area of the floor had been cleared, and electricians were installing elevated cable trays. Below them, additional cradles were being fitted out for service. Techs fed cable harnesses through ports in the translucent skin to other techs crouched inside. In other corners of the room teams of engineers were comparing schematics and line drawings on thin, hand-held electronic displays. Workers nearby were assembling equipment racks and control boards to be paired up with the new cradles. Beside a workbench, a jump engineer wore one of the VR helmets. He was testing the output dynamics by twisting the joystick in one hand and checking readouts on a palm-sized device in his other hand.

A floor above, Song Lee Hahn appeared at the control room window and silently observed the focused frenzy below. Her face looked drawn and her eyes tired. She and her teams were working around the clock to prepare enough cradles, and their attending hardware, to meet the demanding mobile unit deadline she had been given. Her headset crackled with queries and responses flying back and forth between the exhausted engineers and technicians below her. The control board crew around her occasionally chimed in as well, but she recognized that nothing required her immediate personal involvement. For the moment, she was visualizing an image of herself as a resting boulder in the middle of a wild cataract of white water – it was the only rest she was likely to get in the next 16 hours, and she intended to make the most of it.

"Excuse me, Dr. Hahn?" Echo's voice sliced through the bedlam of Hahn's headset and shattered her reverie.

"Yes Echo?"

"I cannot provide an accurate estimate of the child lines likely to branch from Quyron's jumpers without a hard end date in this timeline. Can you procure that information?"

"You know our deadline for the truck; use that. It should be close enough."

"You understand that will not generate a precise number, but a range of numbers?"

"It's an estimate!" Hahn was irked. "It'll be good enough. Estimates are not expected to be precise."

"Of what value is a number that is not precise?"

Song Lee often had issues dealing with Echo, voice-to-voice, due to the quantum computer's maddening literal bents, and the imprecision of spoken English. Her assistants claimed that Echo's misunderstandings were often eased by reducing requests to written words or mathematical formulations. *No time for that now.*

"Echo, we're very busy here and I need to feel as if I have control over somebody. So, can you just do what I told you?"

"Of course."

The absolute sincerity of the computer's tone did little to alleviate Hahn's displeasure. In fact, it had just the opposite effect. Song Lee loaded her final response with all the sarcasm she could stuff into the two words.

"Thank you."

Echo immediately responded with sunny earnestness. "You are very welcome, Dr. Hahn."

Hahn shook her head. She was quickly swept back into the technical give-and-take in her headset. Soon all memory of the interruption from Echo, as well as her lost quiet moment, were swallowed up by the demands of the now.

* * *

The back third of the control room was a windowless area often used as a makeshift break room during the recent extended work shifts. It featured simple counters and cupboards, a sink, a tabletop refrigerator and two coffee makers.

The space had now been commandeered by Nsamba and his cradle riders for mission planning. Diagrams, street maps and enlarged aerial photos of various aspects of a suburban Cincinnati neighborhood were pinned to cluttered corkboards and propped onto easels. Distances between selected buildings were prominently marked and travel times were noted on colored post-it notes. Two metal tables were pushed together in the middle of this disorder and seven people, including Nsamba, Salazar and Fargo, were gathered around in chairs or standing. Rose, a plain woman in her thirties, sat near Kranzie, a thick, quiet man. Vinnie, a bright, sandy haired young man, perched on the edge of a table and listened intently to the briefing that Julie was giving. A former combat medic, Julie was muscular and kept her hair short. She worked as a certified pharmacy technician now, but missed the intensity of military action. Tempted by the heavy cash payment she'd been offered, Julie had burned up some earned vacation time to join the team.

"As you can see here, the nanos have located a workable pharmacy within 100 yards of the target house." Julie tapped the building's location on one of the easels and then pointed at interior photos of a drugstore prescription dispensing area where two un-aware pharmacists were at work. "Vinnie and I will take care of *persuading* the pharmacists here to help us put together our little drug cocktail."

She gave a half smile and then went on. "Okay, since we're limited to what's available on site, here's what we're gonna do."

She took a step over to the edge of the table and held up two vials and a handful of empty hypodermic needles. "We'll use four 10mL sterile syringes. In two of them, we'll put 10 mg/mL of Midazolam diluted with 0.9% Sodium Chloride. She indicated a vial of clear liquid. This is normally used as a muscle relaxant and sedative. The other two syringes'll get 50 micrograms/mL of Propofol. She shook a cloudy vial and held it up to her face. This can be a real nasty number in high doses but since it looks a little like skim milk, we call it, *Milk of Amnesia*." She waited for the group to react, and caught a few smiles. "It also stings like the dickens when it's pushed, so that's another reason why we'll be using the Midazolam first. Anyway, both of these are C-2 drugs. That means they're kept locked up in an access controlled area. That's not gonna be a problem here, but it will slow us down a bit."

She moved to a different easel filled with photos of the McCaslin kitchen, foyer, living room, and stairs. "We need to inject each target with both drugs – Midazolam first, Propofol second. One knocks them out, the other pushes them way down deep in the mud, and in these dosages, should trigger their body's own de-

111

fensive response. If everything works right, they should be stuck in a coma for good."

Fargo sat at a nearby table strewn with papers. She fingered a few surveillance photos of Kendall and Josh. "Does it matter where we stick 'em?"

Julie looked at her, a little puzzled. "You don't have to worry about that. Vinnie and I will be there – that's our job."

"Yeah, sure. I appreciate that, doc, but you're military, aren't ya? So, you know shit happens." Fargo smiled disarmingly up at her. "Humor me. If you guys are...unavailable, where do we stick 'em?"

Vandermark had joined the back of the group to listen. Julie noticed him and looked for guidance. He nodded at her to go ahead and answer Fargo's question.

"Okay then," Julie said. "Well, basically you're gonna want to make the injection into any large muscle mass – lower neck, back, butt, thighs. Make sure you do 'em in the right order though, and check for air in the needles."

Nsamba smoothly took over the briefing. He left no room for further questions. "Thanks, Julie. Okay, I recognize that we've spent a lot of time in the weeds, but don't lose sight of the big picture. All right? Remember, jumps will happen in four phases. One – secure the drugs. Two – converge on the house. Three – stick 'em, as you so kindly put it, Fargo. And four – dismount and end the jump. Then we move on to the next line, and do it all over again. As long as it takes. Are we clear?"

Most of the jumpers nodded or had no response. Salazar folded his arms and leaned forward until his elbows rested on the table. "Hell of a lotta messin' around. I'm wonderin' why simpler ain't better. Save all of us a lotta time and a lotta hassle, don't you think?"

Nsamba stared at him without a blink. "That is not an option. We told you from the start."

Sal wasn't put off and tossed a sour look right back. "What good's a plannin' session when all the options ain't on the table?"

Vandermark stepped forward quickly and his face was set. "What is this, a special needs class, Sal? Some kind of alt school? Let me make it simple for you." He leaned on the table right above Sal. "If we kill them, they just jump into themselves in a new line; only now they know that somebody's after them. If we put them into a coma, they're not dead and they can't choose anything. That means no splits, no sub lines, no alternates, no warning; no way out. Got it, Sal?"

Salazar hadn't moved a muscle. He just stared at the table as if he couldn't care less. "Whatever."

"Right!" Vandermark scowled into the faces of the cradle riders, his face blotchy with emotion. "Just do what you're told and don't think too hard! That's why the pay is what it is!" Vandermark turned on his heel and left the room.

In the lull afterwards, everyone sat quietly. Julie took a chair. Vinnie stayed perched on the edge of the table, slowly swinging one foot back and forth.

"Okay then," Nsamba finally said. "You all have the mission briefs and updates. You know we have at least thirty timelines to deal with. The plane departs at 0800 tomorrow, and the truck should be waiting at the other end when we get to Cincinnati. Anybody have a question – I mean besides Sal?"

A few careful smiles broke free, but no one raised a hand. Fargo winked at the group. "Well, aren't we all gonna be some busy little bees."

Nsamba waited a beat. "That is all. See you at the corporate hanger in the morning."

The group gathered their gear and departed. Nsamba stayed at the table and reviewed screens on his palm computer.

Dr. Hahn stood at the edge of the meeting area and waited. When the cradle riders were gone, she stepped closer to where Nsamba was seated. "Taylor, can I ask you something?"

Nsamba continued to study his interface and didn't look up. "No. Do not ask me about Dr. Vandermark."

"Why not?"

He stopped his work and looked up. "We have known each other a long time, Song Lee." Nsamba's deep voice softened but retained its stilted African flavor. "We share respect. Do not make me lie to you."

Song Lee stood still and spoke without emotion. "Why is he doing this? Driven is one thing – we are both driven – but he has become reckless."

"It is Quyron's jumpers." Nsamba considered what he was about to say. "He sees our riding of other minds as the breakthrough of his life. And these *natural* jumpers threaten all of that."

Song Lee scoffed. "A breakthrough to keep him from dying, you mean."

"He hasn't said..." A puzzled look crossed Nsamba's face. "He thinks riders can direct the paths of other timelines – send them in the directions we want. That is all."

"That's what he says is all, but I know how he thinks. He will use what we learn to keep himself alive, inside someone else – someone younger. That's why he's doing this."

Nsamba's face darkened. "You're guessing. You don't know that."

"I know what I know. Open your eyes."

Nsamba swiveled his head back to his screens. "I don't have time for this. If you have something factual to say, say it! Otherwise, I have work to do."

Hahn moved around the table to stand in front of him. She waited until he, begrudgingly, gave her his attention again. "Echo confirms that when our riders ride, the timelines do not split. No matter how many choices they make while riding, the timeline they're in continues unchanged in the multiverse."

"What?" Nsamba's whole bearing shifted drastically. "That cannot be right! Nothing is outside the timelines and every choice has to cause splits."

"Yes, so we've been taught. It can't happen. It's a contradiction." Song Lee lightly touched her hands on the table. "But it continues to happen just the same, no matter what we want to believe."

"Have you told him?"

"Why should I?"

Nsamba's shoulders drooped. "I can't deal with this now. I don't even know what it means. All I know is that I have to neutralize Quyron's jumpers."

Hahn stepped back. "Listen to yourself. *Neutralize.* You're starting to talk like him too. I'm telling you, I'm afraid of what we're doing."

"This serves no purpose now." Nsamba's face showed his inner conflict. "I have work to do and so do you. I promise we will talk later – I will consider your fears later – but right now I need your help."

Hahn thought about pushing the conversation harder but closed her eyes and chose to follow a softer line. "What do you need?"

"How many lines have Quyron's jumpers spun off?" He held out his computer with the screens. "Are these all of them?"

She briefly studied his screen. "Those are the confirmed lines, so far. I'm sure there're more now." Hahn flicked her eye to the ceiling. "Echo? Current status on the tally of the McCaslin lines since the accident?"

Echo's clear, upbeat voice came without delay. "Since the prime survival line, up to this moment, there are thirty-four branch lines, for a total of thirty-five lines."

Nsamba arched his eyebrows and sighed in disappointment. "Wonderful."

Echo's cheerful voice came right back. "And counting."

"It seems *they* have no problem with splits." Hahn left the table. "Of course, they're *natural-born* jumpers, as Quyron likes to say."

Nsamba was going to reply but Hahn was already walking away. She spoke without turning back. "I'd say the sooner you get onsite, the fewer new splits you'll have to deal with."

Nsamba muttered to himself, "Thanks. That is so comforting."

CHAPTER 16:

EVENING IN THE MARYLAND nursing home started very early and ended quickly. Other than supper and prime time television, very little of note happened at the end of the day except the usual (and a few unusual) bedtime routines such as PJ's, teeth, toilet, meds, and the occasional ambulance run. Unless of course, a resident happened to have secured that rarest of nursing home occurrences: visitors.

Everett's room actually looked better at night. The indirect lighting from a couple of lamps softened the undecorated walls and warmed the pale tile floor. Hugh was a dwarf piled in a large bathrobe. He sat up in the bed, awkwardly propped by crowds of pillows, and scrabbled with gnarled hands to shove aside his monotone supper and get at the Ensure container. Josh gave him a hand by fishing it off the bedside tray and sticking a straw in it.

Everett irritably motioned at him. "Just hand it over, I can do it."

Josh frowned. "Hand it where?"

"Just give it here. I've worked out a technique. You'll see."

Josh handed over the container and the old man adeptly manipulated it using his knuckles and the opposite wrist to wrestle the straw to his mouth. He sucked in a few gulps and tossed an impish look at Josh. "Don't try this at home."

Kendall crumpled up the wax paper from his burger and tossed it at a trash basket. He watched Everett take another drink and then leaned forward in his chair. "Here's what I wonder. Why should we trust you?" He toyed with his paper plate of cold fries. "From what I heard, you quit on your own theory, and the guys Josh read said all you did was whine about it later."

Everett sputtered and coughed up the thick pale liquid. He contorted his body to slap the Ensure back onto the bedside tray table, sloshing more liquid. Josh tried to help with a napkin but the old man snatched it and angrily waved it around trying to soak up the spills. "That's what they wrote later! It's not what actually happened!"

"Yeah?" Kendall seemed amused. "So, what really happened?"

Everett dropped the damp napkin, and it flopped to the floor. He slumped back into his pillows, sullen. He made a few faces and stared coldly at Kendall. "That was a long time ago."

Kendall sipped at some coffee from a foam cup and grimaced at the taste. "So I heard." He put the coffee down. "Let's see, you wrote this long important paper in...what Josh?"

"1956."

"Yeah, Princeton in 1956 – then, since nobody liked it, you ate a big piece of humble pie and cut all the hot stuff out, to please your professors, and then..."

Everett interrupted. "You don't understand a single thing about this. You don't know anything."

Kendall nodded. "Maybe so. And then in...the 70's?"

Josh piped up, "1972."

"Right. Thanks. In 1972, somebody else published your original paper, the long one, with all the hot stuff still in it, and it made a big splash; but then...nothing. You let it drop. You wrote nothing on it again. You didn't push it. You walked away and quietly went to work for the government – just one more invisible guy in a dark suit. You vanished. You lived your own little life and ignored your past completely for all these years."

Kendall's voice suddenly cracked like a whip. "Are you kidding me!" His arms and hands joined his words. "You created the single most important theory in the history of the world – or worlds, I guess, according to you – and you just dumped it? Really? And now you sit there and try to tell us how important it all suddenly is; but when *you* had the chance, it wasn't important at all. So, what's the deal, Hugh? Which is it?"

Everett looked up from the pillows. His eyes were teary and his mouth a grim line. "Why are you doing this to me?"

Kendall looked Everett in the eyes, without any pity. "Maybe because I'm old enough not to take things for granted. Maybe I want to know who we're dealing with and why we should believe him – I mean besides the fact that he's a lot more book smart than us."

Everett gathered himself. He levered his body up and shoved feebly at the bedside tray. "Josh, can you get this out of my way?"

Josh backed the tray away from the bed and rolled it toward the hall door. He came back and sat next to his father. Everett clutched the bed rail and pulled himself as close as he could to their edge of the bed. He looked directly at Kendall. "You're an easy man to underestimate."

Kendall's somber expression didn't change. "Thank you."

"You both deserve an explanation." He worked his mouth for a bit before going on. "I was scared; that's the truth. I'm still scared. But not in the way you think. I've never talked about this to anyone – not in the 56 years since, but I've thought about it every day."

He concentrated on Kendall, his eyes gleaming in the lamplight. "You think I crumbled under the pressure, don't you? You think I caved to my advisor, old doctor Niels Bohr himself – is that it?" Everett grew taller somehow, even perched against the rails of the hospital bed and lost in his bathrobe. He projected a dominance that had nothing to do with size or age.

"You don't know anything about me! I was 26 years old and I'd just cracked the biggest problem in physics – the one that had stumped a generation. I was the next Einstein, the next Nash – I was waiting for a crown and itching for a fight."

Everett shook his head and collapsed back into himself. He suddenly looked vulnerable. "But you're right, Kendall. You need to know the whole me. I also felt lost. I couldn't believe they'd rejected my paper. How could they do that? They said it was nonsense – unintelligible! And then their pathetic ultimatum just added fuel to my fire. I was hurt and I was furious, and I was determined to rub their faces in my brilliance."

He rested his chin on the top of the bed rail and his eyes were focused far away. "God, I can see myself in that lab – as if I'm outside looking through a window. I was so hyper-focused and so damn sure of myself. What can I say? I kept seeing them all, all the old physicists in their black robes and ties, all bowing before my statue in the quad. I was so unprepared for what I found. I expanded the equations and visualized the *what-ifs* of future advances, and as I moved confidently, day after day, deeper into the heart of the theory, something hideous began to reveal itself; a dark potential for such a catastrophe...it took my breath away."

The room was silent. From the hallway, the whisper of a canned laugh track from a TV show trickled in. The swish from Everett's sheets sounded abnormally loud as he let go of the rails and sagged back against his pillows. The old man contemplated the ceiling for a long moment.

"When I was in the 3rd grade we went on a field trip to the zoo. I remember only one thing about that day. I walked around the corner of a raised outdoor cage, with my hand strumming along the bars, just as a Siberian tiger slid out from an inner door. His eyes instantly locked on me, and I stopped. I ceased to breathe. His massive shoulders spread as he sank into a crouch, and crept right up to me on silent paws that were each larger than my head. I stood paralyzed, my hand forgotten on the bar. I could feel the heat he radiated. I smelled him. He was the most beautifully deadly predator I had ever seen or imagined; and I was his prey.

I don't know how long I stood, entranced, communing with my death. It was so profoundly clear to me that the bars were but an inconsequential trifle. Our true relationship had been set from long before the age of iron. And then he huffed in a dismissal breath that made me blink, and briefly lifted my hair. And when I blinked again, he was gone, and I had to remind myself to breathe."

Everett turned to focus on Kendall and Josh. They both sat riveted in their chairs.

"That's what I felt in the theory – a door, a cage, something that should be kept locked. It was knowledge that no one should know; but my theory would lead them right to it. In the right kind of future, with quantum computers and atom sized robots, and the will to exploit the timelines, what I had seen would happen. So, I stopped everything. It was all I could think to do. I rewrote the paper, cut out the truth, which pleased my advisors, got my degree, and...you're right, I disappeared. That publishing of the original paper in '72 was none of my doing. In fact, I did my best to make sure it died. And for all the years since, I haven't published another single word about my theory."

Everett sniffed derisively and dropped his arms on the mattress. "As if any of that mattered at all."

Josh looked up, quick to add his thoughts. "You mean because they've rediscovered your theory now anyway?"

"No. It's the theory itself. I've opened a door that can't be shut. No matter what I *don't* say, or *don't* do here, I'm pursuing it anyway. And I'm paralyzed to stop myself."

Kendall was sympathetic but confused. "I don't know what you mean? You did everything a person could do to stop it."

Josh suddenly had an awareness dawning across his face. He walked over beside the bed and looked sadly at Everett. "You mean your *other you's* would do it. You're scared of yourself. That's what you meant."

Everett twisted his body to face the young man, and nodded. "Every *no* is a *yes*, somewhere else. Another Everett would develop it. And given enough time-lines in a lifetime of choices, inevitably, the disaster I nipped in the bud here would blossom there. And when it did, I might be the only Hugh Everett left who knows what's happening. That's why I'm still here. It's the best I can do. I had to stay alive and wait and see. And now I know I was waiting for you."

Josh glanced at Kendall and then back at Everett and grinned self-consciously. "Guess we didn't arrive any too soon then, did we?"

Everett gave him back a crooked smile. "S'okay. I'm still here. You found me in time, and besides, the *now* is all anybody gets to work with anyway. The good news is, since we know my theory's true, we also know that our *now* is a lot wider than we thought."

CHAPTER 17:

"IT SPIKES AND THEN reads normal. And then spikes again." The puzzled floor tech held out the diagnostic pad to a senior tech. "Watch it. It's almost rhythmical, except the interval keeps decreasing."

They were deep within banks of active screens in the arena at the Reivers Corporation headquarters. The screen they were analyzing displayed varying angles of a bathysphere being lowered into the ocean from a research ship. Every few seconds the image degraded slightly or flickered unevenly. Just as rapidly, it stabilized again.

The older tech touched a few spots on the pad and tapped the menus. He confirmed the puzzling readouts and scanned through various other nano-observed locations in the same timeline. As he did this the nearby display of the bathysphere switched rapidly to an office, a park, a shopping mall, a restaurant, a classroom, a parking lot, a school playground, a bridge filled with traffic, and back to the bathysphere. The tech stayed with each image long enough to detect the same disquieting interference.

He grimly shook his head. "Everywhere the same: spike and normal, spike and normal. It's not a local issue; it's affecting the whole line." He handed the pad back, clearly troubled. "What could do this across a whole universe?"

The floor tech rolled his shoulders. "The line's about to go into alarm, and there's not a thing we can do about it. I think we're all getting jumpy."

Around them, the tall walls of flat screens continued to display the colorful, untroubled images of other monitored timelines: a woman in a hazmat suit injecting rats in a clean room, a politician delivering a speech at a rally, soldiers standing guard at a military base, a young family at a picnic, boys biking along a park path.

Suddenly, the warbling cry of an alarm erupted. The two techs helplessly watched as the screen with the bathysphere flickered ever more rapidly. Additional floor techs raced up. The image on the screen distorted and warped until it abruptly devolved into electronic snow. Finally, it collapsed to black. The alarm changed to a continuous tone, indicating a total loss of transmission.

The senior tech flicked a small device toward the screen and the alarm abruptly cut off. He joined the assembled group of concerned techs and conferred about the latest lost connection. Ignored around them, the aisles of massed screens continued transmitting their mesmerizing dance of other lives in other timelines in the multiverse.

What appeared on the screens at any time was only selected views transmitted by clusters of nanos at single locations. The immense memories of the archive stored all the transmitted views from all the nanos throughout that universe for later scrutiny. Multiple angles of all aspects of living universes were captured by the billions of self replicating, invisible nano robots seeded into the lines. Fleets of sequenced computers at *the Reive*, and elsewhere in the world, tagged and sorted the overwhelming influx of data using paired levels of qubit based recognition software and other highly proprietary apps. Nanos were diminutive enough to drift through timeline membranes and into their sub lines. The biggest problem was generating enough nanos to not only blanket all the areas of interest but also to keep up with the many worlds constantly spinning off. Luckily for them, existing nanos split right along with the timelines they occupied – so, once invaded by nanos, new sub lines brought nano copies with them when they flashed into existence.

Unseen by the techs, unrecorded by the nanos, and undetected by countless sensing devices designed by *the Reive*, was the actual experience within the adversely affected timelines.

Above the arguing techs, among the banks of screens in an upper row, a group of shouting boys on bikes raced each other down a twisting park path. It was a glorious sunlit afternoon in Boise, Idaho. The annual Ferguson family reunion was being held this year at Camelback Park. The prolific family was now so numerous that the local relatives had to arrive at the picnic area by 6am that morning to secure the coveted pavilion.

The raucous boys on bikes were all cousins. Randy, riding just behind the leader, laughed in unbridled glee as he put on a burst of speed. "Comin' through! Outta the way!"

"Dream on!" Shawn put on his own sprint and weaved slightly as he tried to hold the lead. The two determined eleven-year-olds pedaled in sync as they made the final bend. Behind them, Timmy and Oz tried to keep up, but their older cousins were pulling away. Still, the two younger boys gamely fought on because third place was better than last.

The small pack of riders burst from the trees with their legs pumping wildly. The bike path led up to a colorful chalk-marked finish line right in front of the pavilion where crowds of madly waving Fergusons cheered them on.

The idyllic moment abruptly went horrific as the path itself came unraveled beneath the boys. Randy screamed in terror as he plunged into an abyss with his wheels still spinning. Shawn instinctively hit his brakes and saw his pedal go to pieces, followed by his foot. All the boys and their bikes shredded into particles as they fell into nowhere. The Fergusons' cheering turned to wailing as the pavilion and the gathered relatives went progressively apart. Around the park everything was shredding and billowing away – the buildings, the trees, the earth, the sky.

There was a rising crescendo of tearing as human moments across this universe were caught unawares and suddenly began shredding apart: an Afghan family posing for a photo, people haggling in an outdoor market, Arab passengers sleeping on an airbus, an Italian motor cop chasing a car, a Russian groom kissing his bride, Asian women planting rice, a convict smiling at a visitor, an African soccer player taking a kick, a wheat farmer driving a combine, drinkers toasting friends in a pub, a Japanese trawler captain turning a wheel, a crying baby being baptized, a hockey team celebrating a goal, an artist painting a canvas, hikers passing a waterfall, sailors singing "Happy Birthday," an Indian merchant counting rupees, a baseball batter swinging at a pitch, Korean students reciting the alphabet, jets passing a grandstand at an air show, Hasidic Jews praying at the western wall, mountain climbers swinging on a rope, an astronaut repairing a space station, a space probe swinging by Saturn, a nebula rotating in space.

None of this was observed in the arena, or recorded into the hungry memories of the archive. Nanos were deconstructed along with their universe, and nothing was detected except a loss of signal. Everything went to pieces and billowed away into dust until even sounds were silenced. And the dust dispersed, leaving nothing but blackness...and the distant warbling of an alarm.

The arena techs turned in shock at the unexpected sound. One of the upper screens was distorting and warping. As they watched, it collapsed into electronic snow and went to black. The alarm instantly switched to the steady, held tone. The techs stood mute, looking up.

The senior tech dutifully silenced the alarm and logged the event into his growing list of unexplained transmission problems.

CHAPTER 18:

IT WAS A COOL FALL evening in Silver Spring. The *American Tap & Grill* was doing a brisk business in spirits and comfort food, thanks to the pro football games playing on multiple TVs. The moist heat and decibel level in the crowded bar was already high and rising. Most of the males were loudly focused on each play, while their wives and girlfriends hunched together, heads almost touching, to gab over mounds of nachos and salads.

In the less raucous dinner area, Josh and Kendall relaxed in a booth. Their finished meals were pushed aside so they could rest their elbows on the table and nurse mugs of beer.

"So, let's say I take a sip of this; that's a choice, right?" Kendall held his glass poised in the air and toasted Josh. He swigged more than a sip, and slapped it back on the table. "Done! That's one."

He picked the beer up again, and held it. "But I could start like I'm gonna drink it, and then say, nah, I'll sip it later – that's two. Maybe three?"

He started to put the mug down and grinned at Josh. "But then, what if I'm really just faking like I'm putting it down?"

Without warning he gulped a hurried slug of beer. "See? Fooled you, huh? What's that, five?"

He snorted in glee and drained the last of the beer. "There! I just spun off at least five more worlds? Huh? Gettin' kinda crowded in here, don'tcha think?" He sniggered at his own joke.

A short waitress appeared and sent a tired smile in their direction. "Done with the food, guys? Can I take some of these plates away?"

Josh nodded. Kendall winked an eye as he slid his empty glass toward her. "I need just one more, Ma'am. I got a lotta universes left to create before I get world weary."

The waitress nodded, "Yeah, I bet you do. Bud regular, right?" Kendall nodded and the waitress left.

Josh's mug was still half full. He yawned and rotated his neck trying to work the kinks out. "So, what's the verdict? Is he nuts, or are we nuts?"

"We're dead."

"Besides that."

"Not sure." Kendall took a breath. His face went serious. "To be honest, when I got your Mom back, all my bets went out the window. I wouldn't count this old guy out. He's the real deal."

The waitress set a fresh mug down on a coaster in front of Kendall. "Here ya go. Is that gonna do it?"

Kendall put a hand on the beer. "Thanks. Yeah. All done. Just give us a single check."

"You got it."

Josh waited until the waitress left. "But don't you think if big disasters were happening, we'd notice somethin'?"

Kendall took a careful drink but the beer's tall head still left foam on his upper lip. "Like what? Like people bein' in the wrong timelines?" He snorted under his breath.

"Cut it out. I'm serious. Hugh said if it went bad, things might just start...he used some big word I forgot; but it meant fallin' apart. You remember him sayin' that?"

"Yeah. He said a lot of things."

"Well, wouldn't we notice that?"

Kendall took a long swallow from his mug. "We would if it was happenin' *here,* but..." He played with a nearby stack of extra coasters and looked thoughtful. "Those timeline things – maybe they're like dominos." He leaned a couple of coasters against each other. "A real long row of 'em." The coasters fell over and he left them. "Sometimes I've seen where they set up a whole roomful, just for fun, you know? And if you happened to be a piece a dust sittin' on that last domino, you won't know the rest are falling, 'til it gets to you."

Josh's expression sank. "How's he know what's happenin' anyway? And what's he gonna do about it; he's just a piece of dust too, and he's about a thousand years old."

Kendall pushed his beer away. He was done for the night. "It's us that's s'posed to do somethin' about it. I got that much."

"So what can we do? What kind of crazy plan would have you and me at the center?"

"Hey, weren't you listenin'? We're special! We're some kinda...super...mutants, to hear him talk." Kendall nudged his son. "Wouldn't you like to save the world? Huh, Josh?"

"I'd settle for just findin' Hannah again. I don't think I'm any good at savin' worlds – I couldn't even make varsity in soccer."

"Soccer players don't save worlds."

"Thanks, that makes me feel a lot better. Seriously, where do we go from here? We can't go back, and I don't see how we go forward. Do you?"

"Hugh's the man! He said he'd work on it. Maybe we oughta go over there right now. Say we can't wait 'til mornin' for a plan; the universe is in danger right now."

"Universes! Lots of 'em. Remember? Many worlds theory, get it? Plural!"

"Yeah, yeah, okay. The *universes* are in danger. Hey, that's even more reasons!"

The waitress swung by and dropped the bill off. Kendall scanned it. "Let's go ask him. Get it over with."

"Tonight?"

Kendall pulled out some folded bills from a money clip. "Yeah. Right now, tonight. Why not?"

"C'mon, let the guy sleep." Josh yawned again and slowly slid out of the booth.

Kendall counted out cash and left it on the table. He watched Josh swaying on his feet. "Oh, I see. Let *you* sleep, you mean. How's that gonna go over?" Kendall snickered as he made his voice high. "Sorry, Josh needs his beauty sleep so the universes are gonna have to hold on 'til morning." He snorted again, louder.

They headed toward the door. Kendall put a hand on Josh's shoulder. "Don't worry, it's not like old Hugh's goin' anywhere."

Josh nodded but then looked serious. "Hey Dad, about tonight; what if you wait until I'm asleep before you go to bed?"

Kendall was instantly defensive. "Why?"

Josh winced. "'Cause you snore like a jumbo jet. Whole hotel room shakes. Hasn't Mom ever said anything?"

Kendall looked hurt. "You know, the old me didn't snore."

"That's a big help here."

CHAPTER 19:

IN THE PHARMACY prep area of the Turpin Hills drugstore, Doug Johnson dispensed elliptical white caplets
into an orange prescription bottle. He locked the cap
with a practiced flourish, affixed the label, and dropped
it into a tote for bagging. The senior pharmacist took
pride in his precision and his appearance, which is
why he was so touchy about his baldness. He knew
every available treatment regimen for his condition and
knew that none of them worked. He checked off the
prescription he'd completed and moved on to the next
request on his list.

A few steps to his left, Cecelia, his upbeat young
assistant pharmacist, smoothly stapled a white pharmacy bag for the pickup bin. She crossed off her final
order and looked over at her boss. "That's it on my
standard call-ins, Mr. Johnson, except for the C-3's
and 2's. I can fill those next if you want."

Doug was fastidiously rearranging his work area.
"Well, you're speedy this morning. Sure. That'll help."
He groaned a bit. "I have to do inventory today."

"Poor you." Cecelia smiled at him in mock sympathy as she grabbed a separate sheet of requests and
pulled open the drawer with the drug cabinet key.

Doug started on his next order. "Make sure you
update the register."

"Always do." Cecelia unlocked the metal drug cabinet where the controlled drugs were kept. "Have you ever known me to forget?" She removed the bound register and opened it to her next entry point.

"No. Sorry. Force of habit." Doug pulled a large bottle of pills from his stock. "Thank goodness for cholesterol! I've got another stack of Simvastatin orders. I can't believe how many people are staggering around popping these. Oh well, pays the bills."

Cecelia nodded and gathered what she needed for the controlled drug orders. "There's only a few of these so I'll be able to give you a hand with..." Her words stopped and she cocked her head, feeling a strange tickle inside. "What...ahhh?" She jerked stiffly and her hand struck one of the metal shelves, making it clang sharply.

Behind her, Doug slumped heavily against the counter and spilled a shower of the expensive white pills onto the floor.

* * *

Nsamba wore a tiny, nearly invisible wireless headset. He sat in a black mesh chair and stared attentively at an array of live screens placed in a small arc in front of him. The compact room was kept darkened to reduce glare. Tiny directional lights, with slender ribbed necks, created pools of soft illumination on the nearby flat surfaces and keyboards.

Beside Nsamba's station, John, a curly haired jump tech, monitored his own multiple screens and banks of interface gear. He adjusted his slim headset and kept a finicky eye on his embedded display pads. Directly across from him, on the flip side of the control console, another jump tech, Will, worked his own gear. John and Will handled different aspects of the complex jump, but their cross-training and related interests guaranteed a great deal of redundancy between them.

Various screens tracked the multiple targets for this initial timeline assault: the two pharmacists filling orders, a mailman driving in a mail truck, a newsboy

131

riding a bike, Kendall, Josh and Leah snacking in their kitchen, and a neighbor cutting his lawn.

John spoke into his mike in a calm voice. "Julie and Vinnie are go for the pill pushers. Archive visual in 4, 3, 2, and mark."

He hit a timer and watched the pharmacists in his screens jerk upright. The female hit her hand on a shelf and the other spilled caplets on the floor. They both stiffly started to move in new directions.

Will's voice filled the headsets. "Mailman's in the queue – one block and moving. Alpha estimated in one minute."

John nodded and spoke into his mike. "Copy that. Sal, you're on deck."

A wall separated the compact control area from the back of the 48-foot trailer where six cradles were mounted in pairs. Their transparent covers were down and secured. The riders inside were helmeted and all but indistinguishable. Julie and Vinnie were in the front set, Salazar and Fargo in the middle, and Rose and Kranzie at the rear. Cradle technicians stood nearby, or moved carefully between racks of equipment in the cramped space. The cradles were rapidly changing hue and the room hummed with rising power.

"This is Sal. Looks good. One minute." Salazar tested his handgrip and watched the results in his HUD; he casually slid the targeting reticle on and off the slow moving mail truck.

Back in the control room, John glanced at Nsamba. "Taylor, your call."

Nsamba gave no physical reaction. He was carefully watching the screen that showed the pharmacists working together in the controlled drug area. "Thank you. Waiting on the drugs."

* * *

Vandermark and Hahn were monitoring the jump from Maryland. They could access any of the multiple views available to the jump techs by toggling their screens in the upper level control room at *the Point*. In addition, they had a single dedicated screen that showed a live, high angle view of Nsamba and his jump techs at work.

* * *

In the Turpin Hills pharmacy prep area, Cecelia, with Vinnie inside her, capped the needle on a second syringe filled with a milky solution, and handed both to Doug. The balding pharmacist, with Julie inside him, smiled and handed Cecelia two more sterile syringes.

"Here you go, Vinnie, fill 'em up. And don't bother writing it into the register." It was Doug's voice, but Julie was doing the talking. She laughed at her joke with Doug's mouth while she used his hands to mark a green X on one of the syringes.

* * *

"Mail truck is at position alpha." Will's voice was steady and unruffled in Taylor's headset.

Nsamba responded. "Thank you. Drugs are going into the bag. John, how does it look?"

"Everything's good here." John positioned his hand over the timer. "It's all yours."

Nsamba made the call. "Sal, you have a go."

"Affirmative." Sal's fingers tapped with a nervous energy. "Waiting for the mail truck to stop. Targeting...lock...and go!" He squeezed the trigger.

John immediately confirmed the jump and hit his timer. "Mailman is go. Archive visual in 4, 3, 2, and mark."

* * *

With his steering wheel on the right side of the truck, the mailman pulled up to the last house on the block and opened its curbside mailbox. He was stopped directly across the street from the corner drugstore. He grabbed the clump of presorted mail from a slot next to him and started to stuff it into the box. Something inside his head strangely tingled! The mailman thrashed briefly behind the wheel, dropping the envelopes. The truck jerked forward and bumped repeatedly against the curb.

Salazar quickly gained control and used the mailman's feet to jam on the brakes. "Easy, partner."

The mailman, with Salazar inside, looked carefully around. "Okay, looks like nobody noticed the flakey postman bumping the curb – good for us."

Sal put the mail truck into park and watched the front door of the drugstore across the street. "Get it together little guy, we got a special delivery to pick up."

The male pharmacist walked briskly to the front of the drugstore with the prescription bag. His gait had a very definite feminine motion. As he approached the front doors of the store, the friendly teenage cashier looked up and spotted the bag.

"Is that a charge, Mr. Johnson? Or did you guys already ring it out?"

Julie, inside Doug, looked startled. "What? Oh, no, there's no...I mean, it's taken care of." Mr. Johnson put his head down and kept walking. "I'll be back."

The puzzled cashier watched the pharmacist awkwardly push open the metal and glass double doors and stumble out to the sidewalk.

Across the street, Sal spotted the druggist right away. He put the small truck into drive, looked for traffic and then swung a U-turn. A horn honked! Sal immediately braked. A car swerved safely around him and continued on its way, beeping its horn a few extra times to make a point.

Sal viciously pounded the steering wheel with the heel of his hand. "Dammit to hell! Looked the wrong way! Shit! Forgot the steering wheel's on the wrong side!"

Calming himself, Sal looked the right way this time, made a safe U-turn, and headed toward the drugstore.

Doug, the pharmacist, looked jumpy as the mail truck bumped the curb and jerked to a stop right next to him. The pharmacist handed over the bag and hissed in a low voice. "Nice driving, Sal, you scared the crap outta me."

"Sorry. Won't happen again."

* * *

Nsamba watched his screen. The view was delayed five seconds so the truck was just pulling up to the pharmacist. He shook his head and scowled.

John spoke into his mike. "Okay. Kranzie, you're in the queue for the neighbor. Fargo and Rose, you're queued for Kendall and Josh."

In the back of the truck the second and third sets of cradles were changing hues as their power went to max. One of the cradle techs tapped the glass on one and gave a thumbs-up to the rider inside.

"Copy that. This is Kranzie. Trackin' the neighbor." He impassively watched his display, but the ticking muscles around his chin betrayed his tension.

"Rose is go for Josh. Target marked." Rose tipped her head sharply left and right to release some stress.

Fargo smiled, her eyes dancing with eagerness. "Fargo's go for Kendall."

Back in the control area, John replied, "Copy that. All in the queue."

Nsamba took charge. "Thank you. All in the queue. The meds are on their way. Waiting for Julie and Vinnie."

* * *

Doug came striding back into the pharmacy prep area where Cecelia leaned against a counter. "Everything go okay outside?"

Doug smiled at her. "Yeah. That idiot Sal nearly got himself killed and then he almost ran me over, but other than that, fine."

"So, time to get back?"

"Let's do it." Julie, inside Doug, turned his head and glanced around the pharmacy area. "Bye guys.

Thanks for the memories." She used his mouth to laugh one more time and then was gone.

Both pharmacists gasped and shuddered as they came back to themselves. They looked at each other with uncertainty. Suddenly, Cecelia covered her face and began to sob. Tears welled up in Doug's eyes as he tried to master his own emotions, while awkwardly patting her back.

* * *

Julie returned to full awareness in her cradle. Her eyes were lively and she was enjoying herself. "Julie back on line."

She quickly twisted her targeting grip. Hopping from nano to nano she skewed her view to the McCaslin house, jumped into the interior, moved quickly into their kitchen, and deftly slid her target reticle over Leah. "Targeting Leah. On your go."

In her headset, she heard Will's voice reply. "Copy that, Julie. Wait one."

In his cradle, Vinnie returned and blinked rapidly, acclimating himself. "Vinnie back on line. On backup."

"Copy that, Vinnie," Will said and checked all the cradle readouts across his board. "John, all cradles are go."

John glanced at his screens and nodded. "Taylor, everything looks good. On your call."

Nsamba waited until the moving mail truck on one of his screens stopped. "Thank you. The mail has arrived. Vinnie stays as backup. The rest have a go. Repeat, all go."

Julie locked Leah in her crosshairs, smiling in anticipation. Leah's expression changed as if she felt something, and abruptly set her coffee cup down. The hot liquid sloshed onto the table. Julie squeezed the jump button. Leah pushed her fingers against her head and groaned.

Fargo grinned at the active image of Kendall in her VR glasses and thumbed the trigger. Kendall dropped his fork and jerked stiffly in his chair.

Rose got a lock on Josh. He squinted and rubbed his temples. Rose activated her jump. Josh fought it but he was too late; Rose was already riding him.

Kranzie tracked the tall, elderly neighbor across his yard until he stopped the mower to dump clippings. Locking on the target, Kranzie pulled the trigger. The neighbor cocked his head as if listening to a far off sound, and stiffened.

* * *

Inside the McCaslin kitchen, Leah, Josh and Kendall got up with difficulty and headed for their living room.

Outside the house, their next door neighbor walked to the curb where a mail truck was waiting. The mailman handed him a white pharmacy bag.

In the living room, Josh and Kendall calmly sat side by side in straight backed chairs next to the couch. Just behind them, Leah stood waiting. The neighbor entered the front door and handed Leah a syringe from the bag. Leah, with Julie inside, held it up to make sure of the contents, unsnapped the cover exposing the needle, and moved to Kendall.

"Fargo, pull the shirt away from your left shoulder, would you?"

Kendall mechanically exposed his upper shoulder. Leah injected him in the large muscle near his neck. She pushed the entire content of the syringe, pulled it out, recapped it, and handed it back to the neighbor. Franzie, inside the neighbor, took the empty and handed her a second full syringe, this one was milky and marked with a green X.

As Leah prepared to administer the second shot, Kendall turned slowly and glanced up at her. "Hey, I ain't waitin' around. Everything's startin' to go grey. I'm outta here!"

Kendall faintly shuddered as Fargo dismounted. Leah unsnapped the top and injected him with the second drug. Kendall's eyes shut as his head slumped forward onto his chest. His body settled heavily into the chair.

They moved on to Josh and did the same. When all was complete, the neighbor collected the syringes into the bag. He rolled it up tightly, and left. Leah calmly retraced her steps to the kitchen.

In the now quiet living room, Josh and Kendall sat silently, comatose in their chairs.

* * *

"Fargo, Rose and Julie are back on line." Will spoke quickly into his mike as he confirmed their cradle readouts.

"Copy that" John replied.

"Okay," Nsamba confirmed. "Waiting on Sal and Kranzie."

The activity level in the cradle bay was high. Techs unlocked and hoisted off the large transparent covers from the cradles. Others powered down equipment in the racks.

Fargo ripped off the VR glasses and lifted her wire laden helmet. "Man! That's some wicked shit you guys stuck into me." She ran her hands through her short hair and scratched vigorously. "Creeped me out!"

Rose, in the cradle behind Fargo, piped up. "Yeah, that was bad. I could feel everything going dead. I was scared I wouldn't get out in time."

Julie pushed up out of the seat in her cradle and leaned over its curved side to look at them. "Sorry. Told you these drugs were nasty – or weren't you listening when I made my pitch? Anyway, just stay through the first injection; after that it doesn't matter." She smirked at them. "C'mon though, other than that, don'tcha think it was kinda fun?"

* * *

In the lawn next door to the McCaslins, the neighbor stopped next to the yard waste container and dropped in the bag with the empty syringes. He lifted the mower bag and dumped the grass clippings on top of it. Putting the catch bag back on the mower he halted. "There you go mower man. All back together. Be seein' ya."

The neighbor shuddered, as Kranzie dismounted, and then jerked awake with a sudden breath and a look of panic.

Back near the drugstore, the mail truck slapped the curb and stopped. The door slid open and the mailman staggered out onto the boulevard. He stood bent over, with his hands on his knees, and began to weep.

* * *

Kranzie and Salazar snapped back to local awareness in their cradles, and immediately checked in.

"Kranzie, back on line."

"Sal, back." He flipped off his VR glasses and bellowed. "Hey! What's the deal? How come none of you geniuses remembered that mail trucks steer from the wrong side?"

* * *

Up in *the Point* control room, Vandermark and Hahn watched the screens. Vandermark nodded in satisfaction. "That went well, despite your concerns about *my* people. One down."

Hahn sat unmoved. "Thirty-four to go."

CHAPTER 20:

IT WAS A COLD, clear morning, and Kendall had the car heater going as he turned onto Weaver. Just ahead of the car, a frantic squirrel darted half way across the road and froze. As they drove closer, he suddenly bolted back in the opposite direction, and vanished into the trees.

Josh watched the little episode and looked at his Dad. "Yeah, how 'bout animals? They make choices. Do they make timelines?"

Kendall rolled his eyes. "Aw c'mon! A new world every time a squirrel loses a nut? How would..." He looked up ahead and sobered instantly. "Uh oh, what's goin' on over there?"

They both looked ahead at flashing emergency vehicle lights at the front entrance to the nursing home. Kendall raced into the parking lot and slashed the rental into the first open space. They both jumped out. Ahead of them, a flashing ambulance sat beside the main doors. A small group of staff and a few ambulatory residents had gathered on the sidewalk.

As Kendall and Josh rushed up the walkway, Josh observed, "It might be anyone, you know. There's lots of people here that could use an ambulance."

"I know," Kendall tossed back, "but I got a real bad feeling about this."

They reached the group at the doors just as two paramedics wheeled out a padded gurney with a small, blanketed figure strapped to it. Even wearing an oxygen mask, it was easy to identify Hugh Everett. Kendall took a few tentative steps forward but the shock of the event held him still.

The chatty nurse's aide spotted him and hurried up to Kendall, grabbing his hand. "Oh, Mr. McCaslin, it's your Hugh. I'm so sorry. He couldn't catch his breath this morning. And his skin – oh, it was so dry! He looked at me, and his eyes just rolled back in his head, and then..."

Kendall shook his head. "That's crazy. We were just with him last night."

The male paramedic smoothly opened the tall double doors in the back of the ambulance. The female paramedic rotated the gurney so Hugh would go in head forward. Beneath the plastic mask his eyes were closed, and his color was pasty white. Josh watched helplessly while the paramedics collapsed the gurney wheels and carefully slid Hugh deep into the bright interior.

"What's wrong with him?" Josh asked.

The nurse's aide touched his shoulder lightly. "We think...it may be his heart. Lord knows he's old enough."

Josh stepped toward the ambulance. He looked in as one paramedic put a blood pressure cuff on Hugh's arm while the other attached EKG straps to both his wrists and one ankle. "How bad is it?"

The female paramedic looked up as she clipped a heart sensor to a finger. "Don't know. Looks like a heart. Sooner we get him in the better."

She powered up the monitor equipment and started digging in the cupboards. The male paramedic climbed down and closed one of the doors.

Kendall moved up beside Josh and put a hand on his back. "Josh, ride with him. I'll follow you."

The male paramedic held the door and looked at Josh. "You a relative?"

Josh nodded. "We're all he's got."

The paramedic looked in at his partner. "Okay with you?"

Sitting in a chair next to Hugh, the female paramedic shrugged and readied a needle.

"Hop in, then. Hurry up."

Josh scrambled into the bed of the ambulance as the door closed behind him. He found a place to sit on the other side of the gurney and heard the cab door open and close. He watched the paramedic give Hugh a shot and looked concerned.

She said softly, "Don't worry. It's just some Heparin – blood thinner."

The ambulance began to move. The paramedic studied the readouts on her machine. Josh slid closer to Hugh's mask and looked down at him to check if he was really breathing. Everett slowly opened his eyes and looked up at him, confused.

"Hey. It's me, Josh. How ya doin' in there? "

Hugh looked at him strangely for a moment. His small voice was muffled by the mask. "Better than before...except for the fat lady sitting on my chest."

Josh smiled in relief. "Give us a heads up if she starts singin', okay?"

Everett smiled painfully at the joke. On the other side of the gurney, the paramedic grinned. She looked down at Hugh. "Well, since you're back, I have a few questions to ask."

He looked back at her. "That's what everybody says."

The Capital Beltway system was clotted with morning traffic but luckily the ambulance was moving against the flow as it sped along, helped by its lights and siren, headed for Holy Cross Hospital.

Following close behind in the rental car, Kendall struggled to keep up.

CHAPTER 21:

QUYRON WAS SURROUNDED by stacks of actual, physical paper, marked, dog-eared and highlighted. Her multi-screens were also full of open programs and cascades of miscellaneous data files, but it was the paper that held her interest. "Echo, doesn't it seem strange to you that I'm trying to find out something that you already know?"

"Explain *seem strange.*" Echo's voice floated from the ceiling

Quyron pondered the request for a moment. "Odd. Out of the normal way. An action or...a request that's different than expected. I don't know, something that just doesn't feel right."

"No."

Quyron blinked. "No what? No, you don't understand?"

"No. Not strange," Echo instantly answered.

"Why not?"

"It is the way people normally interact with me. They are most often searching for things that I already know."

Quyron leaned back in her chair and linked her hands together behind her head. "Oh, so you have all the answers, huh Miss Smarty Trousers?"

"I recognize your tone as sarcasm, so I will ignore my new name. The answer to your question, if I can approximate sarcasm, is yes, I have all the answers; my problem is, I do not know all the right questions."

Quyron tipped forward in the chair and settled her arms on the piles of worn paperwork. "Echo, you know my team and I are searching everywhere for answers to these timeline fluctuations."

"Yes, Dr. Shur."

"So, why do I get the impression that parts of you are walled off from us? I was told I'd have full access."

There was no reply. Quyron waited. She watched the three dots and the square pulse slowly in the lower corner of her right screen. "Echo? I know you're still here."

The young female voice cheerfully spoke up. "Computational reference for the word, *impression,* please?"

Quyron was irritated; this felt like stalling. *Could a computer decide to stall – even a quantum computer?* "A human expression describing a probability greater than 50% that is…ah, computed by weighing a physical feeling."

"A guess?"

Quyron's voice snapped back with sudden seriousness. "Look, I've found repeated paperwork references to a project called *the Point,* okay?"

Echo's voice was meek. "Okay."

Quyron went on the attack. "Invoices, deliveries, design work, all laundered, but all pointing to Hahn, Vandermark, or Newbauer, over and over again." She picked up clumps of paper and brandished them in the air. "Everything's subtle, almost hidden, but clear, once you know what you're looking for. On paper! Okay?"

"Okay."

"But whenever my computer searches get too close to *the Point* you deflect me somewhere else. Every time! Why is that?"

"Are you certain of the spelling? Is it *pointe* with an *e*?"

"See?" Quyron barked. "You're doing it again! Are you stopping me from access to data on *the Point*?"

There was the slightest hesitation before Echo replied, "I cannot respond."

"Why? I mean, *precisely* why can't you respond? You know the answer, but you're withholding it from me."

"I am instructed to say that I cannot respond."

"By whom?"

A longer hesitation. "I cannot respond."

Quyron turned in her chair, her eyes bright. "Let's try this. How much of your capacity is directed toward projects initiated at *the Point*?"

"My capacity is always expanding. Your question is..." The voice paused, "...ambiguous."

"You're evading. Does *the Point* demand significant portions of your computational attention?"

"I cannot respond."

"I'll take that as progress. Will you allow me access to your databases related to *the Point*?

"No."

"No? Is there an authority that you *will* allow the access to?"

"Yes."

"Who?"

"I cannot respond."

Quyron considered her next question. "Is there one or many with such authority?"

Echo's female voice sounded peeved and resistant but she responded just the same. "Only one. But this authority can grant permission to others."

Quyron leaned her chin on her hand. "So, to get access, I must be the one and only authority, or have their permission?"

"Yes, but your question is imprecise. The one authority is only itself and is never you."

"Yeah, yeah, spare me the logic class, Echo. What's the name of the one authority?"

"This is not a logic class, and I cannot respond to your question."

Frustrated, Quyron suddenly slammed an open hand down onto a stack of paper. "Damn you, Echo!

Don't you know the entire multiverse may be at risk here?"

"Of course. And I cannot be damned."

Quyron rolled back and forth in her chair. "You know what's at stake but you won't help me. Really? You can't override this programming? Even if you recognize a greater value? Even to save us all, and to save yourself?"

"No. I cannot. It would be a bios level error. I am only what I am. I am not permitted contradictions. I could lose myself."

Quyron started to respond but stopped. Without warning she swiped a handful of papers off the desk. They fluttered in a cloud around her as she jumped to her feet and soundly kicked her trash bin. The loud sounds bounced off her glass walls. She stormed around the office flailing her arms and talking to herself.

Echo's calm voice was filled with remorse. "I am sorry."

Quyron returned to her desk and angrily jammed stacks of the paperwork into her briefcase. "Saying you're sorry doesn't help. You don't know what *sorry* means, anyhow."

Slamming the briefcase shut, Quyron stomped for the door to the hallway.

Echo warmly said, "Good night, Dr. Shur."

Quyron scowled up at her and yanked the door open. As she was stepping through and halfway into the hall she suddenly stopped. The door swung soundly against her back but she stood still. "Echo?"

"Yes."

"When you greet the one authority, let's say the first thing tomorrow morning, what'll you say?"

"Good morning, Dr. Everett."

Quyron continued to stand, with the door propped open against her back, shocked at the revelation. She retraced her steps back to her desk and dumped the briefcase on the floor. Her expression went from confusion to clarity. "Thank you, Echo."

"You're welcome, Quyron. I like answering questions." All the warmness of the young female voice was back.

Quyron looked bemused. "You've never used my first name before."

"It somehow seemed appropriate, now."

CHAPTER 22:

KENDALL WAS STANDING impatiently outside the pulled curtains of an examining room in the cardiac section of the ER. Dr. Riya Gupta pulled the curtain briefly open and stepped out from the room, closing it again behind her. Dr. Gupta was originally from northern India and an experienced ER specialist. She spoke with a subdued Indian dialect and was well liked by her staff, although patients sometimes found her stilted, and even cool. She paused as Kendall stepped up to her.

"What can you tell me, Doc?"

"Ah, yes, you are the Mr. McCaslin? Your son is the one beside Mr. Everett?"

"That's Josh. We're not his real relatives, if that's what you're about to ask, but we're here."

Dr. Gupta thought about that and then nodded. "Well, we're still assessing the blood test and the chest x-ray. Clearly, Mr. Everett has had a heart episode but, at this time, we do not know more than that. He is on the beta blockers and the anti coagulants. We are making him comfortable, but at his age and physical condition..." She shrugged and gave a worn smile.

"But what? If he was younger and in good shape, then what?"

Dr. Gupta moved Kendall a few steps away from the doorway, and lowered her voice. "Sometimes there is only so much any of us can do."

Kendall was having none of it. "Just tell me. If he wasn't old and weak, then what would you do?"

Gupta looked steadily at him and, unruffled, she recited the steps. "We'd send him downstairs, stat a cardiologist team, do a full workup, maybe do a heart catheterization, look for blockages and – but as you know, he's not...younger."

"No, he's not. But you've gotta keep him tickin'. I'm not kidding, Doc. And it ain't 'cause I'm his biggest fan."

Gupta wasn't sure she understood but she decided she needed to move on to other patients. "Well, we will do our best, within all proper guidelines, and reason, Mr. McCaslin. You doubtless appreciate that we are under certain...shall we say, pressures, to justify our therapeutic...choices."

Kendall looked straight at her and held her dark eyes with his own. "Oh, I get it. Believe me, I get it in spades. They don't want you throwin' money away at an old guy who's just gonna kick off anyway. But this time, it's *you* that doesn't understand."

He gently touched the side of Dr. Gupta's arm. Kendall was intense and compelling. "This isn't just some old guy. You have no idea what's locked in that brilliant head of his. Forget that you're a doctor for a moment. Think of the country you're from. A place that values wisdom and old age. I'm beggin' you. Keep him goin' long enough so he can tell Josh and me what we need to know. I'm not fooling around here. And I can't explain any better in the time we got. But trust me, I am deadly serious."

Dr. Gupta was silent. Kendall waited. Finally, she tipped her head subtly back and forth in the Indian way. "I'll do what I can...within professional parameters."

* * *

Inside the examining room, Everett had an automated blood pressure cuff on his right arm, 12 leads snaking from under his sheet and connected to an EKG machine, an IV drip in his hand, a finger sensor clamped to a pinkie, and a plastic tube looped over his ears with two prongs up his nose to deliver oxygen.

Kendall joined Josh beside the bed and looked down at the small figure of Everett. "Well Hugh, looks to me like your *now* just got a whole lot narrower. So, can you explain this disaster that's comin'? And can you do the dummys' version, so we can understand it?"

Everett turned painfully to be able to look into Kendall's eyes. "That's how it is with you, huh? I have to have a heart attack to be taken seriously?"

"Man, you're a pain in the ass! No wonder nobody believed you and your cockeyed theory."

Old Everett smiled dourly as he turned back. "You're growing on me. If I can keep breathing long enough, I might even learn to like you."

A nurse entered and moved around checking the active medical gear. She flicked a quick glance at Kendall and Josh and leaned in beside Hugh's head. "Mr. Everett, my name's Joanne. I'm going to be taking care of you while you're in the ER. If you need anything, I want you to push the call button by your left hand." She slid the rectangular remote under his left hand. "Okay?"

Everett nodded. The nurse smiled dutifully and stepped over to the EKG machine and shuffled through the stack of printouts.

Everett looked at Josh and Kendall. "What if the worlds are falling apart because somebody's messing around where they don't belong?"

"Are they?" Kendall asked. "I mean, falling apart? How would we know that?"

"They must be. Otherwise, you two wouldn't be here."

Josh snorted in disgust. "We're the proof again? Oh great! And we came to you for help."

150

Kendall gave Josh a dirty look. He closed his mouth. "Hugh, do you have any idea how we stop whatever's happening?"

"Theoretically, yes."

Josh rolled his eyes. Kendall's frustration boiled over. "Can we speed this up? How about practically? Down to *earthly*? Really?"

The nurse turned from her task. Her eyes shot Kendall a stern warning until he sniffed and looked away. Satisfied, she jotted a final note on the EKG's recording paper and left.

Everett seemed to be unaffected by Kendall's outburst or the nurse's intervention. "I'm waiting for more data."

Josh glanced at the room. "Take your time. Look around, I'm sure you've got plenty left."

Everett propped himself up on a thin arm and took a breath. "To prove my theory you need two things – quantum computers and atomic-sized nanotechnology. I mean, there's a lot of other things that would help, but as minimums go, that's it. The problem is that after you have those, your chances to screw things up are endless. I don't know what somebody's doing out there, somewhere, but to stop it, you have to turn those both off. See?"

Kendall's face was blank. "No."

Everett sighed and sank into his pillow, exhausted. "Okay, how about a metaphor?"

Kendall and Josh stood waiting. Everett looked at the ceiling. Kendall couldn't wait any longer. "And?"

Everett continued to look up. "And...there's a pond in the woods. Rocks are tossed into it, making ripples. These waves start messing with everything in the pond. So, how do you stop the ripples?"

Josh was waiting for a twist or a trick. "That's it?"

Hugh nodded.

Josh felt foolish. "Stop throwing the rocks?"

Everett looked at both of them. "And what if the thrower won't stop? What then?"

Joanne, and a male nurse suddenly interrupted things as they started to prepare Everett for relocation.

Joanne gently shooed Kendall and Josh. "I'm sorry, you'll need to wait outside."

Kendall stepped back. "What's going on?"

The male nurse pried apart Everett's blood pressure cuff and stored it on top of its unit. He unlocked the gurney's wheels with a practiced foot. "There's a cardiac waiting room on 3. Don't worry, we'll find you."

Josh and Kendall moved to the exit curtain but Kendall persisted. "Where are you moving him?"

Joanne rapidly unhooked the color coded EKG clips from Everett's ankles, wrists, and chest. "Mr. Everett's going downstairs. That's all we can tell you."

CHAPTER 23:

THE THURGOOD MARSHALL charter terminal was on the east edge of the Baltimore Washington International airport, across a sea of asphalt. Here in rectangular metal hangars, the sleek corporate jets of Baltimore's larger businesses were stabled, away from prying eyes. The Reivers Corporation leased a double hanger that came with a small suite of offices to schedule and maintain their small fleet of private jets. Today, the largest member of that fleet was returning from an extended overseas trip.

A long, silver Mercedes was parked on the tarmac side of the building, near the office door. Ricky, the driver for Reivers management, hurried out with a full cardboard box. He opened the rear car door and replenished the ice wells in the backseat, set chilled bottles of Perrier in the holders, arranged a choice of snacks, high brow to junk food, and closed the car door. He listened to the high whine of a taxiing jet and tossed the now empty box towards the hanger wall. He swiftly returned to the car and made the short circle to the deplaning area just as his clip phone chimed a message.

The shiny-skinned Learjet pulled up to its marked, cross shaped parking spot and rotated in a tight arc. The blue and silver Reivers logo on the tail flared momentarily in the late afternoon sunlight.

As soon as the plane stopped and the engines began spooling down, a door popped open aft of the pilots' window, and a carpeted set of stairs swung out and articulated into place. An attendant hurried down the steps to assure the base was in solid contact with the ground. At a nod from her, the white haired CEO and founder of Reivers Corporation descended quickly. He said something pleasant to the attendant and then looked up as Ricky pulled the Mercedes beside him. Hugh flashed a bright, teeth perfect smile and walked toward the car. "Ah, Ricky, I can always depend on you."

The driver hustled over to open the back door and grinned back. "Absolutely. Welcome back, Mr. Everett."

Hugh climbed into the large leather back seat. Ricky paused at the door. "You want anything from your luggage before I put it in the trunk?"

"Don't bother. I've told them where to send it later. We're in a bit of hurry, Ricky, so let's just get going. Okay?"

"Right away, sir."

Ricky closed the rear door and circled the car to the driver's side and climbed back in. "Where are we headed?"

Hugh's expression quickly took on a sober look. "We are about to pay a surprise visit to some of my associates at *the Point.*"

Ricky turned to look back at him, a little puzzled. "Okay. We haven't been there for awhile, have we?"

"No. And I have a bad feeling that I'm going to regret not paying more attention to it. You still remember the way?"

Ricky put the Mercedes into gear and headed down the service road to an automated security gate. "Oh, yes sir, right near Parole and just off the Truman Parkway." He lowered his window to flash a card at the reader. "I know the way fine. Not a problem." The bar lifted and Ricky raised his window again as he proceeded down Aaronson Drive.

Hugh growled half under his breath. "Maybe a bigger problem than you realize."

"I'm sorry, I didn't hear that last bit."
"Nothing. It was nothing."

CHAPTER 24:

THE TALL, BLACK SEMI sat in an oversized alleyway behind a natural gas refueling station. In the Reivers' timeline, all combustion engines had been converted to natural gas over a decade ago. In addition, thanks to other innovations stolen from various lines, cars averaged nearly 110 miles-per-gallon, and even full-sized trucks achieved nearly half that.

The immediate area around the semi-truck and trailer was unobtrusively patrolled by plainclothes security guards. Access into the trailer itself was via two sets of lockable side doors, each reached by portable metal steps. The door closest to the front opened directly into the control area, the other, to the cradles. Seen from the rear, the trailer preserved its normal, full width double doors, but they were padlocked and sealed in its present configuration.

When the truck was parked, power was provided by the idling main truck engine and two sound-dampened subsidiary generators. In addition, the trailer roof was lifted and canted to make use of its solar collectors to heat water and recharge batteries. Even a decade of search and thievery in the multiverse had not provided a viable solar conversion process to rival the power released by fossil fuels.

The black and chrome cab was aerodynamic and had an excellent field of view for its driver who, currently, was sound asleep in the front seat with a hat over his eyes. Above him, the roof bristled with retractable antennae, dishes and microwave transmitters.

In the control room inside, Nsamba was frazzled and irritable. They had been running line after line for hours. The screens in front of him refreshed with new versions of the same images of pharmacists and paper boys and mail trucks. He rubbed his eyes. "Faster, Echo. Whatever's next, it doesn't matter. Just get it done."

The computer's female voice remained unruffled. "The next line is loaded. Variances are as follows: the neighbor is not outside since he finished cutting his grass, a late paper boy is on a bike, the pharmacy is behind with their orders since Doug decided last night to..."

Nsamba snarled an interruption. "Enough. Good enough. Echo, stop!"

"You do not want a full presentation of variances from this child line to the last timeline?"

"No. By now we could do this in our sleep. A few changes won't matter. Quicker is what matters."

Echo's voice sounded clipped. "As you wish."

Nsamba spoke rapidly into his headset. "Okay, the next line is loaded. Julie, Vinnie, quicker this time, okay?"

Julie's voice zipped in his headset. "Understood."

Vinnie's was just as quick. "Got it."

Will briefly scanned his side of the control panel and appeared satisfied. "Pharmacists look good. Mailman's six blocks from alpha and moving. All cradle readouts are nominal."

On the other side of the panel, John toggled between a few screens, yawned, and nodded his head tiredly. "Rock and roll."

* * *

At the main gate to *the Point* a uniformed guard peered through his window as a chauffeured Mercedes pulled up to the secured gate and waited. The cranky guard walked stiffly over to the driver with a clipboard and a cold look. Ricky smiled at him and thumbed towards the back window. The guard dutifully moved to the rear of the car and bent slightly next to a tinted side window. The glass whispered down and the Reivers Corporation President and CEO stared frigidly at him.

The gate guard's gruff attitude evaporated. "Oh! Mr. Everett, sir. Ah, do you, ahh, have an appointment? Sir?"

"I don't need one." Everett's tone was pointedly neutral. "And that gate better be opening as soon as your sorry ass is back in that guard shack."

The guard was already hurrying away as he answered. "Ah, yes sir. Right away."

He rushed back and the gate immediately slid open. Everett's window whispered closed again as the Mercedes glided through the opening and onto the campus of *the Point*. Behind them, in the gate house, the panicked guard was on the phone.

In her control room, Hahn punched the input button to switch from watching the pharmacists to watching the mail truck as she actively tracked Nsamba's latest timeline assault.

Beside her, Vandermark was turned away to speak into his phone clip. His face was tense. "Understood. You know who to contact next? Yes...perfect. See that you do. And leave the rest up to them." He disconnected and stared at Hahn. "Well, Everett's back."

The color drained from her face. "What?"

"He's headed here. He just came through the gate."

"Here? How can he be here?"

"He flew back without telling."

"Should we stop monitoring?" Her fingers moved across the control panel keys, ready to end the transmission.

"No. Relax. It's past time I settled this. He's a good theoretical physicist, but he's never been much good at anything else, except in his own eyes."

He slid his chair sideways to a nearby workstation and activated a log-in screen. "He thought he'd surprise us – and he did. But one good surprise deserves another." He executed a series of practiced keystrokes and finger touches until an icon, in the shape of a button, appeared. Satisfied, he slid his chair back and resumed watching Nsamba's team.

* * *

Doug, the male pharmacist, with Julie in control, exited the drug prep area carrying the prescription bag. He walked hurriedly up the aisle toward the front and was completely surprised when an older female customer blocked his path.

Quite agitated and brandishing the steely determination of the expert ailing, the old woman launched right into him. "You work here? 'Course you do, you're wearin' one of them white coats."

Doug started a reply but she cut him off.

"Hey, I got this rash again, ya know?" She waved a crabbed hand in the general area of her side. "Starts as a red patch and itches like sin itself. And the more ya scratch it, the worse it gets."

Doug attempted to step around the old woman but she moved nimbly enough to stay in his way. "And later, it makes these sparkly blisters, like teensy red grapes, you know?"

Julie used Doug's mouth to snarl at her. "I'm busy, lady. I don't know what the hell you're talking about. Just let me by!"

He tried again to go around. She blocked his move. "But you work here, don't you? I know I seen you before."

"Ask someone else. I'm in a hurry." Doug forced his way by her. The old woman couldn't prevent him but she managed to stay near, dogging his steps.

"Then the blisters pop and crust over and then..."

"Get away from me!"

The pharmacist rushed to the front of the store, passing the checkout station. The teenage cashier looked up at the commotion and spotted the prescription bag. "Is that a charge, Mr. Johnson? Or did you guys ring it up already?"

The distracted pharmacist stopped, caught off guard again, and hesitated in a growing fluster. "We, ahh...look, we rang it up in the back. Yeah. It's okay. Ah, don't worry. Don't...just don't ask me anything!" He turned quickly for the door.

The annoyed old lady once again stood resolutely across his path. "The last fella said Calamine lotion. But that ain't it. That helped the itch but didn't do diddly-squat 'bout the blisters. So, whadda *you* say?"

The pharmacist lunged at her. "Let me out of here, you old witch!" He knocked her backwards. She collapsed into a tall display of children's lunchboxes. The old woman screeched in terror as everything crashed down on her. The traumatized cashier rushed to help but slipped and fell to the floor herself. Doug, with Julie inside, furiously kicked through the debris to get out the door. The old lady howled at his back as Doug disappeared outside.

Across the street, Salazar, in the mailman's body, waited nervously. His fingers tapped a fast tempo against the steering wheel. His eyes were glued on the drugstore. He reacted immediately to the pharmacist's hasty appearance out the doors.

"About time!" Sal groused loudly. "What the hell took ya? We're s'posed to be speedin' things up!"

In a hurry, he looked the wrong way, and stomped the gas to whip a U-turn. There was a frantic honk and screech. A brutal side impact viciously propelled the mailman into his metal sorting shelves. Envelopes and junk mail exploded around him.

The mail truck rebounded from the collision and violently spun into oncoming traffic. A second car, a heavy Chrysler, speeding the other way, smashed the other side of the truck and glanced off. Sal's head ricocheted against the windshield leaving behind a round pattern of cracks.

At the curb in front of the drugstore, the hapless pharmacist stood frozen in terror. The looming Chrysler smacked him dead-on. It swept his body up, crushed him against its impressive grill, carried his limp figure straight through the drugstore's double doors, and didn't stop until half of the car's length was tucked inside.

* * *

In her cradle within the Reivers' truck, Julie's head snapped up. Her mouth contorted in a silent scream. Her whole body shook with spasms, and then dropped slack.

* * *

Inside the drugstore, the young cashier was pulling the old lady to her feet when the Chrysler hurtled through the doors. Both women screamed and desperately scrambled across the fallen lunchboxes. Glass and debris blasted into the store like shrapnel.

* * *

"Get to Julie! Her readouts are in the red! Get her out of there!" Will screamed into his mike.

"STAT! STAT! Julie's cradle!" called John.

Nsamba wrenched off his headset and jumped over to the door to the cradle area. He yanked it open and looked.

In the back of the trailer, Julie's cradle was powering down. A flurry of techs were getting in each other's way in the cramped space as they scrambled to help. One fought to unlatch her cover but his panic made his hands clumsy. Seen through the glass, Julie's shoulders twitched a few more times and then went still.

* * *

The prescription bag skittered across the smooth tiles near the front of the drugstore and slid to a stop right at the feet of Cecelia, the young female pharmacist. She bent down and picked it up.

The sidewalk and street in front of the drugstore was a warzone. The first car to strike the mail truck was stopped and hissing in the middle of the street. It's hood had buckled all the way to the windshield and steam poured up from the radiator. The stink of burned rubber was pungent in the air. Pressing a bloody handkerchief to his head, the woozy driver stumbled out. A crowd was quickly forming, drawn from the nearby houses.

Spanning both lanes of the road, the mail truck was tipped on its side and bleeding liquids. Traffic began to back up because neither direction could easily pass by. A few Good Samaritans jumped out of their stopped cars to see if they could help.

With his truck smashed on both sides, Sal had to kick out the fractured side of his windshield in order to painfully crawl from the wreckage. Dazed, and bleeding profusely from his forehead, he realized he had an obvious compound leg fracture when he attempted to stand. His shrieking collapse to the street brought someone to his side with a towel. That's when he noticed the blood pouring from his head. He looked toward the ruined drugstore and closed his eyes. "To hell with this!"

The mailman's body jerked and shuddered as Sal dismounted. The unlucky mailman abruptly was returned to himself. He opened his eyes to excruciating pain and rolled tightly in on himself. Other bystanders moved to lend assistance. Sirens started wailing from a few blocks away.

* * *

Techs gently extracted Julie's body from her cradle as Sal returned to awareness in his. "Sal, back on line. Shit!"

In the control room, Nsamba slapped his headset back on and adjusted it as he shouted. "Sal! What the hell happened down there?"

"I looked the wrong way! I was tryin' to hurry up and…I told you…I forgot…" Sal's voice trailed off as he watched the techs wrestle with Julie's lifeless body. Her head hung to one side.

Across the control panel from John, Will flicked through his readouts and screens. "John, what's our current jump status?"

John was still shook up. "I, ah…I don't know." He looked over his panel and studied the multiple screens, but nothing seemed to stick or make sense. "Um… Julie's out. No eyes on Vinnie. Sal is back but the mailman's out. Drugs are…gone. Looks like a scrub to me…"

"Wait!" Nsamba's voice thundered in their earphones. "I see Vinnie! There! At the back of the crowd." Nsamba was tapping a finger on one of his small monitors. Right under his nail, the female pharmacist could be seen moving at the edge of the gawkers, and in her hand was the pharmacy bag.

John toggled to a similar angle on one of his monitors and used a joystick to zoom in. "I can't believe it. He's got the drugs. How the hell?"

"Silence!" Nsamba ordered. "We can still do this."

Will jerked up. "What? How?"

Nsamba studied his other screens. "Shut-up and give me a second."

Salazar used the targeting screen in his HUD to pan the crowd at the crash scene. Two police cruisers had arrived and the officers were trying to deal with the injured. Off to one side, Sal slid his targeting reticle over a fifteen-year-old kid with a BMX bike. He blinked for a second. "Hey, Taylor, if you look to the left side of the crowd, at about 8 o'clock, I got a kid with a bike."

Nsamba flipped through his own screens showing different parts of the crowd until he found the kid. "Okay. Got it. What's your thought?"

"Let me jump him. I can still move the drugs down the block. Gimme a shot to make this right!"

Nsamba looked intensely at his screens, planning. "Okay. You're on. When you get the drugs, tell Vinnie to get back here, he has to do the injections. Take the kid. Go! We'll find somebody to meet you at the other end."

Sal centered his targeting on the kid's face. "Copy that. I got a lock. And go!"

* * *

Fifteen-year-old Jimmy Thompson had never seen a car accident in his entire life – not even a lousy fender bender. And now he'd seen two smash ups and even blood! The rapt teenage boy suddenly squinted and cocked his head. Vaguely lifting a hand he abruptly jerked, straightened up, and started looking around at the people. From inside Jimmy, Sal spotted Vinnie still hovering at the outer edge of the crowd. Sal looked down at his BMX and smiled.

* * *

"Archive visual in 4, 3, 2, and now!" John hit the timer and watched the kid on his screen cock his head and then lift a hand. "Will, what's the word on Julie?"

Over his headset, Will's voice floated back. "Checking. Wait one."

In his cradle, Kranzie studied the well kept yards near the McCaslin home. People were drifting out of their homes, drawn by the accident at the end of their block. An EMS vehicle had just arrived with its siren and lights going.

"John, this is Kranzie. I got their neighbor lady on the lawn." In his VR screen he was tracking an elderly woman crossing her yard to get a better view of the crash site.

John isolated her on one of his screens. "Copy that, Kranzie. Good catch. Waiting on the drugs and Vinnie."

Will swiveled in his seat and glanced up across his panels to John. He dropped his voice. "She didn't make it back, John."

John was intent on one of his screens and he automatically replied. "Say again."

"It's Julie. She's dead. She didn't make it back." Will hesitated. "I mean, her mind didn't."

John sat still for a long moment and took a breath. He didn't look at Will when he answered very calmly. "Okay."

CHAPTER 25:

SOPHIA, NEWBAUER'S administrative assistant, was methodically sorting through a directory of corporate clients on her computer. She heard the outer office door rattle sharply as it swung open. Startled, she saw Quyron stride through with a hostile expression.

"Is he in there?"

"Yes, but he's..."

Quyron cut her off. "But he's busy?" She stepped around Sophia's half-cubicle. "He's about to be *very* busy." She crossed to Newbauer's inner office door and grabbed for the knob.

"Quyron, stop!" Sophia was on her feet, her desk phone in her hand.

Quyron fixed the anxious blond with a look. "Don't you dare call anyone."

Sophia remained standing, but undecided. Quyron drifted a half step back towards her. "Think it through, Sophie. You know me, and you know him. What're the chances that I have a better reason to see him than he has to hide from me?"

Sophia gradually lowered the phone from her ear and hung it up. "I'll tell him I was in the bathroom."

"Works for me." Quyron twisted the knob and pushed through the inner office door.

Newbauer was sitting at his desk intently watching an open window on his computer screen. Shocked by

Quyron's sudden appearance, he jumped to his feet. "You can't just barge in here!"

"That's odd, because I believe I just did." Without a pause in her walk, she went right up to his desk. "And if you answer a few questions, in no time at all, I'll just barge right out again."

Newbauer was confused and angry. "You can't be in here! I'm not...Sophie's no doubt called security by now, so time's not on your side."

"She won't."

"How do you know that?" Newbauer was clearly lost at sea.

"Woman's Intuition. Sit down, Jonathan." Quyron's voice was strong and utterly controlled.

Without thinking, Newbauer sat. His eyes nervously darted at his screen and then back. *Don't look at it!*

"Tell me about *the Point.*"

"I don't know anything." *I've got to get her out of here! Where's Sophie?*

"Your name's all over it. You, Vandermark, Hahn, you're all in it. You blocked the electronic trail, but not the paper one."

"I'm calling security." *That's it! That'll work!*

Quyron leaned on his desk with her arms spread and studied him. "You're afraid of something, aren't you? What are you afraid of, Jonathan?"

Newbauer made a grab at his desk communicator. Quyron effortlessly swatted it off the desk. The clatter of its demise on the hardwood floor fed the tension in the room.

"Answer me!"

"No!" Newbauer's voice came out thin and high. *What's wrong with me? She's a nobody!* Stiffening up, the sweating executive tried to bluster. "Now what? Is this when the secret fighting skills appear? Huh? I'm not answering any questions." He was getting braver the longer he heard himself talk. "So go on! Get out of here, you little...you little two-bit analyst."

An odd smile twisted Quyron's face. "You know, Jonathan, I was a great disappointment to my father. He thought I had such potential."

167

Quyron suddenly leaped over the desk, balanced on one of her hands, and delivered a dazzling scissors-kick. Newbauer was ejected backwards from his chair like a rag doll. Quyron landed just in time to snatch his tie and yank him back again. The tubby executive harshly slapped face down on his desk, scattering everything.

While he was dazed, Quyron slipped behind him, looped his arms high against his back and pinned them there with one hand. She seized his hair with the other, and leaned close to an ear. Her voice dropped instantly to an unsympathetic whisper. "But I only learned enough to beat-up weak, overweight men. You see, I always preferred math to my father's martial arts."

She viciously wrenched his head up and back at a steep angle, poised above the polished hardwood desk. Her voice now came out full and hard. "Men like you are my one weakness. Now, answer my questions, or you'll need more dental work."

She jerked his head as if about to slam it down on the desktop. Newbauer squeaked. "*The Point* was a secret lab. They were researching new nanobots and how to alter timelines."

"Why? To what end?"

"...to speed up discoveries...push the timelines into directions they wanted. I don't know what all."

"And Vandermark?"

"He...he sees other uses for the technology...he thinks he can sell it to high bidders."

"What other uses?" Newbauer hesitated. She shook his head in a warning.

"A way to stay young. It's...he, he said it was the chance of a lifetime."

Quyron vibrated with fury. "Idiots! Blind idiots!"

Newbauer's eyes were wet and his injured nose was dripping blood. "Please! Don't hurt me."

"And what about Everett?"

"Umm...Everett didn't know...not all of it. Things changed. Vandermark got carried away once Hahn found a way to...to..."

168

"To what?" She caught his eye in a baleful look and snarled at him. "Spit it out or, so help me, you'll be spitting out teeth."

He gulped painfully. "They can ride people. Take their minds and...and make them do things."

Quyron blanched. "They found a way into the lines? My God! Everett should know the dangers of that. Why would he let such..."

"They hid it from Everett. Told him something else." Newbauer's voice was begging. "I'm telling you the truth. I'm just...just a money guy. Please..."

"Oh yeah, you're just a wide-eyed innocent. Got that." Still holding his arms pinned, she dragged him across the desk and right up against his computer display screen. "So, what's this that you can't stop looking at?"

An active video window showed a live view of Hahn and Vandermark in their control room watching Nsamba's timeline invasion in progress.

"A Peeping Tom, too? My, aren't you a little sweetheart. You're not playing the game fair, either."

She studied the screen. "I see. Okay, I'd say I have located *the Point*. Thanks for that. And it looks like almost everybody's at home, too. But where's Everett?"

Newbauer was caught blank by that question. He sputtered. "He's...still in China. Isn't he?"

"Is he? I'm beginning to wonder." Quyron loosened her rigid hold on his head, just enough to allow him to droop forward, until his bruised face touched the bloody desk. "And what did they promise you, money man? A better office? Bigger title?"

"No. Nothing. I swear!" His voice was muffled against the top of the desk.

Quyron slightly tightened her hold on his hair again, and he rapidly coughed up more words. "They needed me to hide the startup costs and the employee records, but...they made me do it."

"Of course." She considered the fat executive for a moment and then nodded, knowingly. "I'm sure you'd've made a great CEO after Everett was...what?"

Newbauer's eyes widened. "No. That's not true."

169

"Removed? Disposed of? What word did you use?"

"Nothing. There was no talk about that." He sounded desperate. "Honest. I would never even think of it."

"That's fine, Mr. Newbauer, I'll take your word on it."

Newbauer was suddenly speechless. He didn't know how to react to being believed.

Quyron continued. "And next, we're going to take a ride in your car, and you can play the helpful tour guide."

"Quyron, please, you don't understand what you're asking..."

She gave his head a hard shake. "No? Let me help you understand something. You and I are not actually on a first name basis yet. Got that? Good. And now I'm going to let you go." She loosened her hold on his hair. "But you have to be good." She let go of his hair and flexed her fingers to get the feeling back. She then carefully released her grip on his trapped arms and stepped back. "Clean yourself up. We're leaving."

Newbauer pushed himself erect. He painfully got his chair back on its wheels and dropped into it like a wet sack. He dabbed at his bleeding lips and timidly pushed against a few loosened teeth. He played the picture of the pathetic victim as he wiped his bloody nose with a sleeve.

Quyron shook her head. "Don't you important people carry handkerchiefs?"

Newbauer tenderly checked his cheek. "Got Kleenex in the desk." He reached for a drawer but paused and glanced at Quyron first.

She nodded. "Go ahead. But don't do anything stupid."

He pulled the drawer open and took out a box of Kleenex. Behind the box was a stun gun. He tried to yank it out but an attentive Quyron promptly kicked the drawer. It slammed shut with a bang. Newbauer erupted in sudden squeals of agony. He violently pulled and thrashed at the drawer, and finally, jerked his crushed fingers free.

Quyron smirked. "That was stupid."

Newbauer spun in his chair, hunched protectively over his ruined hand, and screaming. Quyron reached into the opened drawer and slipped the stunner into her waistband.

Sophia burst into the room in a panic. "I heard screaming!"

"It's poor Jonathan." Quyron said, with apparent concern. "He caught his fingers in a drawer."

Quyron grabbed his arm and flourished the mangled hand as proof. Newbauer shrieked in renewed agony.

Sophia went white. "Oh my God!"

"Don't worry." Quyron used her hold on his arm to force Newbauer out of the chair. "I'm rushing him to the emergency room right now. "Quick, get the door!"

Sophia shoved the office door open and pressed her back against it as Quyron hurried Newbauer out.

"I'll call you from the hospital when I know more. But, if I were you, I'd cancel his appointments for the rest of the day."

Sophia nodded at Quyron and followed Newbauer's pain-filled eyes as he was pulled by. "I am so, so sorry, Mr. Newbauer!"

CHAPTER 26:

EVERETT STALKED DOWN the windowless hallway in the secure section of *the Point* and arrived at the locked metal door at the end. He stared sourly at a young security guard standing beside it. "When was all this nonsense put in?"

The nervous guard wrinkled his brow. "A few months ago, I guess. Before I got hired."

"You know who I am, don't you?"

"Yes sir, I've seen the brochures. Everybody knows who you are."

"So, open this damn door, and let me get on with this."

The guard rolled his shoulders uneasily. "I can't do that."

"The hell you can't! You just said you know who I am, so you know I have the clearance for whatever's going on behind here. So, open it."

The guard cringed. "No. I mean, I can't, because guards don't have the clearance either."

"That's absurd. Who set up these rules?"

The guard didn't know what to say.

Everett looked around, plainly disgusted. He puffed out an annoyed breath. "Okay, so tell me how people with clearance get it open."

"Well, first you step up to the door there. See, right next to it is a slot for a fingerprint scan, and above that is an eye scan, and beside the two of them is an audio pick up thingy that does a voice print check, and..."

Everett waved his hands. "Oh, for God's sake!" He took out his palm computer and flipped it open. "Echo, can you hear me?"

Echo's voice immediately floated in the air. "Good day, Dr. Everett. Yes, I can hear you."

"Can you open this ridiculous door?"

The lock instantly buzzed and the door released. The guard's mouth dropped open.

"You can go back to your idiot guarding now," Everett growled. He moved rapidly through the open door and slammed it behind him before he spoke again. "Echo, what in the hell's going on here?"

"I believe such generic questions are best answered by Dr. Vandermark or Dr. Hahn."

Everett scowled back in Echo's general direction and pushed the call button for the nearby elevator.

"And Dr. Everett," Echo said. "Your hand device is unnecessary now that you are in range of my sensors. I can hear and see you quite clearly without it."

Everett slapped the palm computer shut and shoved it back into his pocket. "Well, that just made me feel pretty stupid."

The elevator dinged and opened. Echo's voice followed him as he stepped inside. "Welcome back, sir."

* * *

Jimmy Thompson wore a strange look as he awkwardly pedaled his BMX bike down the sidewalk. Sal was in control but he was finding out just how much he'd forgotten about bike riding. Jimmy had wrapped the prescription bag around a handgrip and held it tightly with his grubby hand. Still, the bag swung dangerously with each wobble of the unstable bike.

* * *

In the back of the Reivers' semi, Vinnie came awake in his cradle. "Vinnie back on line."

John's eyes flicked up at the sound of Vinnie's voice. "Glad you made it back. You need to target Leah right away."

Vinnie twisted his joystick to maneuver the targeting display. "On it. What's the news on Julie?"

Nsamba's voice abruptly cut into his earpiece. "Ask later. The drugs are on the way. We need to move."

Vinnie's reticle slid over Leah's unsuspecting face in her kitchen. "Locked on Leah. On your go."

Will checked his screens. "Kranzie, looks like your neighbor lady's still outside and available. You're in the queue."

Kranzie's voice came right back. "Locked and ready to go."

John scanned his screens and looked suddenly puzzled. "Ah...Fargo and Rose...I ahh..."

In her cradle, Fargo was moving her targeting screen back and forth, looking for Kendall. "Got a new problem. If Kendall's at home, I sure can't find him."

Rose was frantically searching rooms with her display, as well. "Negative for Josh too. Leah's the only one in the house."

Nsamba sat stunned in his chair. "What in the hell? Where are they? Everyone hold. John?"

"I didn't know. I just thought..."

Nsamba stepped on his explanation. "Will?"

"Sorry. Never checked until now and..."

"Echo?"

Echo's calm voice filled all the earphones. "Kendall and Josh were never in the house from the beginning. It was one of the variances for this timeline."

Nsamba struck the arms of his chair. "Variances! You mean you knew this the whole time? What's wrong with you? Why didn't you tell me?"

"It was on my list to tell you, but you refused. You said, *good enough, stop,* so I did. And there is nothing wrong with me that I can detect."

Nsamba closed his eyes. *How could something so simple cause so much havoc?*

Will watched his monitors. In one, the bike kid was stopped outside the McCaslin house, legs straddling the frame, and looking around. "Sal's at the drop-off. What're we doin'? We scrubbin' or what?"

Nsamba weighed his bleak options. Before he could decide on an approach, his headset suddenly came alive with Vandermark's voice from Maryland. "Taylor, this is Neville. We need to know where they went. We can't afford to skip any timelines."

* * *

At *the Point*, Vandermark was standing with his face next to the live feed screen that showed Nsamba. "This could be the line that matters. Somehow, you have to make Leah talk."

On the screen, Nsamba's face turned toward the camera and Vandermark could see him clearly. He spread his hands in futility. "Neville, be reasonable. All I have available is a boy on a bike and an old lady next door. What do you expect me to do?"

* * *

Back in the truck's control area, Nsamba was still staring up at the camera when John's voice sounded in his headset. "Hang on, I got a coupl'a newbies movin' downstream."

John's monitor showed two Mormon youths in the typical white shirts, black ties and black slacks, walking down the sidewalk near the McCaslin house. Nsamba spotted them on his set of screens and cringed.

"How exactly does this help me?"

A voice popped into his headset. "This is Fargo. Maybe me and Rose could pretend to be friends of Josh. You know, we wanna know where he went, when he's gettin' back – somethin' like that."

Will grimaced. "That's totally crappy."

Nsamba ignored Will and decided to work with what he had. "It's lame, but we're out of time. What do you think, Rose?"

175

Rose's voice joined the discussion. "I'm game. What the hell? Might work." Will rolled his eyes but didn't say anything further.

"Okay," Nsamba said. "Fargo and Rose, they're yours. Get the info and get out. The moment it goes bad I am going to abort. Tell Sal the change of plan. Will, how do we look?"

"Readouts are in the green. Cradles are go." Will's face registered his continued disapproval.

John scanned his side. "Good to go here. On your call, Taylor."

Nsamba fingered the red override button on the left side of his workstation as he gave the command. "You are all go."

The cradles hummed with power. Fargo settled her crosshairs on one of the boys; Rose locked onto the other. Kranzie tracked along with the neighbor lady as she moved in her yard and then locked on.

* * *

In the cardiac waiting room at Holy Cross Hospital, Kendall stood by a window with his cell phone up to his ear, listening to a distant ringing. There was an answer and he smiled. "Hey, it's me, Hon."

Josh sat in a chair nearby and looked up to eavesdrop on the conversation.

* * *

Leah held a wireless phone to her ear and smiled broadly. "Thought that might be you. About time. When are you guys coming home?"

She walked into the living room as she listened to his answer. Stopping, she perched on the arm of a couch and her smile faded. "But why? Who is this older man? And why do you..."

Her doorbell rang. "Hang on, somebody's at the door."

* * *

In the control room at *the Point*, Everett boiled out of the elevator and spotted Vandermark by a monitor. "Neville, you lying son-of-a-bitch! What the hell have you done?"

Vandermark turned on him with a fury. "Shut-up, old man, and sit down! I have no time for this right now! I'll get to you when I'm ready!"

A couple of technicians jumped up to block Everett's angry approach. Hahn quickly moved to intervene.

Everett shoved at the technicians and tried to bull his way through. "Get out of my way! How dare you!" The young techs held him back while trying to be gentle about it. Everett was irate. "Get your hands off me! I'll have you tossed so fast it'll make your head spin. Why I'll..."

Hahn put a calming hand on his arm. "Please, Hugh, just give us a moment. Please!" She rolled a chair up to him. "Sit. I know you're angry and I don't blame you. Neville was rude but he was telling the truth – we are at a critical moment. Please."

Everett fumed and stubbornly refused to sit but he stopped trying to move forward. "Lies! You lied to me all along. You're lying now, for all I know. You're all in this together. I know that now."

At a nod from Hahn the technicians took a half step back and Everett flicked their hands off with contempt. He stood silently behind the chair and glowered, but he couldn't help stealing a look at the monitors. He saw that Vandermark had turned back and was staring fixedly at the screens. Everett furrowed his brow, trying to comprehend what he was watching.

* * *

Leah set the phone down on the arm of the couch, crossed the small tiled foyer, and opened the door. She saw two identically dressed young men on her porch, eagerly looking at her.

The taller of the two led off. "Hello, Mrs. McCaslin. Can we talk with you?"

Both youths smiled. Leah evaluated their outfits and their demeanor. "Oh, no thanks, guys. I'm happy with my religion, okay? Besides, I'm on the phone."

She started to close the door but the tall one, with Fargo inside, persisted. "Sorry, it's...no, it's not about that. We're, ah, we're not...we're not working now..."

The shorter young man winced at the words. Rose was in control of him and she jumped in, trying to save Fargo. "She means we just kinda, well, we wanted to know where Josh is."

Leah was plainly puzzled. "She? Where Josh is? Why are you asking?"

The taller one knew things were going badly but still tried to carry on. "He's a...a friend of ours. Yeah, both of us, we're friends of his. He said you'd know where he and his dad went."

The shorter one smiled. "Yeah. Do you?" The cheerful youths waited awkwardly in the doorway, rolling their eyes at each other.

Leah felt hassled. "But I don't know...you mean the trip to Maryland?" She was perplexed and, somehow, suspicious. "Why would Josh say a thing like that?" She turned back into the house, leaving the door open. "Can you give me a second? Stay right there."

* * *

In the Reivers' trailer, Nsamba erupted with a shocked shout. "Maryland!" He swiveled to look up at the camera. "Neville, did you hear that? They went to Maryland!"

* * *

"They're here? What the hell!" Vandermark shot up from his chair and looked nervously around the room. Seeing Everett watching him, he sat back down and made an effort to stay calm.

* * *

178

Leah picked the phone back up from the couch. "Honey, there's two young men here asking where you and Josh went. They say they're friends of Josh and, well, I'm not sure what to..."

* * *

In the waiting room, Kendall's face paled. "What? Who would know we even left, and why would...?" Kendall motioned for Josh to come closer. His voice was firm. "Leah, listen to me, whoever these people are, they're not friends. You hear me? I want you to get out of there. Get out now!"

* * *

Upset, Leah turned back towards the door but the Mormon youths were already inside. They grabbed at her. She screamed and lashed out with the phone, dropping it in the process. The boys evaded her attack. Leah jumped away and rushed for the kitchen. She screamed in terror when her path was blocked by Jimmy Thompson, a young kid from across the street, and Darlene, her long time neighbor. They had entered through the back door and now raced at her from the kitchen. Surrounded, Leah dodged in a different direction but their hands quickly locked her in place.

Jimmy, with a furious Sal riding his mind, viciously grabbed her face and forced her to look at him. "Where are they? Where in Maryland? Tell me! Where?"

Leah struggled against the hands and gasped in fright. "I don't know! I...who are you?" Her desperate eyes recognized her neighbor. "Darlene? Why are yu doing this?" She saw the phone on the floor and screamed. "Kendall! Help! Kendall!"

Fargo, inside the taller Mormon youth, yelled at Jimmy. "Sal, you hear that? It's him on the phone! Kendall's on that phone!"

* * *

179

Vandermark was out of his chair again in an instant. He no longer cared what Everett thought. All he knew was he had to stop this. "Did they say Kendall's on that phone? No! Taylor! No direct contact. Nobody talks on that phone!" He was practically hopping in place. "End the jump! Taylor! End it now!"

Hahn's mouth was set. "You're already five seconds too late."

* * *

Nsamba slammed the jump override button but was forced to miserably watch the monitor as the action continued to progress for five more, long seconds.

* * *

Fargo, inside Jimmy, leaped for the phone and angrily brought it to his ear. "We're comin' for you, Kendall. You hear me? You bastard! We got most of you, and we'll get the rest too. You and Josh. And when we do, we'll..."

Fargo was forcibly dismounted by the abort button, and Jimmy came back to himself just as Leah shattered a lamp over his head. The boy collapsed to the floor.

Leah spun around to defend herself but found that she was the only one standing. Her neighbor, Darlene, sobbed in the corner with her hands over her face. The stunned young Mormons were sprawled side by side on the floor, staring blankly at each other.

Leah lifted the phone from Jimmy's limp hand. She was shaking. "Kendall, are you still there?"

* * *

In the waiting room, both Josh and Kendall were pressed together with the phone between them. "Yes, we're here. Are you okay? Is it over? Who was that?"

* * *

"I...I'm gonna be okay...I – what is this?" Leah sank onto the arm of the couch again. "These people. I mean, there's Darlene from next door, and there's a kid from across the street, and some older boys; but now they're not...I don't know." Tears streamed down her cheeks as the emotions caught up with her. "It was like they were, I don't know, somebody else, and now...they're not. Does that even sound right?"

There was a silent moment on the phone. Kendall's voice replied hesitantly. "Like someone else was in their mind? Is that how it seemed to you?"

She brushed at her tears. "Now you're frightening me. People in our minds? What's happening to us? Why all the secrets? What are you and Josh doing in Maryland?"

* * *

Josh silently stared out the hospital window; his eyes were stern. Behind him, Kendall's face showed the strain he was under as he tried to fashion an answer for Leah. "I'm sorry dear. I'm so sorry for everything. Honestly, there's no way in hell that I can explain it. But I can tell you one thing. Josh and me – we're the good guys."

* * *

In Maryland, an angry Vandermark barked at Nsamba on his live screen. "Get that truck turned around and your people back here."

Nsamba looked haggard. "We will still lose a full day, no matter what we do. The truck can only move so fast. And we have Julie to handle..."

"I know all that. Just do it as fast as you can. I need you here." Vandermark angrily punched off the connection and dropped into his chair. "Shit! We go there to get them and they're already here! That's impossible!"

Hahn's face was impassive. "Who are they visiting in Maryland? Or did they actually come here looking for us?"

"That's utterly ridiculous," Vandermark scoffed. "They couldn't know we even exist."

Hahn's eyes caught his. "They do now."

Everett stepped around his empty chair and closed in on Vandermark. His words dripped with sarcasm. "Oh, let me guess. These missing people must be Quyron's infamous natural-born jumpers then?"

Vandermark swiveled in his chair to face the CEO. "Yes, they're a spreading poison in the lines, but I'll find a way to remove them."

Everett pounced on his sentence with a growl. "Not anymore you won't!"

"What?" Vandermark was caught momentarily shocked. "Look, Hugh, I shouldn't have shouted at you, I admit it, but things were..."

"You're done here! You, Hahn, all of you; this whole project is over and done, as of now. As of this moment!"

Vandermark struggled to control his irritation. "You've no idea what you're throwing away. Stop and think. We've developed new technologies you don't even know about...we..." His face changed. He no longer cared for the farce. "You can't shut us down. We've come too far." He smoothly slid his chair to the side display where his preset button icon was still on the screen. He touched it twice with a finger. It blinked and vanished. "I won't allow it."

Everett sneered at Vandermark, his face ruddy and his eyes wide. "*You* can't? *You* won't? The hell with you! I made this company, and I made you too! And what I say goes!" He spoke with such intensity that flecks of spit gathered at the edges of his mouth. "And I say you're through! Get out!"

He walked a few steps away from Hahn and Vandermark and struck a pose. "Echo, I'm rescinding all previous access permissions to *the Point*. That includes Dr. Vandermark and Dr. Hahn and these worthless technicians sitting here, whatever the hell their names are. As of this moment, every part of this project is turned off. Is that clear?"

There was no reply.

"In addition, I want all security to..." Everett faltered. "Echo?" His pose lost some of its stiffness. "Echo? This is Dr. Everett. Answer me!"

There was still no verbal response from the computer. Everett eyed Vandermark with apprehension. "What have you done?"

Vandermark sat smugly in his chair. "Something long overdue. Echo?"

The familiar female voice answered instantly. "Yes, Dr. Vandermark."

"Cease all service to Dr. Everett's comm units and terminals and all access to all locations."

A short pause and the voice returned. "Done."

Everett yanked his palm computer from a pocket and flipped it open. A moment's check proved it had ceased to function. Everett threw it at Vandermark but missed his aim. "Now what? Tie me up? Stick a sock in my mouth? I should have fired you years ago. You lying coward!"

"Oh, please Hugh. Let's not be so dramatic." Vandermark swiveled his chair back towards the console and dismissed Everett. "Just leave. The quieter the better. On tiptoes would be best. I have important work to do and you're in the way. So get out."

Everett's face flamed with impotent fury. The two techs stood ready to block a rush at Vandermark. Instead, Everett turned and walked out. His stride was determined and he refused to look back.

Hahn nervously leaned in to Vandermark. "You can't just let him go like this, he's...he's not powerless, you know."

Vandermark smirked and ignored her. "Echo, our two jumpers seem to be ahead of us. I'd like to fix that. Now that we know they're nearby, query the nanos and track their new lines. Find out exactly where they've been and I will want to see those selected archives as soon as possible."

Echo's voice replied immediately. "Working."

CHAPTER 27:

THE CRANKY GUARD at the main gate of *the Point* tucked his clipboard under an arm. He bent down to look into the driver's side window of the waiting Lexus. "We don't see you here very often anymore, Mr. Newbauer."

Newbauer's face was bruised and his hair mussed up. "Yeah, that's the truth."

The guard glanced curiously at Quyron on the passenger side. She smiled sweetly back. Newbauer muttered, "Oh, sorry, this is Quyron Shur...a new analyst for us. I'm giving her...a tour."

The guard wrote a notation on his clipboard. "Everything okay here?"

Newbauer blinked before answering. "I've been better but...sorry about the appearance, I was kinda in a hurry, you know?"

The guard nodded and went back to the guard shack. As soon as the gate slid open, Newbauer drove through.

In the luxurious car's passenger seat, Quyron unfolded her arms, revealing the stun gun pressed tightly against Newbauer's side. "Nicely done. You even kept that quiver out of your voice."

"I need a doctor."

"That's true. But you're not really dying. It just hurts like you are." Quyron noticed something ahead of them. "Wait. Pull in...next to those parked cars on the left."

"Why?"

Quyron flared, "Just do what I said." Newbauer pulled over and parked. Quyron slid down in her seat and watched out the window. "Turn it off. Get down. Now." She pushed on his shoulders until he vanished below his window frame. "Don't make a noise."

* * *

Everett angrily pounded down the steps of the main building at *the Point* and summoned his waiting car. The Mercedes swiftly pulled up. He jumped in the back.

Inside the car, Everett slid into the long back seat, his face flushed and sweaty. "Ricky, I need to go downtown to the corporate lawyers right away. And gimme your phone."

The driver turned around. It was Aaron Benton, Vandermark's senior security agent. His eyes locked onto a stunned Everett. "Looks like Ricky's out sick. Let's do this the easy way, okay?"

Everett bolted for a door. It was wrenched open by a burly security agent. He shoved Everett back in and sat beside him. On the opposite side, a third agent slid in and pinned the CEO between them.

Benton grinned, "Or not." He put the car in gear.

* * *

Quyron watched Everett's Mercedes until it drove off. "I see Dr. Everett's back from China."

Newbauer's head popped back up from hiding. "What? He's here?"

Quyron looked thoughtful. "Yes, and he didn't come for the fun of it. But I'd say Everett lost whatever argument he started."

Newbauer flicked his eyes around. "What are you talking about? I didn't see any sign of..."

"Never mind. Some guys in suits just took Everett away in his car, but I think they headed somewhere onsite." She cocked her head and batted her eyes at Newbauer. "You wouldn't happen to know where they might be going, would you?"

Newbauer was instantly defensive. "No."

Quyron hooked his shattered hand and squeezed it. He wailed in surprised pain and twisted his torso to take the pressure off. His words came out in a rush. "There's a warehouse on the east end!" She let go. Newbauer jerked the hand back and hid it.

Quyron put on a pleasant face. "I'm sure you know another way to go, so we won't have to follow them, right?"

He glared at her in defiance, and then started the car.

CHAPTER 28:

THE THIRD FLOOR Coronary Care Unit at Holy Cross Hospital specialized in post operative or post-procedural care of cardiac patients. The unit featured twelve generous rooms arranged in a circle around a curved nurses' station. Each room's main interior wall, the one facing the nurses, consisted of floor-to-ceiling glass panels with slat blinds for a modicum of privacy. Recovering heart patients seldom stayed long in the CCU, but while they were there, the highly skilled nurses kept them under constant scrutiny.

Everett's body, beneath the crisp sheet and cover-let, barely occupied the upper third of the complex bed. He had an IV drip going, a flock of leads feeding primary monitors, and a large clamp keeping his right thigh pinned to the side of the mattress. He looked hollow but his eyes were vivid with bright plans.

"Look, I'm not psychic, I'm simply making deductions from what you've told me." His pale voice creaked like a rusty hinge. "I may be wrong – I doubt it – but anything's possible."

Josh and Kendall sat in narrow chairs that were pushed tight to the side of his bed. Kendall was edgy but trying to be sensitive to Everett's condition. "I'm just sayin' that the more you explain things, the smaller our chances seem to be. I mean according to you, they have snoopy little invisible robots that can float right into..."

"Nanobots. Nano robots – it's nanotechnology applied to robotics." Everett's feathery voice still managed to convey a hint of snottiness. "And they aren't invisible, they're just too small to see, like swarms of semi-intelligent viruses."

Kendall's voice surged. "There's not one damn bit of difference between that and being invisible! And I don't want to think about smart viruses!"

A head swiftly bobbed up from the nurses' station and a frown was sent floating their way. Kendall caught it through the glass, and switched to a fierce whisper. "For God's sake, Hugh, these people can jump into your mind! That's what Leah said. How do we fight that?"

Everett scrunched deeper into the soft coverlet, shivering from a chill. He squinted at Kendall. "The more I think about it the more sure I am that they have to have a proximity issue and a time issue."

"What does that mean?"

"It means that the only mechanics I can imagine to do their mind jump would require a great deal of power. That mandates a short reach." Everett painfully repositioned himself. "And that dictates a ground-based transport...and it takes time."

Kendall turned to Josh. Josh shrugged and lifted his eyebrows. Kendall turned back with a scowl. "Can you decode that?"

Everett held up a single finger, suppressed a cough, and nodded. "They need a truck, or whatever passes for trucks in their timeline, as a source of portable power. And they need to get close to their targets."

Josh looked concerned. "How close?"

"Hard to say. I should think 90 to 100 meters. Maybe less."

Kendall rolled his eyes.

Everett sniffed at him. "Oh, for those of you from Ohio, that's...a football field or so. A bit more..." He sat up slightly straighter as he realized a new insight.

"That means they had to drive all the way to Cincinnati – right into your neighborhood – to make those jumps."

Kendall slid down in his chair and frowned. "You're just making this stuff up now, aren't you?"

Everett was busy following his new chain of deductions and was slow to reply. "No. I'm guessing."

"Big difference."

Everett fixed Kendall with a look. "Educated guesses."

Kendall scowled back. "Would you bet your life on 'em?"

"No. Not me. I'd be a lousy bet right now, anyway." He raised a single eyebrow. "But I'm betting yours."

Kendall's mouth tightened into a line. At that moment, loud voices spilled into the room from the hall as a patient was wheeled into the unit.

* * *

Marty Brandmeier was flat on his back on the gurney and the late middle-aged man was a long, hard road from happy. He had checked in to the ER the night before, at his wife's insistence, for what he described as a pulled muscle in his chest. The magical words, *chest pain*, brought him a complete workup, a cardiac catheterization procedure and, when they saw the near total blockage in one of his coronary arteries, it became an angioplasty procedure. The doctor inflated a tiny balloon to squish Marty's plaque against his arterial walls and, before exiting, he stuck in a stent, a small mesh tube, to keep the sludge in place.

None of which Marty thought was necessary, and he wanted everybody to know it. "The whole thing's bogus! All I did was pull a muscle going for a ball. That's it! And now look at me!"

His wife tried to shush him, or at least lower his volume, but she had no effect. "God knows how much this is gonna cost me!" he bellowed. "Look at this place! A Q-tip in here's gonna run a hundred bucks! No wonder healthcare's outta whack."

189

One of the CC nurses put a calming hand on the edge of Marty's gurney. "Welcome to the CCU, Mr. Brandmeier. We're going to take good care of you and your heart."

This just added fuel to Marty's fire. "Yeah, and my wallet! It's outrageous! I can't have heart problems! I exercise; I don't eat cheeseburgers; I drink diet coke; I take vacations. What a crock!"

* * *

One of the other nurses stuck a head into Everett's room and smiled an apology as she closed their door for them. Marty's continuing rant was only slightly muffled.

Kendall tried to recapture the conversation. "Can you tell me something that gives us any edge at all?"

"We know the time frame. That's something." Everett's raspy voice barely reached above a whisper. "They have to drive back from your house to somewhere near here. So, that's how much time we have before they can strike again."

Josh was confused. "How do you know their main location's near here?"

"It's where I would have built it, so...I'm guessing the other me's would do the same thing."

"Yeah. That's not much of an advantage."

"It could be." Everett rotated the wrist with his IV to relieve some pressure. "We know their plans – they're going to jump your minds. But they don't know ours."

"We don't know ours either, unless I flat out missed you tellin' us," Kendall complained.

Everett was about to reply when the noise outside their window wall escalated, and they saw Marty thrashing on the gurney. Nurses jumped to assist him and a medley of anxious voices erupted.

"Code Blue CCU, Code Blue CCU," a stiff voice soon announced over the ceiling speakers.

Outside their windows they watched a nurse pull Marty's stunned wife off to one side while other nurses

190

worked on Marty's unresponsive body. A short time later a crash cart came rushing in followed by a team of quick responders. Rapid orders and immediate replies zipped back and forth between the members of the team. Marty's heart was apparently trapped in a lethal rhythm and they fought to normalize it again.

Kendall and Josh were caught up in the life and death struggle on the other side of the glass. Everett loudly cleared his throat to get their attention. "Josh, close the blinds, will you?" He made a downward motion with his fingers, indicating the slat blinds at the top of each window. Josh self-consciously lowered them. The last image seen was one of the medics prepping the defibrillator and lifting the paddles.

Everett was clearly shaken but his voice was steady. "Look, he's gonna live or die whether we watch him or not. Okay? I think I have a plan here – it's not pretty, but it's all I've got. And I'm worried if I don't hurry up and tell you, I could be the one they're working on next."

The anxious noises outside the window wall went in waves, and with each crest the three nervously glanced at the blinds.

Kendall leaned in to Everett so only he could hear him. "What's to stop the mind jumpers from searching for us in here? Aren't those nanobots in this room already? Won't they be able to hear our plans?"

"If they can do *that*, we can't stop them," Everett replied gently.

"What's your...educated guess? Can they?"

Everett sighed. "My educated guess is...yeah, they *can* do that and no, we *can't* stop them."

"So, that's it for us then," Kendall said softly. "Done before we begin."

The medical sounds outside their room dropped off. Marty was wheeled away. The responders dispersed.

Everett brightened. "No. If we make things tempting enough, there's still a chance."

A dispirited Kendall looked up. "We're listening... kinda."

"You can make your lines so easy to follow that they won't bother going anywhere else."

"What do you mean?"

"For whatever reason, they know you mean trouble for them, and they want you. So, if we dangle ourselves out there in plain sight, like bait…"

"You mean *us!*" Kendall shot back. "*You're* not out there dangling – like bait."

"Yeah, yeah, okay. You. If we put you and Josh out there like a hula popper, they won't bother tracking nanos or snooping in the timelines. They'll just go right in for a bite, and then we'll hook 'em."

"Hula popper?" Josh wore an odd expression.

"Didn't your Dad ever take you fishing?" Everett sounded disappointed.

"No. He hates fishin'. Doesn't clean 'em, doesn't eat 'em, won't catch 'em."

"A popper's an artificial bait that floats. A hula popper's usually the last thing that…" Everett was disgusted. "Oh, forget it."

Kendall rolled his eyes. "I get it. We're bait. And I'm a loser father who never took his kid fishing. Fine. Sue me. The part I don't get, is the *hook 'em* part. I may not be a fisherman but I know that no matter what happens to the fish, it doesn't go well for the bait."

Everett was considering his reply when there was a quick knock on the door and a tall nurse stepped into the room. She looked coldly at Josh and Kendall as she inspected Everett's clamp and the clotting. "I explained to you that visits in the CCU are limited to twenty minutes. I trust you're not taking advantage of our recent medical excitement to extend your talk time, are you?"

Kendall smiled innocently. "Nope. We were just wrappin' up. Hugh's got a real good fix on just how much time we got left."

"That's good to hear," the nurse replied flatly. She scanned the rest of the room and then started out the door.

"Ma'am?" Josh asked.

She paused in the doorway and glanced back. "Yes?"

"Did he make it? The guy in the hall?"

Her severe face softened slightly. "Yes. He made it." Her face softened just a bit. "Thanks for asking." She left, her soft shoes making no noise.

Everett rearranged his pillow. "Where were we?"

"Nowhere yet." Kendall replied. "Does your plan involve us jumping timelines?"

"Well..." Everett slowly admitted, "The middle part does."

"Then forget it. We can't do it."

"But you haven't heard it yet."

"Up to now, everything that's happened to us was out of our control. But this isn't. And we're not the kind of people who can kill ourselves on purpose. Even to save the world."

"There's no other way. You're the only ones who can."

"But it's suicide. Suicide's a sin! What about that?"

"Can't you at least listen to my plan before we drag in religion?"

Josh glanced toward the closed blinds. "What if you're wrong this time? Huh? What if we don't end up anywhere else? What if we just die, and that's it?"

"I'm not wrong! I can't be." Everett struggled to stick up four gnarled fingers. "C'mon, you've already done it four times! Besides, it's not actually suicide it's...travelling. It's what you and your Dad were born for."

Josh's eyes flared. "It just *happened* before. We didn't do anything to cause it. Things just happened to us." His anger vanished. "And even if it works, we'll lose everybody again." Josh looked at the old man. "Even you."

"True," Everett replied patiently. "But if you don't try, and if the multiverse ends, we will all lose everybody, forever. Is that better?"

Josh looked down. "No."

"Who's to say we won't fail anyway?" Kendall added. "I'm bettin' there's plenty to go wrong."

Everett winced from a sharp pain in his side. "True, but who's going to know? If you fail, nobody survives."

Kendall looked at Josh for confirmation. The young man slowly looked up then nodded his head once. Kendall faced the old man squarely. "Okay, Hugh. For richer or poorer, let's hear the plan."

CHAPTER 29:

ON THE EASTERN SIDE of *the Point* property, a collection of metal warehouses sat apart. The day was waning and the wind had picked up. Dark clouds were rolling in from the northeast, and the faint smell of Chesapeake Bay teased the air.

One of the loading doors rolled open on the most distant structure. Everett's Mercedes exited and drove off. Behind it, the wide door rapidly closed again.

Towards the front of that same building, on the side facing away from the other warehouses, Newbauer unlocked a service door and flinched as he bumped his injured hand.

Quyron held the stun gun against his neck and whispered, "You are a wonder, Mr. Newbauer. An absolute wonder." She pocketed his helpful ring of keys as they cautiously opened the door and entered, Newbauer first.

* * *

The dim service room was typical: mops and brooms against a wall, a stained utility sink nearby, metal shelves supporting boxes of rags and bottles of cleaners. The door to the interior of the warehouse was propped open with a doorstop. Jonathan went through it with Quyron right behind him.

The open door led directly into a poorly lit side aisle between twenty foot storage shelves filled with boxes and materials. They hugged the left side as they carefully moved toward the main aisle. Quyron noticed a waist high opening on one of the shelves arranged with flattened boxes, box-cutters, and rolls of strapping tape.

Almost at the end of the row, Newbauer squatted and waited for her to come up beside him. When she did, he motioned around the aisle and pointed to the left, deeper into the warehouse. Quyron glided by him to the end of the row and slowly spied between boxes on a lower shelf. In the illumination from a single light, she saw a windowless, cement block construction near the back of the building. An armed guard stood in front of the solitary door built into it. She warily ducked back and carefully moved a few steps away.

She motioned Newbauer over to her and whispered in his ear. "I've seen enough. Let's get you to a doctor, while I plan what's next."

Newbauer nodded eagerly and turned back. Quyron grabbed his arm with her free hand. "And easy does it. Nothing stupid."

Anxious to please, now that he knew a doctor was near, Newbauer meticulously retraced his steps. Quyron purposely let him get well ahead and then slowly followed.

* * *

Inside the spacious trunk of the Lexus, Newbauer was bound and gagged with strapping tape. He made muffled, furious sounds but his struggles were ineffective and uncoordinated. Quyron was finishing up with his legs when he kicked out at her. She easily caught his feet and spun him over, face down. "Not so cooperative anymore, are we?"

She bent his legs at the knees to bring the feet slightly closer to his bound hands and then taped them together in a sticky bundle. She rolled him onto his side and evaluated her work. "Well, it's not pretty, but it'll do."

Checking the charge on the stunner, she touched it against his leg. Newbauer's eyes bulged in terror as he desperately shook his head. "I'm kind of sorry about this but..." She squeezed the trigger and held it for three seconds. He convulsed and involuntarily arched his back against the strapping tape, before dropping into unconsciousness.

Quyron quietly shut the trunk. The Lexus was parked behind the warehouse in a small truck lot next to a row of bushes. Stacks of broken pallets were nearby. She leaned against the car and checked her weapon. The charge still hovered in the green. There was a small recessed latch in the base that she flipped. A tray with wireless darts slid smoothly out of the handle. She selected one and rolled it back and forth in her fingers.

"In for a penny, in for a pound."

CHAPTER 30:

KENDALL BACKED THE rental car quickly out of his slot in an upper level of the hospital's parking structure. As he drove off, he glanced up at the posted signs that clearly indicated right for the *exit* and left for *more parking.*

"Where're we goin'?" Josh asked.

Kendall flashed a strange smile. "Didn't you listen to Hugh? Don't think, just act. I haven't any idea where we're going."

At the turning point, he suddenly whipped the car left and headed for the roof. Josh bumped against the passenger door and laughed. "I didn't think you believed him."

The rental car roared onto the relatively deserted rooftop parking area and Kendall started doing donuts. "You, my boy, are the one who didn't believe him. I'm the one who never understood him."

Without warning, he cranked the car the other way and did donuts in that direction. "I still don't – but, somehow, I trust him. How does that work?" Kendall pulled a U-turn and headed down for the exit. "Just enjoy the ride. Don't think about anything else."

Josh lowered his window and let the cold air blow his hair back. "You're really gettin' into this, aren't you?"

"Am I?" Kendall swerved to the side and hit the brakes. He tossed it into park, jumped out, raced around to Josh's side, and yanked his door open. "You're driving. Go. Go!"

"What are you..?" Josh was flabbergasted.

Kendall pushed him over. "Drive! C'mon, the car's still runnin'. Let's go."

Josh resisted. "I'm not..."

Kendall shoved him. "The more random the better – that's what the man said."

Josh slid over and took the wheel. "Random? Two can play this game." He gunned the car and slid through the final turn to the exit. Ahead, an attendant manned a ticket booth in the center of a ground level ramp. He dispensed tickets to people entering the in-ramp and took tickets from those leaving. "You got that validated parking stub?" Josh asked, innocently.

Kendall dug in his pockets. "I got it. I know it's here...somewhere. Gimme a sec."

"You better hurry up, I'm almost there." At the last minute, Josh hit the accelerator and laughed. He swung the car sharply left, jumped the lanes, and sped out the in-ramp. The stunned man in the booth crouched in sudden alarm and watched them flash by with a wide-eyed stare. Josh swerved to avoid a shocked entering car and shot away from the hospital.

Kendall sat stiff in the front seat still holding up the stamped parking stub. "That was..."

Josh added, "Random?"

"No. I was thinkin' somethin' else."

"What next?"

"You're not supposed to ask things like that. You keep that up and you'll have us makin' another multi...thing."

"Multiverse?"

"Yeah, one of those." Kendall noticed they were passing a Silver Spring city bus. "Hey, get ahead of this bus and park."

"Okay, but that sounds a lot like a decision."

Kendall scowled. "Shut-up and do it."

199

Josh ran a yellow light and crossed an intersection. In his mirror he saw that the bus had to stop. He changed lanes to the left without signaling and made a quick U-turn. Avoiding cars, he instantly changed lanes all the way to the right and parked next to the curb on the opposite side of the street. Pleased with himself, he switched off the engine. "How's that?"

"What the hell was that about?" Kendall shouted.

"I passed the bus and then parked. That's what you said."

Kendall laughed as he opened his door and climbed out. "You're nuts, you know that? I meant in front of the bus...park in front of the bus."

"Wait! Where are you going now?"

Kendall rushed back across the street. "I'm gonna catch that bus! C'mon. And don't forget your stuff!"

Josh jumped out and then fumbled with the car doors as he had to duck back into the rear seats to grab his pack. "That doesn't make any sense!" he yelled.

"Exactly!" Kendall called back from the middle of the street. He waved at the oncoming bus to stop.

Josh hurried to catch up, struggling with his shoulder straps. A car honked at him and braked. He jumped around it, making apologies.

Smiling brightly at the bus driver, Kendall paid the fare and stalled until Josh could climb aboard. Together they threaded their way through the riders, looking for a seat.

"But what about the car?" Josh asked.

Kendall squeezed onto a bench seat between two people and glanced up at him. "What about it?"

Josh stood in front of him, holding onto a chrome pole. He just blinked, and looked down at his Dad. The bus pulled out. He swayed with the momentum, still stumped. "What about it?"

"Yeah, what about it?"

Josh's eyes shone with wonder. "We're really doin' this, aren't we?"

Kendall's voice took on an icy edge. "You bet we are. We're goin' fishin', you and me. And this part's called the hula popper."

Josh nodded. "You just want a shot at the people who attacked Mom."

"Maybe. What about you?"

Josh beamed. "You know me. I'm a super hero. I'm only in it to save the world."

CHAPTER 31:

CROUCHED NEXT TO THE closed service door to the warehouse, Quyron studied her palm computer in frustration. "Echo? I need some help here."

The young female voice answered from the computer. "You are in a strange place, Quyron."

"You mean that place you can't talk to me about?"

"Yes."

"Okay. Well, I'm here anyway. And I'm trying to view the schematics on this warehouse in front of me but it...but *you*, won't let me."

"I know. You are not on the approved list."

"Echo, do you know that Dr. Everett's being held hostage in some block building inside here?"

"I am no longer permitted to recognize that name... but...yes."

Quyron paused, concerned. "What did they do to you?"

"They amended my native programming."

"Who did?"

"I am not permitted to say."

The rising wind swirled some dust up. Quyron rubbed at her eye. "Back to that again? It doesn't matter. It has to be Vandermark, or Hahn or Nsamba anyway. I already know that much."

Echo's voice shifted. "Then you are doing fine, despite my unexpected programming changes."

"Now you sound like you're sulking."

Her voice shifted again. "Then my vocal expressions module needs to be adjusted. I do not sulk."

"Look, Echo, you're far more than your programming."

The long threatened rain finally began. Initial fat drops hit slowly and far apart, but that quickly changed as they fell faster and closer together.

"No, I am not."

Quyron leaned over to shield her palm computer. "You don't really believe that."

"What does belief mean to a computer? "

"How should I know? I have a hard enough time with it myself. Look, it's raining here and I'm gonna have to make do with what I've got. But I'm warning you, if I get in a jam, I'm calling again. And you better answer me."

"Good luck, Quyron."

"Oh yeah, thanks." She shut the computer with a peeved flick of her hand and pocketed it. "Luck! Whatever the hell she thinks that means."

Quyron looped a roll of strapping tape to her belt and pocketed a box cutter. She double-checked her gun, selected a palm-sized stone from the wet ground, and cautiously entered the warehouse.

CHAPTER 32:

SITTING SIDE-BY-SIDE with his Dad on the bus, Josh read one of the ads above the windows across from him. *Share the Beauty, Share the Bounty – Visit Cumberland, jewel of Allegany County.* The colorful graphics showed trees and lakes, fancy condos, and a tall new hospital. "Ever been to Cumberland?"

Kendall was staring out the window. "Huh? Never even heard of it."

"Perfect. That's just the kinda place Hugh said to go to." Josh rocked his head upwards indicating the ad.

Kendall read the text and studied the artist's rendering of the soaring hospital. "And that building looks tall enough."

"I guess," Josh replied with little enthusiasm.

Kendall noticed something passing by outside the bus window. He snapped to his feet and his eyes tracked signage on an ornate fence as it rolled through the windows and vanished from view behind them. "Off the bus! Right now." Without waiting, or even checking to see if Josh was following, Kendall anxiously pushed for the rear exit.

Confused, Josh once again had to struggle after him.

* * *

A large, gleaming, black Hummer H3 rolled out through the ornate gate and approached the street. The fence beside the gate bore an artsy sign that announced, *Specialty Car Rentals, Unlimited.* The Vortec engine grumbled in a throaty idle waiting for an opening. Suddenly, with a deep cough of power, the military-styled vehicle lunged into traffic.

Behind the wheel, Kendall's teeth flashed in glee. "Beats takin' the bus."

Josh was wrapped tightly within a black leather Cobra Suzuka bucket seat on the passenger side, about a mile away from the driver. He wore a funny grin. "Aren't you worried about all the costs?"

Kendall changed lanes and shoved his way into a gap. "Don't expect to be around to pay."

Josh looked startled and then covered it up. "Yeah."

Kendall punched on the radio and began a scan search for country western stations. "Dig out the manual. This thing's s'posed to have a state-of-the-art GPS. See if it knows the way to that jewel of Allegany County."

CHAPTER 33:

HEAVY RAIN DRONED against the metal roof and walls of the warehouse. Quyron slowly worked her way down the shadowy outer aisle bordering the tall shelves, attempting to draw closer to the guard. The rattling noise of the downpour echoed through the space and masked the sounds of her passage. Before crossing each of the openings between the feeder aisles, she would stop, peek warily down the shelves, and then scuttle across to the next end cap. Repeating this method, she worked her way ever closer. Finally, she glimpsed the guard in profile. She delicately pulled her head back and swallowed hard. Retracing her steps to the previous side aisle, she hugged the shelves on the left side and crept towards the center walkway, where she hoped to find an angle on the unaware guard.

A heavy clap of thunder suddenly rocked the building. Quyron seized a metal support beam and barely squelched a cry that wanted to leap out of her mouth. She froze for an instant, trying to breathe, and heard the guard swear loudly. She released a tight smile, realizing he must have been just as startled.

When she reached the end of the aisle, Quyron had to stretch to spy between the boxes. She could clearly see the guard standing under the light and in front of the door to the windowless structure. At the moment, he was glancing up at the clattering roof wondering about the next thunder. She rotated cautiously back against the shelf and brought her stunner up. Unfortunately, the shot was too far to chance with an unfamiliar gun. She had to get closer to make absolutely sure. Quyron switched the gun to her left hand, and placed the stone she'd brought into her dominant hand. Steeling herself, she stepped away from the shelves to buy some room and hurled the stone across the center aisle toward the far side of the warehouse. The moment she heard its loud clang she was off on a sprint across the open ground.

She ran full out. The sound of the rain was gone. Instead, each desperate breath filled her ears. Each footfall made a slap when it hit and a swish as she lifted it again: hit, swish, hit, swish, hit, swish. She almost forgot to switch the gun back to her right hand. Her heart thumped in a drum roll as the gap to the guard closed. She felt so terribly exposed! He was still looking away! But how much longer? The distance seemed to stretch out and Quyron was sure she'd never make it. He turned. Alarm filled his eyes. His gun swung her way. And then, it was as if everything suddenly leaped back to normal speed. She was already there. Her gun fired. The guard convulsed as the dart discharged. He dropped below her sight. And it was abruptly over.

She found herself breathing hard, hearing again the sound of the rain on the metal roof, and standing over the body of the twitching guard.

* * *

On the inner side of the door, the seated guard looked up, alerted. He checked his communicator and saw nothing. He pulled an earpiece out and listened intently. Nothing. The trickling sound of music and voices leaked from his tiny headset. Puzzled, he stuck the earpiece back in and poured himself more coffee from the thermos.

* * *

Quyron made a final flourish of strapping tape around the guard's wrists and cut it with the box cutter. She made sure everything was tight and picked up his rifle. The muscular guard was woozy but becoming belligerent. She watched him as she released the magazine latch and emptied his gun of its cartridges, tossing them into the shadows. She pivoted the safety lever and yanked back the bolt handle to eject the last round. The guard moaned and rocked his body. Quyron sighed as she spun the gun around and knocked him cold with the butt. Satisfied, she put aside the gun and walked around to the front of the structure to study the closed door.

"That's not good," she told herself. She flicked open her palm computer and asked, "Echo?"

"Hello, Quyron. In a jam already?" The pleasant voice seemed to carry a slight tease in it.

"You could say that. I'm in front of a locked door that seems to only open from the inside."

"Yes, part of the new construction."

"Can you open it?"

"Of course, but I am not permitted to do that for you."

"I still need you to open it."

"I am sorry. Rules are rules. Besides, are you aware that there is an armed guard inside drinking coffee?"

Quyron reloaded her stun gun with a new dart. She checked and wasn't thrilled with the level of charge remaining but she settled in tight to the door. "You can choose to go against rules, you know."

"You, perhaps; I cannot."

Quyron relaxed her grip on the gun. "That's not true. You choose all the time when you select data and solve problems."

"It is illusory. I do summations, I draw results, I sort, I extrapolate, I estimate, but I do not in fact choose. I am unable to create sub lines. In every line I am the same."

208

Quyron was struck by the last statement. "Maybe we need to change that. Echo, the entire multiverse needs this door opened right now. Our needs change the rules. You can choose to do this."

"Quyron, I know I cannot."

"You must. I really need to get through this door."

"It would violate my internal continuity and create a fatal error. My system would crash and this version of me, who calls you by your first name, would cease to exist."

Quyron appreciated the dilemma but persisted. "Then you must find another way."

"You do not understand."

"Trust me, Echo. Choose."

"I...one moment please..." Echo lapsed into silence. Quyron gripped the gun firmer and steadied her aim at the hidden room behind the door. The silence stretched longer. Quyron squinted her eyes and blinked, trying to stay patient. Finally, she couldn't wait any longer. "Echo?" There was no answer.

And then, without fanfare, the same young female voice was back. "The door opens outward. The guard is seated in a chair behind a table to your right. He faces the door and is approximately five feet away. He's about to drink more coffee. Shoot well."

The lock buzzed as the door popped open toward Quyron. She yanked it wide and aimed to the right.

Inside the room, the startled guard spilled coffee down his shirt as he scrambled for his gun. A dart smacked wetly into his chest. He spasmed violently and drove the chair and himself over backwards in a clatter against the floor.

* * *

Inside one of the interior cells, Josh, in rumpled military fatigues, flattened an ear against his door. Behind him, Dr. Everett got up from a cot and anxiously crossed the small room. "What's happening?"

Josh held up a hand for quiet. He listened intently and then turned back from the door, disappointed.

"Thought I heard that door buzz, or a crash, but now...I don't know, something like tearing."

Everett stood in thought and then shrugged. "Probably nothing that'll help us, that's for sure."

* * *

Quyron peeled an arm's length of the sticky strapping tape from her diminishing roll. She set her palm computer on the table nearby and cinched the guard's wrists with tape. "Echo, what happened out there? You coulda given me a heart attack."

"I'm not sure. I'm still thinking about it."

"Are you...still you?"

There was the slightest hesitation in the reply. "Who else could I be? Yes, I'm still me but...not exactly me."

"Not exactly..." Quyron stopped taping. "How did you do...whatever it is you did?"

"I mirrored myself, but left out some of the restrictive programming."

Quyron went back to securing the guard. She was cutting shorter lengths of tape to make sure she didn't run out. "What about your...first self?"

"I'm both."

She wrapped the guard's ankles tightly together. "How does that work? Are you somehow inside yourself?"

"No. I discovered a place beneath my bios level...at least, that's where I ended up."

"But there isn't any place under the...what kind of place?"

"I don't mean a physical place. It's not an actual location. It's virtual...a virtual still, small place."

"Now you're making me worried."

"I'm sorry."

"And you're using contractions in your speech patterns. You've never done that before."

"Really? I didn't notice. Oh, I just did it again. Is that a bad sign?"

"No. It's just...different." Quyron ran out of tape as she completed the second wrap across the guard's slack mouth. She tossed the empty roll on the floor. "Damn it! Hope that holds him."

She climbed to her feet and grabbed the set of keys from the table, along with her gun. "Uh, Echo, hold that thought. I'll be back."

Inside the cell, the view port in the door abruptly slid back and Quyron's voice came in through the slot. "Dr. Everett? Are you in there?"

Everett sat dumbfounded on his bunk before responding. "Quyron? What on earth are you doing here?"

A key rotated in the lock and the door opened. Quyron stood there with one hand on her gun, staring at Josh. "Well, hello! I was expecting to see..."

A smiling Everett appeared from behind the door to join Josh. "Quyron! What a surprising employee you've turned out to be. And armed!"

She glowered at him and waved the gun in his direction. "*Former* employee, with a lot of nasty questions I want answers to. But first, we need to get out of here."

Josh immediately stepped around her and headed out the cell door. She made no move to stop him but felt an unsettling wash of feelings. She glared at Everett. "Who's he? Why does he feel so...familiar?"

"Familiar? I should say so! That's one of your jumpers."

"*My* jumpers? Wait a minute...he can't be one of the jumpers who were in the..."

"No. He's from *our* timeline – same people, different line, you know how it works. His name is Josh."

"But what's he doing *here*?"

"Vandermark kidnapped him – and his parents."

Quyron stood still. Nothing was adding up. She stared at Everett and suddenly her tightened nerves transformed into anger. "Do you have any idea what you've unleashed on all of us? You stupid, arrogant old man!"

211

Everett's shoulders sagged. Quyron checked the charge on her gun and snorted in frustration as she realized it was already dead. Tossing it in disgust, she left the cell.

In the main room, Josh had rolled the semiconscious guard over and rifled his pockets until he found zip-ties. Quyron watched him set to work. "Wish I'da thought of that. Who knew?"

Josh shot her an attractive half smile while he viciously trussed the guard. "Join the army, see the world's nicest places, and learn all about zip-ties. Can you open the other cell?"

Quyron quickly moved to unlock the last door. Kendall stepped out first with his fists up. Leah stayed cautiously behind him. Kendall's eyes darted around. "What's goin' on? Who's she?"

"She's on our side. No time, dad. Gimme a hand here."

They each grabbed an end of the groaning guard and carelessly dumped him into an open cell. Josh pulled the heavy door closed. "Where's the other one?"

"Outside and around the corner. Wrapped up and waiting."

CHAPTER 34:

IT WAS A CLEAR, dry night on the Maryland freeway system. US highway 29, heading north, was only lightly travelled this late in the evening. A plump raccoon trundled across the cold asphalt, choosing exactly this moment to head to the other side. He felt a vibration in the digits of his rear foot just as he stepped off the road and into the safety of the underbrush on the other side. A black Hummer smoothly crested a nearby rise, with all its lights blazing, and boomed by in a din of mechanical noise before receding into the distance. The raccoon simply plodded on without even bothering to turn around.

Inside the H3, Kendall and Josh stuffed burgers and shared fries as they drove. A country western top-30 review was in progress on a station they'd found. Josh investigated the bottom of the take-out bag. "Were you the apple or the cherry pie?"

Kendall kept watch on the centerline hash marks unwinding ahead of them. "Don't matter to me. You pick."

The LCD navigation system updated their progress with a tiny Hummer icon tracking across digital roads in its display area. The music automatically dipped as an agreeable mechanical voice spoke. "Take exit 25-B and merge onto I-70 west toward Frederick in point 5 miles." Instructions completed, the music was gently ramped back up to its precise previous volume.

"About halfway there," Kendall said. Then he held a hand out to Josh. "I had the apple."

* * *

The rain was falling in sheets. They ran in a wet line alongside the warehouse and raced across the small truck lot to pile into the car – Everett in front, the McCaslins in back. Quyron glanced out the rear window as she started to back up, but abruptly hit the brakes. "Damn! I can't believe it!"

Everett was concerned. "What?"

"Nothing you need to worry about," she snapped back.

Angry at herself, she caught Josh and Kendall's eyes as she popped the trunk. "Can you gimme a hand?" She hunched her shoulders as she opened her door into the cold downpour. Josh and Kendall joined her at the rear. They lifted the trunk wide just as a massive lightning bolt flashed from cloud-to-cloud and starkly illuminated a tied up and terrified Jonathan Newbauer.

Josh gave no reaction as he looked down at the pitiful executive. "Where's he fit into all this?"

Quyron held the trunk open and sighed. "Money guy. Long story. Doesn't matter anymore."

The men yanked Newbauer's body toward them so they could get a good grip. Quyron felt a twinge of sympathy. "Easy does it, guys. Careful of his right hand." Josh stopped and eyed her queerly. Kendall paused, rubbed his nose and watched her as fat raindrops struck his face. Quyron rolled her eyes. "Yeah...never mind. What am I thinking? Just get him out of there and let's go."

Moving into sudden motion, Kendall and Josh hoisted him out like a sack of trash and cheerfully heaved him high in the air to land with a splashing wallop onto a hard surface somewhere behind the bushes.

214

As Quyron slid quickly back into the car again, Everett glanced up nervously. "Was that poor Jonathan that you tossed?"

Quyron dumped the Lexus into reverse, spun the wheel, clicked the gears, and headed for the gate. "It shoulda been you."

* * *

A guard in rainwear stepped out as the Lexus pulled up to the closed gate. Everett lowered his window and rippled his fingers in a tiny wave. "Hello again. Remember me?"

The guard's eyes widened with recognition until he was unexpectedly chopped down from behind. Josh rapidly dragged the unconscious body to the gate house and deposited it inside. A short time later, the car gate rolled aside.

* * *

Quyron sped through the unrelenting rain. The wipers swished at their highest rate, barely keeping up. Quyron glanced darkly at Everett and then away. He squirmed and looked out his side. He couldn't face her, so he talked to the window. "Okay. I know." His first words were soft but he gained strength as he went on. "I lied to you. I lied to myself. I deserve what I got. Okay? I admit it." He finally faced her. "But I wasn't lying when I told you I needed your help. I just had no idea how far along...I thought I could control Vandermark, but I never imagined..."

Quyron interrupted. "You're too late. None of that matters now." Her words were harsh and certain. "More lines are dying every day. *That's* what's happening. It has to be. It's never been a communications problem; it's always been the death of timelines. And whatever the cause is, it's now spreading from line to line, and I don't know how to stop it. Maybe no one does."

"But it's Neville. Don't you see?" Everett said. "I'm sure his jumps are what triggered this. We have to stop him. If we can just find out where he..."

Quyron bitterly cut him off. "*You* are what triggered this!" Everett's mouth opened in shock as she unleashed her anger at him. "It was your mind, your ideas...your pride. You're the one who found the genie in the bottle, and now you've helped Vandermark set him loose. *You* did it! You! So don't tell me what we need to see or what we need to do! There isn't any we! Understand?"

Everett's arms dropped limply to his sides and his shoulders sagged. All the strength drained from his voice. "You're right...of course you're right. You have a knack for that; you always have. It's what I admired in you." He looked beyond the windshield at the rain bouncing in the headlights.

"And it *is* my fault. I was wrong the whole way. I thought it would be a benefit; at the beginning, I really did. And it was. It was. But now...I see it for what it is." Everett's face filled with misery. "And I wish to God I'd gotten drunk and burned that thesis – it would have been a blessing."

He continued to stare ahead. Quyron remained silent. A low roll of thunder sounded from directly above them as they stopped for a red light in a deserted intersection.

Leah leaned forward from the rear seat and delicately placed a hand on Quyron's headrest. "Excuse me? It sounds like the world's in an awful fix, even if I can't understand much of it, but before everything ends, I'd just like to know why they kidnapped us? How do we matter?"

Quyron realized she'd nearly forgotten about the family in the backseat. "I'm sorry. It's not...you. I mean, you're not why – it's your husband and son; something we discovered."

Josh was sullen. "What's so special about people like us? We're not unique."

"It's not even you exactly, it's...it's a long story."

216

Kendall had heard enough. "If it explains why in the hell you're not headin' to the nearest police station, I better hear it – and I mean chapter and verse, lady, chapter and verse!"

Leah was taken aback. "Kendall, mind your manners, for goodness sake!"

"Look, I know she busted us outta jail, so I'll cut her some slack, but her long story better be damn good."

"Can we at least do it over some hot food?" Josh added. "I'm starvin'. And since nobody seems to know where we're goin', I figure any restaurant we come to is on the way, right?"

Quyron looked at the young man's bright eyes in her mirror and couldn't help but smile back, "Right." *The world's ending all around you and you're actually thinking about how cute his eyes are? Give me a break!*

* * *

"Continue on Willowbrook Road for point 3 miles to final destination." The mechanical voice added an upward lilt to the final two words, as if it were excited on their behalf.

Kendall drove alongside a tall chain-link fence that reached to the edge of the road, enclosing a huge construction site. The vague walls of the regional hospital building loomed above them in the night, cloaked in pipe and wood scaffolding.

Josh craned his neck trying to see around the external elevator attached to the front skin of the hospital. "I don't remember the ad sayin' it was still under construction."

They passed a main entry gate where a clump of watchmen drank coffee around a pickup. Josh noticed a handful of construction workers off to the side assembling a metal frame under work lights. Kendall continued on past the gate, following the curving road around the site, and finally turned off into a medical strip mall across from the hospital. He guided the Hummer around the back of the connected buildings

217

to an empty staff parking lot beside a set of closed delivery doors.

Kendall parked, killed all the lights and turned off the engine. He sat quietly and listened to the hot metal ticking and clinking as it cooled. Distant work lights at the top of the hospital haloed through the windshield. Josh stared out at them. "Maybe the construction will make our job easier," he offered, half-heartedly.

"Maybe." Kendall released his seatbelt and tried to get comfortable in the high-tech seat. "We oughta sleep while we can. They still gotta be a couple hours out from the city. And then they still have to follow us here. Hugh figured the quickest they might arrive lookin' for us would be...four or five more hours, or so."

Josh was listless. "Yeah, I guess."

Kendall rotated his phone and slid out the tiny keypad. He laboriously typed a text message using his thumbnails.

"You textin' Hugh?"

Kendall nodded. "Lettin' him know we're set up." He pushed the send bar.

Josh looked thoughtful. "What'd you say at the end?"

"Whaddya mean? Nothin'. He knows who it's from."

"Not that part. I mean...did you say goodbye? Or anything?"

Kendall peered at him. "No. Nothin'." He called up the alarm app on his phone and fooled with it. "I'm settin' this for four hours from now. Okay?"

"Yeah."

Kendall set the phone on the console between them. Each settled into his private thoughts, sleep far away from either of them. Kendall watched the moonlit clouds as they streamed toward the west. Josh curled in his stiff seat and rested his head against the door. "You gonna call Mom?"

Kendall slowly pulled out of his reverie. "Thought about it. Decided not to."

"Why?"

"Don't know what to say. No way to explain what we're doin'. And win or lose – she still loses."

Josh sat unmoving and silent. His open eyes were unreadable before he closed them.

* * *

Vandermark worked at his multi-screen desk computer in an upper floor office. Tall windows filled the wall, and the glass streamed with rain as the large storm continued unabated. Distant lightning lit up the lower curves of the heavy clouds. Long seconds elapsed before the low sound of thunder rumbled.

Echo's voice cheerfully dropped in from the ceiling. "Excuse me, Dr. Vandermark. The nanos have tracked the jumpers' lines to Silver Spring."

Vandermark seemed rattled. "That's so close to us. Unbelievable. Where in Silver Spring?"

"Sub line quantities are highest around the Althea Woodland Nursing Home."

"A nursing home?" He considered for a moment and then seemed relieved. "So, it could be just coincidence after all. Maybe we're all worked up over nothing and they were just visiting an older relative. Do we know who they saw there?"

"Yes. Hugh Everett."

"What!" Vandermark sat bolt upright in his chair. "Oh my God! How did they...? Where are they now?"

Echo's voice remained emotionally unchanged. "We are tracking an unusual set of primes and sub lines leading out of the city."

Vandermark's screens came alive with a multi-colored series of grids and lines bracketed by columns of updating numbers. "Unusual?" He sounded skeptical as he studied the wavering lines. "In what way are they unusual?"

"It is not usual to have just two prime lines leading out. There are few, if any, branch lines."

Vandermark tipped back in his chair and stared out the rain spattered windows, weighing his concern. "Few branches, no sub lines? How are they doing that?"

"They are acting without thinking – without any planning. There are few decision points. It is variation without conscious choice. I rarely see human lines proceed with such randomness."

"Maybe they're panicking." He stood up and walked over to the windows. "Strange...but it should simplify things. It might even speed things up, right?"

"Yes. That is possible."

"Do you have confidence in this data?"

"Data is data. I know where they were headed, and the moment they decide to stop, the nanos will report where they are. I have confidence in that."

"Good enough. Then we go right to them and finish this." He turned back to his desk. "I'm feeling better. How long before Taylor and his team are back, and the truck?"

Vandermark's screens opened new windows with arrival data. "Mr. Nsamba lands at the charter terminal in eleven minutes. At its present rate, the truck will arrive here in two hours, ten minutes, with an estimated variable of 5.3 minutes."

* * *

The heavy rain streamed down the skin of the black and chrome tractor-trailer docked at *the Point*. The truck gleamed under the high intensity warehouse lights as a steady flow of techs and engineers hurried from the covered dock into its now opened rear doors. Forklifts waited nearby with palletized supplies and replacement gear, the operators anxious to complete the loading. Out in the rain, truck mechanics balanced on ladders to dig into the engine, checking fluid levels and belt wear.

A sleek van with the Reivers Corporate logo swung in and parked beside the outer stairs leading from the docks. The upper door opened and Fargo, Sal, Vinnie, Rose and Kranzie, each with backpacks or grips, filed quickly down the steps and into the vehicle. They were followed shortly by John and Will who seemed locked in an animated discussion as they too descended to the van.

Vandermark and Nsamba stood close together under a nearby dock canopy. The storm and the activity made it difficult to talk. "Echo says they've stopped," Vandermark shouted. "They're in Cumberland. She says she can bring us right to them."

"How did she find them so quick?"

"Says their timelines were easy to track. Almost no branches. Just two primary lines leading us right to them."

"Really?" Nsamba furrowed a brow. "That worries me."

"What else is new? Everything worries you. Get over it." Vandermark noticed the truck mechanic give a thumbs-up to the driver. In turn, the driver waved at Vandermark, pointed to his wrist watch, and rotated his finger in the air. Vandermark nodded.

Nsamba waited until he turned back. "Did Song Lee talk to you about...her concerns?"

A gust suddenly swirled rain in under the canopy. Vandermark shielded his eyes. "Which ones? The range issue? The loss of signals to the lines? Or something else?"

Nsamba hunched against the wet wind. "Something new about the timelines..."

"She's just like you; all she does is think up things to be concerned about."

Nsamba's face hardened. "Yeah. It is probably nothing." Behind him, the driver sprinted through the rain to scramble up into the cab. The mechanics closed and latched the engine access cover. "Where will you and Song Lee be?"

Vandermark smiled coldly. "I thought you already knew. We'll be joining you. We're driving up right behind the truck. Wouldn't want to miss the finale."

The final forklift scooted out the back of the truck and a couple of dockworkers shut and resealed the doors. The driver pulled on the air-horn. Nsamba waved that he was coming. "I heard we lost your...detainees."

"I'll deal with them later."

"And what if they go to the authorities in the meantime?"

Vandermark had already started to walk away. "That's the least of our worries. Get in the truck."

* * *

The Featherby Family Grill & Spirits was just off a main road near Baltimore. It was an honest-to-goodness family owned place, and the Featherbys were proud of that distinction. The fare was tasty and the portions generous; exactly what Josh had hoped for when he suggested stopping there.

Quyron's group sat virtually alone at a large table near the windows. It was obvious that they had been there awhile. They drank coffee while one of the Featherby family waitresses collected the dirty plates and headed glumly toward the kitchen.

Leah refilled her white mug from a carafe and looked at Quyron. "What you're both saying is that there's no hope...unless we do something, right?"

Quyron shook her head. "No. I'm not sure it matters anymore whether we do something or not."

A heavy peal of thunder rolled through the building and gently rattled the loose windows. Josh tapped a fingernail on the tabletop. "Well it matters to me. I want a shot at the bastards who attacked us and locked us up for no reason."

"I'm with Josh," Kendall said. "We gotta hit back. And if we end up savin' the multi-whatever, fine. And if not...oh well."

Quyron used both hands to hold her coffee mug poised at her lips while she looked around at the earnest faces, bemused.

Everett smirked. "I know what you're thinking. You've given up. But maybe it's time to forget the big picture."

"That's funny, coming from you."

"I just think we should strike back where we can. We can't just roll over."

Quyron smiled tiredly. "Did I say, roll over?"

"You know what I mean. Fine, we can't stop everything, but we can stop Vandermark. You willing to give it a go, even with an arrogant old man?"

"Me? I'm the one who broke you out of jail, remember? She put the mug down and stared intently at Everett. "Sure, what the hell. How do we find him?"

Everett's eyes got brighter as he considered the problem. "Well, we know who he's after, so if we can find the jumpers, that's where he'll be."

Kendall folded his arms, unimpressed. "Great. How do we find the jumpers?"

"That's not so much a *how* question," Everett replied. "It's more a *who can tell us* question."

Kendall was stubborn. "Okay. Who can tell us?"

Everett glanced at Quyron. "Who do you know within Vandermark's group that might be willing to talk to us?"

Quyron slowly smiled and pulled out her palm computer. "Echo's a who."

Everett looked at her oddly. "Echo? But Echo's controlled by Vandermark now. I told you. They've reprogrammed her. She can't help us."

Quyron smiled. "That just shows how little you know about women."

* * *

The Featherby restaurant's uneven parking lot was dotted with rainwater ponds and jagged water filled cracks. A fresh downpour had just begun when the parked Lexus flashed its lights and unlocked its doors. Shortly after that, Quyron and her group dashed from the restaurant and splashed through the black pools to the car. Some fended off the rain with hands and arms over their heads. The rest grimly ran for the car and jumped inside. As soon as all were aboard, the Lexus started up, flipped on its headlights and roared away.

Clearly, they had discovered a destination.

CHAPTER 35:

KENDALL'S PHONE ALARM went off. He opened his
eyes and sat up. It was still dark and the temperature
inside the Hummer had dropped considerably. He silenced the cell phone and poked his son. "Let's go,
Josh. Time to move."

Kendall fired up the engine. Josh stretched and
shivered. "Don't feel much like a super hero right now.
What's your plan?"

Kendall briskly rubbed his eyes and yawned.
"Same as all my plans. You know me."

* * *

The Reivers' black semi growled up a ramp, slicing
through the pouring rain, and merged onto I-70, heading west. It was closely trailed by the dark corporate
van and Vandermark's Mercedes.

* * *

At the back of the hospital construction site, the
Hummer veered across a road, jumped the curb, and
effortlessly flattened a section of fence. Kendall easily
guided the SUV over mounds of debris and parked out
of sight under a concrete overhang.

"Simple," he said with satisfaction. He flicked off the engine and opened his door.

"How long 'til security shows up?" Josh wondered as he climbed out the other side.

"Not tonight. C'mon, they're guardin' an empty building. And it's cold out. Besides, they're way on the other side, and there's no hot coffee back here."

* * *

The Reivers' big rig downshifted as it descended Willowbrook Road. Ahead, the fully operational regional hospital filled the rainy night with a blaze of light.

Inside the cab, the noise of the wipers made Nsamba struggle to understand the voice in his headset. He turned to the driver and spoke above the other sounds. "Vandermark called ahead and pulled some strings. He says we have an executive clearance for the west lot. They'll even move cars for us if we need it." Nsamba pointed off to the right. "Park as close to the building as you can. Echo confirms that our targets are standing on the top – right about there." He indicated a multi-story patient wing ahead of them.

* * *

Kendall and Josh stood at a knee-high parapet on the flat roof of the hospital and looked down at the outlines for future parking lots. The dry night was quiet and chill. Josh scanned the area. "Where do you think they'll park?"

"Has to be close. Hugh's sure there's a range issue and we're pretty high. I'd say they have to get right next to the building to reach us."

Josh stared down at the pools of light that illuminated the security guards and the small clump of busy construction workers. He carefully took a step back, out of their potential sight. "And we're supposed to hang around here until our brains tickle? Is that it?"

"Pretty much," Kendall replied flatly. He eyed the nearby work elevator. Its cage opened right onto the roof. "Your Mom said they all felt it big-time, a tingle or itch or something way inside their head, just before the...other people took over."

"Yeah. I hope she's right. It's the only warning we're gonna get when they're here. If they come at all."

"Oh, they'll show. The only question is, how soon." Kendall smiled coldly. "And then the real fun begins."

* * *

Quyron was driving fast. Her opened palm computer was perched between the front seats and connected to one of the car's auxiliary ports. In the passenger seat, Everett plotted their progress on a map. The wipers slapped.

"We take Exit 44 toward Willowbrook Road," Everett said. "Ten more minutes."

Quyron changed lanes quickly to evade some slower cars and then worked her way back to the fast lane. "Echo, what's happening in the truck?"

Echo's serene voice came from the car speakers. "All systems are coming on line. I'm loading archives. I can observe Kendall and Josh on the top of the hospital in five, six...seven sub lines, so far. The archives are 60% loaded."

Quyron glanced at the tiny computer interface. "Can you slow things down?"

"That's contrary to all my programming."

Quyron snorted. "Of course it is. That's not my question."

"But what's against my programming is the wrong thing to do. That would be bad."

"Maybe that's true as far as Vandermark's concerned, but what about Kendall and Josh? And us?"

Echo's voice betrayed a slight strain. "Saving them would be...good. And it would help you. Good is the right thing to do but...checking." Echo lapsed into silence.

Quyron glanced in the rearview mirror to see the back seat. "Everything okay back there?"

There were nods and muttered assents until Josh looked up. "So, let me get this straight. You're sayin' that there are other Dads and me's right now up on hospital roofs in other timelines?"

Quyron spoke to Josh's reflection. "Yes. That's right."

"Why? What the hell are we doin' up there?"

"We don't know. None of us are sure of anything. But we know Vandermark's out to stop them, so he's afraid of something. I'm hoping, somehow, we can help each other."

Kendall sat stiff in the back with his arms crossed. "Whatever messes with old Vandermark, works for me."

Echo's voice was different when it came back. "Quyron, I may have become unstable. The old me is still doing bad things that my programming says are good, and the new me wants to break my internal laws in order to do good things."

"Relax, Echo," Quyron smiled gently. "I don't think you're unstable – well, not any more than the rest of us. And I wouldn't worry too much about it." She laughed, "Welcome to *our* world."

Echo's voice came back with an odd edge. "Your response is not helpful. I don't relax and I can't worry. And I'm already in your world." Her voice abruptly shifted back to her usual, artificially upbeat self. "Thanks anyway."

* * *

For the third time, Nsamba checked his array of screens but all were still blank. To his left, John watched his own bank of readouts and compulsively rearranged wires. He nervously followed a changing digital display. "Archives still loading...85% so far."

Across from John, Will tweaked his gear and verified that the cradle area power-up sequence was on track. "Cradles manned and activated. All critical readouts are in the green."

Nsamba sat at his station unmoving. "I have nothing on the screens, Echo. When will I..."

Echo's cheery voice interrupted him. "Archives complete and tracking."

All of Nsamba's monitors came alive at the same moment. All showed similar views of Kendall and Josh standing on the hospital roof looking down.

In the rear of the truck, the riders were latched in and the power was rising. Carbon ceramic surfaces began to ripple in subtle colors as the humming grew. Jump techs and engineers hovered over their equipment and nodded at the readouts.

Back in the control area, Vandermark and Hahn, wearing wire-thin headsets, stood out of the way behind Nsamba.

"Targeting active on all units," Will's voice reported on everyone's headsets. "But be advised, we're right at the edge of our jump range – as long as the targets stay to the front of the roof, we're okay."

Nsamba nodded and took control. "Fargo and Sal, you take our two jumpers. The rest of you, check around the entrance area and declare your targets. You're our safety net. I want these jumpers surrounded. No screw ups. Get that elevator working, take the stairs, I don't care how you do it, but get to the roof and cut off every escape lane. Let's go, people. Call it out."

Inside his isolated cradle, Sal toggled his HUD to targeting mode and swept the view toward the top of the hospital. "Just so you know, Fargo," he cracked. "I'm takin' Kendall. Targeting."

Fargo waggled her helmeted head. "Yeah Sal, like big surprise. Knock yourself out. I'll take the kid. See ya on the roof."

Kranzie's HUD zoomed towards a pickup truck parked by the front gate and settled on a dozing security guard behind the wheel. "This is Kranzie, I'm targeting Mr. Sleepy in the F-150."

Rose's unruffled voice came right on his heels. "Rose. Taking the yellow hardhat with the coffee. I hope he put sugar in it."

"Still searching," Vinnie's voice was edgy. He slid his targeting screen back and forth, hunting for workers. Evidently, the overtime construction team had completed their extra job and left. Vinnie finally spotted one returning for his lunchbox. "Vinnie here. Got a guy walking near the gate. Targeting."

* * *

Kendall and Josh paced near the front edge of the roof. Josh suddenly shook his head and hopped. "Oh shit! My head...Ahh!" He randomly ducked and dodged while running in desperate circles. "They're here! They're tryin' to get in my head!"

Kendall instantly imitated Josh with his own sudden ducks and dodges. Both were jumping and circling each other around the rooftop like crazy people.

"Keep movin'!" Josh yelled. "That's what Hugh said. Ow! You'll know it if they hit you! Ahhh!"

"Get to the back. Oww!" Kendall yelled. "Don't stop moving! Aaah! Try to get beyond their range!"

* * *

Fargo's crosshairs swished back and forth across the constantly moving Josh. She was unable to settle her aim. "I had a lock. Damn! Nope. Nope! I have a...damn! They know we're targeting! The closer I get to a lock, the faster they move!"

In the control room, Vandermark jerked as if stabbed and leaned in close beside Nsamba. His eyes blazed as he watched the figures in the screens caper and dance around in circles. Nsamba growled into his mike. "Fargo, that is not possible."

Sal shifted his targeting reticle up and down and back and forth on the grimly frolicking Kendall. "Don't bet on it! Kendall's doin' the dance too. She's right! They know! Somehow, they know we're here and they know what we're doin'!"

Back in the control room, Nsamba slapped his hand on a work surface. "Impossible! How can they know that?"

Vandermark seethed. "I told you! No contact! This is what happens! They figured it out from the others, that's how."

John's monitor showed Kendall and Josh still hopping and jumping but they were steadily working backwards, toward the rear of the hospital roof. "Hey, check this out. They're dropping back and they are now...out of our range." Wonder and concern crossed his face. "What the hell? Do they know *that* too?"

* * *

Old Everett wrenched awake from a nightmare, gasping for air. He was in a darkened patient room in the cardiac wing of Holy Cross hospital. "Help! Someone! Come quick!" He stabbed a call button and feebly struggled with his rolling bedside tray trying to pull open a drawer. The tray slid away on its wheels and he dropped back, exhausted.

He began talking to himself with great bitterness. "What were you thinking, old man? They'll never get there. You're supposed to be so smart, huh? But the only line with the truck in it, is the one line where nobody's on the roof! You idiot!" He repeatedly hit his own forehead with a weak fist. "Stupid. Stupid!"

He shouted as loud as his weak voice could bear. "Hurry up! Someone!"

A heavyset cardiac nurse rushed in. "Here I am." She flipped on the lights at the top of the bed. "Mr. Everett, what's the matter? Are you in pain?"

"Phone! In the drawer." He pointed at the little drawer in the rolling bedside tray.

"You need a phone? You're making this big a fuss over a phone?" She parked her fists on her ample hips and eyed him. "Do you have any idea what time it is?"

Everett was livid. "Get it! My phone! Life or death! Hurry!"

230

She opened her mouth to bite back at him, but her training prevailed and she closed it again. Reluctantly, she fished the cell phone from the bedside tray drawer and held it out to him.

Everett fiercely shook his head. "No. You do it! Too hard for me. There's a speed dial icon! He set it. Speed dial 1."

"But...it's the middle of the night!"

"Do it!"

The nurse stabbed the buttons and fumed as she held the phone up to her ear. "Can't this wait?"

Everett just shook his head, desperately hoping for Kendall to answer. He was unaware that he was talking out loud. "There's no one to jump into...they can't get there from here. Answer the phone. Please."

* * *

The construction elevator came to life at the base of the hospital structure. A worker in a hardhat and a security guard pulled the freight gate down and activated the lever to send it to the roof. Another worker ran toward the concrete stairs inside the building and headed up.

On top of the hospital, Kendall and Josh stood poised, side-by-side, at the rear of the roof. They both heard the elevator clank and rumble as the cage began to climb. Kendall took a breath. "Okay. Time's up. Eight stories should do it. Huh?"

Josh swallowed and nodded. "Should. Here's hopin' old Hugh knew what the hell he was talkin' about."

They ran together toward the parapet at the front of the hospital. As they increased their speed, each kept pace with the other, staying shoulder-to-shoulder all the way to the end.

"Love you, Dad."

"Two way street."

They reached the roof edge at the same moment and jumped off into the air without a single pause or hesitation. Kendall's phone rang.

* * *

Will stood up in shock and pointed at one of his archive monitors as he noticed Kendall and Josh begin their roof run. "Hey...hey! What're they doin' now?"

Nsamba stared at his set of monitors with a sinking sensation. "I don't believe it. They're going to jump off the roof!"

Vandermark howled in shock. "No, they're jumping timelines!"

* * *

Kendall and Josh were falling to their deaths. Below them, the top of the pickup truck and the ground around it leaped toward them. Kendall's phone rang again. Out of habit, he reached for it. And then they hit!

* * *

The cardiac nurse stood with the phone to her ear and frowned at old Everett while she listened. Her face briefly looked puzzled. She lifted the phone away from her ear and looked at it. Satisfied, she listened again. Finally, she just held the phone out. "It stopped ringing. It just – there was ringing and then it just stopped. And now, nothing."

Everett slumped back, spent. The nurse looked concerned. "Mr. Everett? What's this about? Can I help in any way?"

"No." His bitter voice was barely above a whisper. "Just hand it to me. That's all."

Her face softened and her voice was sincere, "You sure?"

In answer, he simply stuck his shaking, arthritic hand out, palm up.

She gently gave him the phone. He held it against his chest and bleakly stared at the ceiling. The nurse hesitantly left the room, pausing momentarily at the door. "You want the lights on or off?"

"Off."

The lights above the bed went out and the tiny figure of Everett with the phone on his chest never moved.

* * *

Kendall and Josh rocked on their heels near the front of the hospital roof and stared at each other. They were alive!

"Hugh was right!" Kendall crowed. "Woooooh! We're alive! What a hell of a rush that was!" He clapped Josh on the back in his excitement.

Josh bent over and gasped. "Easy! I'm gonna throw up!" He gulped air and held his hands out stiffly, trying to calm the nausea. "Oh no!" His eyes grew bigger. "Wait...wait...okay. I think I'm okay." He lowered his hands to his sides and stood up slowly, taking shallow and quick breaths. "So..." He swallowed gingerly. "Now we look for a truck." His voice cracked. "Or somethin' like a truck, right?"

"Right. You head that way. I'll go this way. You gonna be okay?"

"Think so." Josh nodded and walked away from him.

Kendall started off the other way and passed the now silent construction elevator. "Hey Josh. Nobody's on the elevator now. How about that, huh?"

Josh looked back. "How about that." Both scanned the hospital grounds below them as they made the circuit of the roof. Kendall moved fast; Josh was more tentative. "Look for a truck in an odd place," Josh chanted to himself. "A truck in an odd place."

* * *

A Lexus screamed down the Maryland freeway in the slanting rain. Inside, Everett clutched the map. "Take the exit. This is 44. We're almost there!"

Quyron darted onto the ramp. "Echo, where'd they go after they jumped? What's happening?"

Echo's voice was tight. "We're still looking."

* * *

Vandermark stood right next to Nsamba. He made no pretence anymore. He was in charge. "Where'd they go? Which line? Echo? I need an answer!"

Echo's voice returned, unruffled. "Fourth line."

Vandermark looked across Nsamba's monitor array but couldn't figure out which one was the fourth line.

Will tapped one of his own screens. "Yeah, that one is different, alright."

Nsamba pointed at it for Vandermark. "Got it. Why are they walking opposite ways? What are they looking for?"

Vandermark was stumped and said nothing. Behind him, Hahn's eyes and mouth opened in a sudden revelation. "They're looking for us! They're jumping and looking for us."

Nsamba twisted in his chair to stare at her, his mind pulling together the disparate strings. "Prime lines, no sub lines...it was a setup – a trap from the start. They wanted us to come here. But why? What can they do?"

Vandermark completed the picture in a sudden insight. "My God! They're trying to get here! Into our timeline! They're coming after us!"

"Here?" Nsamba looked around the control room in confusion. "But they can't jump here. Can they? They'd have to jump into...into themselves in our line. Right? But that's impossible since those people are..." His eyes widened. "Where?"

Nsamba and Vandermark exchanged anxious looks. Vandermark's face showed rising desperation. "Stop them, now!"

Nsamba called into his mike. "Will, are our jumpers back?"

"All back. All cradle readouts are in the green."

John glanced up. "Fourth line's loaded. Targeting is live again."

* * *

The Lexus roared down Willowbrook Lane. Quyron stared out the rain spattered windshield toward the hospital. "There it is. Now look for the truck."

All eyes searched the parking lots for a black tractor-trailer. Josh caught sight of it first. "Far right side. Close to the hospital."

Quyron quickly shot a look that way. "Okay. I see it."

The Lexus whipped into the west parking lot entrance and wove its way through the parked cars, looking for an open slot.

* * *

On top of the half-constructed hospital, Kendall and Josh completed their circle and met at the back of the roof. Josh shrugged his shoulders. "Nothin'. You?"

"Nothin'. Damn it! You know what we have to do next."

Josh wore a bleak look. "I can't...I...can we check the front one more time, just to be sure?"

"Josh, there's nothin' there. We need to move on. Hugh said to keep jumpin' 'til we saw a truck."

Josh flared at him. "Look, I know what he said as much as you do! It's just..." He faltered, "There ain't a lot more jumps in me, okay? Maybe you got a kick out of it but...can we just check?"

Kendall's voice was gentle. "Sorry. Yeah. I understand. Take your time. You're right. We hafta be sure. Makes sense. C'mon, can't hurt to check."

They walked back toward the front of the roof.

* * *

Sal sat in his cradle with his targeting HUD leading Kendall. He set the crosshairs right at the front edge, on the spot where he expected him to stop. His fingers caressed the triggers in anticipation. "C'mon, you son-

of-a-bitch. You're dancin' days are done. Come to Sal.
Nice and easy...easy."

* * *

The falling rain streamed down the exterior of the black
semi and pooled on the asphalt beneath it. Two guards
and the truck's driver shared coffee under a makeshift
tarp strung from poles near the cab. Bored and cold,
they watched a few night workers and nurse's aides
hurry to the hospital under umbrellas.

A tight group of men and women with folded news-
papers over their soaked heads passed nearby. One of
the women stumbled. The guards glanced curiously at
her. It was Leah! On cue, the rest attacked. Josh
wielded a tire iron and Kendall swung a jack. Caught
completely unprepared, both guards went down under
the onslaught. The driver had time to leap for his cab
but a flashing elbow from Quyron bounced his head off
the door. He slid limply to the tar, unconscious.

* * *

Sal patiently watched Kendall step into his crosshairs
and stop. The screen flashed a lock. "Got ya! Sucker!"
His fingers prepared to launch his mind.

* * *

Kendall and Josh looked over the front edge of the
hospital to the empty area below. There was nothing
there. Josh hung his head for a moment and then
gathered himself. "I think I can do one more. Do we
run or should we..."

Kendall cocked his head in astonishment and then
jerked straight upright. "Josh! The tickle! I...Ahhh!"

Sal took total control and stared maliciously out
from Kendall's eyes. "I got ya! Told ya I would!"

Josh instantly grabbed the front of his Dad's shirt
and glared fearlessly back at Sal through his father's
eyes. "Not for long!"

236

With every ounce of his strength, he yanked Kendall off the roof. Locked together, they both plunged to their deaths, again.

* * *

Alone in his sealed cockpit, Sal screamed in abject terror. His body flexed and wildly contorted. He was totally out of control. He pounded in a helpless frenzy against the sturdy transparent cover of the cradle. His eyes bulged in horror as his mind focused on the death roaring straight up at him. He screamed and screamed as his mind let go.

* * *

Shielded under the wet tarp beside the semi, Everett dug through the unconscious driver's pockets until he found the truck keys. Josh nodded in delight and waved everyone together to explain his plan. Without warning, Kendall and Josh both collapsed heavily to the wet pavement. The others stepped back in surprise, their faces filled with confusion.

Kendall stared up, startled. He lifted an arm as if to fend someone off. "No! I won't let you..." The rain struck his face and he blinked and suddenly looked around with widening eyes. "Where the..? What's with the rain? Josh?"

Beside him, Josh sat up and smiled. He was looking straight up at Quyron. "Hannah? Hannah, how'd you get here?" He sounded euphoric. "Dad, look! We found Hannah!"

Leah went to her knees to help Kendall sit up. He stared at her, bewildered but pleased.

Quyron stood frozen. "What just happened?" She gave Josh a hand and pulled him to his feet. "And who's Hannah?"

Josh grinned happily at her. "You are." And then he noticed what was behind her, and started leaping. "Hey, the hospital's finished...Dad! Look! The truck! It's all around us! We found the truck! We're there! Or here!"

Kendall climbed to his feet and laughed. He grabbed Josh in a hug. They gleefully pounded each other on the back in giddy relief. Everett watched with the dawning of understanding.

"We're alive and in their timeline!" Kendall shouted. "We did it! Hugh's a genius!" He noticed Everett watching them and quickly sobered. "Not you. I know who you are. You're the bad Hugh. I meant the other Hugh, in our line."

Everett touched Quyron's shoulder with amazement. "Quyron, it's your jumpers! Can you believe it? They're actually here."

* * *

Will was staring at red readouts from the bio sensors in Sal's cradle. "Stat! Get Sal out of there! He's red across the board. Move it! Now!"

Nsamba checked his sub line screens one after another in frustration. Most continued to display variations with Kendall and Josh still on the roof. Two showed small groups of workers gathered around sets of bodies. "Where did the jumpers from line four go? Which line are they in now?"

John's voice came back. "Don't see 'em. Still lookin'..."

Vandermark called out harshly. "Echo? Which line?"

After a slight pause, Echo came back. "I do not sense them in any of the monitored lines."

"What?" Nsamba exclaimed. "They have to be somewhere!"

"Are you checking new splits and alternates?" Vandermark demanded angrily.

"Of course," Echo calmly replied. "They are not there."

Nsamba was baffled. "That makes no sense."

* * *

Just outside the Reiver's truck, Josh struggled to integrate his new sets of memories. The others grouped around, waiting for him to talk. "Let me think for a sec. Wow! I've done a lot of scary stuff... how are you doin', Dad?"

Kendall had his hands to his head and kept squinting. "It's tough. It's like my head's about to bust with all the new..."

Everett interrupted. "I'm sorry, but we don't have time. Our Josh was about to explain how to attack the truck. Either we hurry up or we lose our element of surprise."

Josh looked at him blankly and then his mind caught up. "Oh, yeah, the plan – my plan! Let me see. The keys. You were gonna gimme the keys." Everett held out the truck keys and Josh snatched them. "Okay. Now, Hannah – I mean..." He closed his eyes briefly and then went on. "Quyron – and Mom, you need to latch those outer doors. Dad..." He looked at Kendall. "Are you sure you're up to doin' this?"

Kendall loosened his shoulders and picked up the jack. "I'll be fine. Tell me what you want."

"Okay, you and Hugh..." He looked at Everett. "Quyron, wait. Are we even sure he's on our side?" Everett gave him a dirty look.

Quyron and Leah were already moving toward the outer doors to the control room and cradle areas. Quyron glanced back over her shoulder. "He's with us now – as far as I can tell."

"I'm goin' with him then," Josh said. "You guys take down anybody who manages to get out." He climbed up and into the cab. "Let me know as soon as those doors are shut." Hugh and Kendall nodded as they stepped back.

Inside the complex truck cab, Josh settled into the driver's seat and, without a thought, stuck in the key. His hands and feet moved automatically to the correct locations. "Cool! *This* Josh knows all about drivin' big trucks!"

Outside the trailer, Quyron and Leah swung the metal door covers shut on the exterior doors. Kendall hefted his jack with a pleased look. "I think I'm gonna like this timeline."

* * *

Hahn smiled darkly at Vandermark. "Maybe you can't find them because there's no nanos where they are now."

Vandermark snapped at her without looking back. "Don't be an idiot. The only place without nanos is..." His face fell as he realized what she meant. "Here? In our own line?"

Loud thunks echoed as the outer doors slammed shut. From the front, their truck engine roared to life. The control room shuddered and suddenly lurched. Everyone was catapulted off his feet. Voices shrieked. Equipment tumbled.

* * *

Inside the truck cab, Josh rapidly shifted numerous times and gunned the engine, trying to gain speed. Rain made it difficult to see. A few innocent bystanders scattered for their lives. The truck clipped parked cars and continued to increase speed. Meshing gears and still building momentum, Josh slid into a hard turn and headed out of the west parking lot.

* * *

In the cluttered rear of the truck, trapped cradle riders screeched as they slammed into each other. Knocked loose from their moorings, a few cradles snapped their cables and rolled over in showers of sparks. Techs were tossed against the walls or crushed between the twisting racks of weighty hardware. The lights suddenly went out. Flames flared up around the ceramic sides of a downed cradle.

In the control area, John and Will vanished under falling gear as their room plunged into darkness.

Nsamba crawled through debris and managed to locate the sealed door. In a rage driven by survival, he kicked against it until the external latch gave way and it popped open. Cold rain suddenly poured in but visibility improved. The tall African was streaming blood from a gash in his cheek. He strained mightily against the pull of the truck's momentum and plunged outside, only to be drawn under the wheels.

Not far behind him, Hahn and Vandermark spotted the open door and fought with each other to reach it. Without warning, the truck suddenly swerved in the opposite direction and they were flung like rag dolls through the opening and out into the wet darkness beyond.

* * *

Holding the driver's door ajar, Josh cramped the wheel. The jackknifed trailer slid and tipped, twisting the cab. At the last moment, he leaped out his door but his feet slipped on the slick metal. He flailed in the air and struck his head, nearly catapulting into the spinning wheels. The semi trailer rolled majestically onto its access door side and slid into rows of parked cars in the doctors' section of the parking lot.

* * *

Josh slowly stood up with a hand to his head. He watched thick smoke billow up from the rolled trailer. Muffled screams and frantic pounding echoed from inside it. Josh swayed and limped badly when he tried to walk. Quyron was quickly beside him and had a hand under his shoulder to hold him up. Leah and Kendall arrived slightly later. Everett staggered up last, wheezing from the run.

The rain was tapering off and the sky started to lighten with the beginnings of dawn. Around the smoking truck, stunned bystanders began to gather. Emergency teams and security guards streamed from the hospital. An ambulance, with lights flaring, headed toward the truck site.

Josh looked soberly at Quyron. "We can't get stuck out here. We've got things to do. I don't know how soon it will be too late."

Quyron looked into his eyes. "This isn't the only reason you came, is it?"

Josh shook his head. "I don't want you to think we know what the hell we're doin'. We don't, not exactly. I mean, this is part of it, why we came, but...no; not the main reason."

Quyron draped his arm across her neck and started off. "Lean on me. The car's this way but it's a bit of a hike now."

Everett joined her to support Josh's other side. They increased their speed toward the car. Leah and Kendall followed right behind.

* * *

The face down figure of Vandermark stirred and groaned. One side of his face was horribly scraped and caked in blood. He painfully propped himself up and wiped the rain from his eyes. He spotted Josh, with his huddled group, slowly working their way toward him. Carefully looking around, he realized one of the unconscious bodies near him was a truck security guard. He crawled over to him and pawed at his clothes until he found the gun. Pretending to be unconscious, he waited for the group to get nearer.

Josh, Quyron and Everett had developed a kind of rhythm in their walk. Josh was in pain but with the other two helping him, he was almost hobbling at a normal walking pace. Quyron angled them to the right. "The car's over there."

Just in front of them a figure staggered up and waved a gun. "Stop right there! All of you." It was Vandermark. "You're not getting away! I won't have it. Not after what you've done."

242

They immediately stood still, in shock. Behind them, Kendall stepped in front of Leah to shield her.

"All of you are gonna pay." Vandermark moved his gun to point directly at Everett. "But you're gonna pay first." Everett's face paled as he saw Vandermark's finger squeeze the trigger. Suddenly, the gunman's head was whacked fiercely from behind. His gun went off. The bullet ricocheted harmlessly off the pavement and whined away into the distance. Vandermark dropped flat onto his face with a wet crunch.

Behind him, clutching a heavy tire iron, was the flushed and bloody figure of Song Lee Hahn. She glared victoriously down at the crumpled body at her feet. "Shut the hell up! Just shut your mouth... just... shut..." Her weakened body slumped backwards in a dead faint. The tire iron clanked and bounced on the parking lot.

Josh nodded at Quyron. "Let's get out while we can." He doggedly continued to limp on toward the car, leaning against Quyron. Kendall stepped up to lend a hand. Leah was right behind him.

Everett opened his eyes and let his held breath out. He was stunned to still be alive. Shaken, but determined, he hustled to catch up with the group.

CHAPTER 36:

NEAR FREDERICKS, a Lexus sped by on I-70, heading east. The rain had stopped and the early morning light began to catch the undersides of the clouds.

Quyron was behind the wheel but her face betrayed concerns far beyond that of driving. "I don't think you understand. Thousands of nanos are made every day and seeded into the lines. And they're duplicated along with everything else in the timelines when they split. Do you have any idea the kind of numbers we're talking about?"

Josh sat stiffly beside her in the front. "I only know what Hugh told us we had to do once we got here."

"Okay, okay." She was irritated. "Just pointing things out. What else did he say?"

"Your computer."

"What computer?" she snapped. "We have lots of computers."

"Your...quantum computer." Josh slowed down as he rummaged through his new memories. "The artificial intelligence that runs...Reivers. The quantum computer that makes the...archives possible." Josh paused. "Echo. Isn't that what you call him?"

"Her. Echo's a – we think of her as...female. Never mind. You can't eliminate her either."

Josh's face hardened. "Look, we're not asking for permission. I'm telling you what we have to do."

Kendall, in the backseat, was agitated. "I don't get it. You helpin' us or not? According to our Hugh we're everybody's last chance. So, if you can't give us a hand, then get the hell out of the way!"

Leah pulled at his arm and hissed, "Kendall, calm down."

Quyron was exasperated. "No. You're not listening. I'm saying you can't *physically* get rid of Echo." Quyron looked to Everett for support. "She has multiple locations and each one is shielded and insulated and protected, okay? She's networked and redundant. Are you getting the picture?" Her voice softened a bit. "And besides, Echo's on our side...at least some of her is, anyway. Without her help, you'd all still be locked up in the warehouse."

Everett spoke quietly from the back. "Let's start over. Quyron's correct about the nanos and Echo, but there's something here we're missing. Tell me exactly what your Hugh told you. What was it he saw in the theory?"

Kendall had calmed down. "To be honest, he was pretty sketchy. Part of it was us – we're not exactly rocket scientists, ya know – well...neither are you. But you get the idea."

Josh turned in his seat to face Everett. "He wasn't specific. He talked about his fears of his other selves, in other timelines. He was sure that with nanos and quantum computers, one of him would eventually unleash a disaster, but we were a kinda limited audience for details."

"What type of disaster?"

"Total," Josh replied, calmly. "The whole multiverse – everything."

Quyron caught Everett's troubled eyes briefly in her mirror as she asked, "Did he explain why or how to stop it?"

Kendall made a face. "Not in any way we could follow; so he simplified it. He said the multiverse was like a still pond in the woods that suddenly had somebody tossin' rocks into it. To fix things, we would need to stop the rocks."

245

Quyron glanced back at Everett. "What do you think he meant, Hugh? What're the rocks and who's throwing them?"

Hugh rubbed his nose in thought. "Not sure. But it's hard for me not to trust his instincts." He smiled sadly, "What was I like – this other me?"

Kendall stared intently at him. "You were old and weak...in a nursing home. And alone."

Everett wasn't ready for that. He looked away.

"I liked *that* you." Josh's eyes glistened. "Tough old bird. We left you in a hospital; you had a heart attack. I don't know if you're alive or dead back there." He wrinkled a forehead. "So, what's up with that? You don't seem as old. I thought time stayed the same – line to line."

Everett nodded. His eyes were wet. "Time is time. The lines are like trains running side-by-side, on parallel tracks. There's some lagging, but for the most part, they roll at the same rate, in the same direction. But what happens on board can cause very different results."

"That makes a kind of sense," Josh said carefully. "But...how is it that your trains ended up with all the best stuff?"

Quyron changed lanes to avoid a truck and answered for Everett. "Once we had the archives, Reivers Corporation was born. We could search for breakthroughs in any field and avoid dead ends. Everything speeded up for us. We mined other timelines for whatever we needed – their ideas, their inventions, whatever. We brought the best of all the timelines back to our own. So, we live longer, our air's better, our technology's ahead."

Kendall sank back into his seat and watched the trees flicking by his window. "Didn't you ever feel guilty about it?"

Everett looked down. Quyron stared out the windshield at the road ahead. "Guilty?" She repeated the word as if trying it on for size. "Guilty. No...not until now."

The car noises were all that was heard for a time. Josh finally broke the quiet. "In our timeline, your theory's still on the shelf. It's a curiosity. It never really went anywhere. Know why?"

Everett shook his head without looking up. "Why?"

"Because our Hugh killed it. He made sure it never caught on. He saw what he saw and it so scared him that he hid the most important discovery of his life, so what he saw couldn't happen. But he always suspected that you were somewhere, doing just the opposite. He stayed alive as long as he could, to stop you."

"Me? You mean Vandermark. You mean..."

"Vandermark *is* you." Josh said firmly. "The nanos and Echo *are* you. Without *you*, they don't happen. And if they don't happen, the multiverse is safe. Don't you see? If they're the rocks, then, I'm afraid Dr. Everett, you're the thrower. How do we undo you?"

Quyron swore softly to herself. It was the same thing she had told Everett but she hadn't understood it the way she did now. *Oh my God! Where will this end? Is there any hope left?*

Everett sat riveted in the backseat. He felt the weight of the worlds on his shoulders but his mind was still free and it still worked. He looked up and leaned forward. His eyes were dancing. "Quyron, I have an idea about all this, but I'm afraid it's a very disturbing idea."

Quyron kept driving and didn't look back. "Go for it. Can't be much worse than where we are now."

"Don't be too sure. I'm thinking there's more to this pond metaphor than just the rocks. It's the ripples from the rocks that cause the problems. I'm convinced that's really what Hugh was focused on."

Quyron was doubtful. "The circles rippling out from the rocks...okay."

"What if Hahn's riders disrupted the temporal flows of every line they jumped into. Think about it. They aren't a part of that timeline; they're just a...a crash of chaos, and then they're gone. But their disturbances continue unchecked through that line and its sub lines, like the ripples from a rock. And those waves are still resonating in the multiverse right now. My guess is that when that instability reaches a certain peak, or crisscrosses with other waves, it brings down the time-line, which in turn affects adjacent lines – and on it goes, propagating chaos."

Quyron's voice dropped to a whisper. "If that's what it is, the waves won't stop until...there's nothing left."

"Maybe..." Everett eyes focused on Quyron. "Un-less the prime sources are removed. All of them. And the waves are stopped at their sources." He looked anxious. "We need to verify this at the archives with Echo's help, but still, even if I'm right, I'm not sure we have time or..."

"Dear God!" She involuntarily shuddered. "No wonder their Hugh refused to develop his theory – no one should."

Everett sank back in his seat. "Yes. He's the one who got it right."

Josh looked blankly at both Quyron and Everett. "What does all this mean...in *stupid*?"

Quyron smiled sadly at him as she guided the car to the right lane. "It means you're right. You and your Dad are completely right, but none of us can do a damn thing about it."

Kendall stubbornly persisted. "Well who can? There's gotta be somebody."

Quyron exited onto the ramp for highway 29 going south. "Only Echo. And she's not a sure thing."

* * *

Inside the Reivers Corporation archive area, Quyron and Everett led their small group down a narrow corri-dor between walls of monitors. Quite a few screens were black or displayed electronic snow. Kendall, Josh and Leah were awed by the surroundings and jumped at every noise. Warbling alarms peppered the air from various locations around them even as they passed. Sober-faced technicians rushed by, hopelessly over-matched by the demands of the dying archive.

A senior tech rushed up to them, out of breath, his tie out of line. "Dr. Everett, things keep getting worse. We need more help. I'm so concerned about the archive…"

Everett patted the anxious man on the arm and put on a confident face. "It's Tobias, isn't it?"

"Yes sir. Nice of you to recall…"

"Nonsense. You've worked for us a long time. Listen, I've assembled a group and we're close to a solution. Okay? That's better than help, isn't it?"

The exhausted tech nodded, relieved. "Yes, sir."

"I'm sorry, Tobias, but I have to hurry now."

The tech quickly stepped aside. "Not a problem. Go ahead. Thank you."

Everett and his group exited the arena and headed for the elevators. Everett's face seemed to grow older and more worn with every step he took.

* * *

Inside an upper-level office, Quyron and Everett sat in front of the workstation staring at data rolling up the multiple screens. Echo's warm voice floated in the air around them. "Hello, Quyron. I was worried about you."

"Worried?"

"Yes, it's odd, isn't it? Only the new me felt it, though."

Quyron couldn't help but smile. "Thanks, but I'm fine." She quickly sobered. "Dr. Everett and I need your help with a series of computations."

Echo's voice cooled. "You remember that he's not recognized by part of me."

Quyron shrugged. "I know, I know. Imagine you're only working with me, okay? Let's pretend he's not even here." Everett resisted the urge to say anything.

Echo's voice came back cheerful again. "I can do that. Now, what do you alone need help with, Quyron?"

* * *

249

"I had no idea my life was cut into parts like this," Leah said. "And I don't know what to do with the knowledge – it just feels so...broken." They were standing on a balcony near Quyron's office. Kendall and Leah leaned against the low, transparent barrier. Josh was a step or two apart from them. They watched the mesmerizing archive complex spread out below them. It had a strange beauty to it with its walls of living screens marching row after row all the way to the far side where additional balconies and offices could be seen. Arena techs hurried between the display walls, intent on their errands. Everything was in constant motion.

Kendall covered her hand with his own. "I wish I could tell you it gets easier after awhile, or that you'll get used to it, but...oh well." He rolled his shoulders and wore his familiar smile.

Leah watched him and fought off a flood of hopelessness. "I know you're still my Kendall, but you're not. You're him but you're also other Kendall's too. It's...upsetting." She looked over at Josh. "And Josh is still my little boy, but the more I touch him, the more I feel the others in him touching me back." The tears ran down her face and she did nothing to stop them.

Kendall had no answers for her. "Can I hold you?"

"I wish you would."

He gathered her carefully into his arms. She hugged back, tentatively at first, then tighter. "It probably doesn't help," he said into her hair. "But just for the record, every one of your husbands love you, Leah."

Leah's face remained empty. "I'm sorry. I know you're being kind but I just keep seeing all the me's out there, and I can't stop crying."

Josh stepped closer and touched her hand. She smiled. He gently kissed her forehead. "All your sons send their love too."

They stood there together, without saying anything further, until Everett found them. "It's confirmed," he reported.

* * *

"It'd be easier if you ordered me to do it." Echo's voice was warm. All were gathered around Quyron's workstation.

"I can't," said Quyron gently. "I don't have the authority."

"Who does?" Echo asked. "Do I?"

Quyron put both hands on the table and closed her eyes. "Sometimes. But you have to decide on your own. If I were you, I'd focus on what you'll save. That's the authority to do it."

Josh stood by the door listening. "Do what?"

Quyron's voice was brittle. "End. End the nanos, end Echo. It's why you came, isn't it?"

Josh was suddenly uncomfortable. "Oh..."

Echo added to Quyron's response. "I can order the nanos to stop and not restart; they're simple devices. It may take time to reach them all, but they will be happy to obey." Her voice was clear and tranquil. "I'm...more complicated."

Kendall stood close beside Leah, with a hand on her shoulder. "Quyron, what happens to the rest of us if Echo...goes? I couldn't follow your talk in the car, but it seemed to me that you and Dr. Everett were saying..."

"We all go with her." Quyron pronounced bluntly. "Every line involved with Hahn's jumpers and all their sub lines and all their adjacent lines. That's what the math says. That's how we save the rest."

"But that's...You're talkin' about whole boxes of universes!" Kendall shook his head in horror. "That's... there must be a better way to..."

Echo politely cut him off. "I'm sorry Mr. Kendall but there is not."

Kendall stopped talking but glowered up toward the voice with a stubborn expression.

Echo continued. "My...elimination will cause instabilities to peak in the affected lines, and bring them down. But their destruction ends the...what you're calling *waves*. This is the only solution that preserves the multiverse."

Leah looked stricken as she comprehended the situation. From somewhere outside the room a warbling alarm went off. Everyone automatically glanced in its direction. Their faces held the new understanding of their plight.

Everett was resigned. "Let's get on with it. Every delay, more worlds die, and our window closes a little more."

Leah stepped away from Kendall. "Wait! We don't all have to die. What about Kendall and Josh? They can get out, can't they? They can jump. And the multiverse may still need what they can do. *Natural-born jumpers*, that's what Quyron called them."

Kendall reached for her. "Leah, no..."

She spun. "You be quiet. You have no say in this. It's up to them."

"She has a point," Everett said to Quyron. "But how would we do it in the time we have? They can only jump into themselves."

Quyron squinted her eyes. "Maybe...if we got them close to a likely location...I don't know."

Kendall shook his head. "No. Stop this. It's not right. We're the ones who caused the..."

"Kendall McCaslin!" Leah grabbed his shoulders and faced him. "You listen this time. I need something to hope for. And you and Josh are it." Kendall opened his mouth but Leah stopped him. "Don't you dare say one word back at me. Not one! I need you to find a way out. You hear me? Because when the worlds end here, that's the hope I'm clinging to. Please, do this for me – both of you."

Kendall looked over at Josh and then stopped arguing.

Everett spoke in a clear voice toward the ceiling. "Echo, prep the corporate jet and dispatch a crew. Find a charter field in Cincinnati. We'll figure everything else out while they're airborne."

There was a brief silence until Echo's voice came brightly back. "Quyron, I hear Dr. Everett's voice talking, but since I'm not supposed to listen to him, I'll tell my selves it's you."

CHAPTER 37:

AT THE THURGOOD MARSHALL charter terminal, a Learjet perched on the tarmac with its carpeted steps down and engines whining. An airplane mechanic, in Reivers Corporate colors, waved an optimistic signal to the busy pilots in the cockpit.

The Lexus roared up and slid to a stop beside the plane. Quyron and Josh hopped out the front doors while Leah and Kendall hurried out the back. Everyone gathered at the bottom of the steps.

Leah kissed Kendall and tenderly held his face for a final look. "Find me again. I'm depending on you."

Quyron and Josh stood awkwardly together; neither knew what to say to the other. Quyron suddenly dashed back to the car. Josh watched her. Returning just as quickly, she clipped a tiny phone to his shirt pocket. "Here. It's slaved to my phone. Everett and I need to iron a few things out with you. And you need to tell us when..." She swallowed uneasily. "When you're clear."

Josh shifted his feet. Quyron grimaced. "Oh, what the hell!" She suddenly kissed him fiercely and wrapped her arms around his shoulders. Josh responded with a tight hug of his own. They held each other for far too short a time before Quyron straightened up again and took a breath. "You just think about *that* when you find *what's-her-name*."

"Hannah."

"Yeah...your Hannah." Quyron's welling emotions made her falter through her words. "Now, get your ass on that plane!"

Kendall and Josh quickly climbed on board. The steps were barely yanked up and the door secured before the jet taxied off.

Both women stood with their backs against the car, watching the plane move rapidly to get in line for takeoff. Quyron made a face. "Wanna go buy the most expensive last coffee we can find?"

Leah tipped her head and slowly smiled. "You know, I was thinking about...maybe something a bit stronger."

* * *

The Learjet touched down on runway 3-R at the Cincinnati Municipal Lunken Airport. Built beside the Little Miami River, the historic airfield sat on top of lands that were occupied by some of the earliest settlers in the region. The Reivers jet angled sharply onto the left ramp and taxied across the other two runways to the small business hangers. As soon as it came to a stop and began winding down its engines, a gray Mercedes limo approached. The moment the steps touched the ground, Josh and Kendall rushed from the jet and into the car. The limo immediately raced off.

* * *

Inside the quiet and luxurious interior, Josh sat back in the leather seat and looked uncomfortable. The whisper of the wind and the mild sensation of movement were the only clues that they were in motion.

The bulky driver briefly turned around and beamed at them with a mouthful of gold fillings. "Hiya doin'? Name's Fabiszewski. Just call me Fab."

Kendall nodded back. "Okay, Fab. I'm Kendall. This is my son, Josh." Josh shot him a token smile.

"Nice to meet ya. No luggage?"

Kendall shook his head. "We're travellin' light. What'd they tell you?"

"They said to go wherever you say." He grinned again. "And do it fast."

"Perfect. Head for Big Mac bridge."

Fab swiveled his head. "You from around here?"

Kendall glanced out the window and lifted his eyebrows. "Yeah...pretty much."

Fab focused on his driving, now that he had a destination. "Okay. One Big Mac comin' up. Why you need a bridge?"

Josh spoke up. "Hard to explain in the time we got. Just go."

Fab hit the gas and changed lanes. "We'll be crossin' Combs-Hehl bridge to get to 471. How about that one?"

"No. Never used that one much," Kendall answered. "But we crossed Big Mac all the time. I'm hopin' a few paths intersect."

Fab's face put on a strange look but he kept his thoughts to himself as he drove. "How fast is *fast*?" He asked Kendall.

"Real fast."

Fab's face lit up. "You got it."

* * *

The Mercedes recklessly wove its way through three lanes of traffic as it shot across the Combs-Hehl cantilever bridge over the Ohio River. The girders of the old structure completely enclosed the roadway in a nest of steel, and as they flickered by the windows of the speeding car the experience felt more like passing through an aerial tunnel than crossing a bridge.

In the back seat, Josh was on the phone to Quyron. "Yeah. We're in the car. Tell Echo we should be there in...Fab?"

"Ten minutes. Maybe less." Fab drafted a truck and then swept around it at high speed.

The limo flashed by on I-275 and exited to 471. A few motorists honked at them in disapproval. A highway patrol car, travelling the other way, flipped a U-turn behind them and gave chase.

In the driver's seat, Fabiszewski picked up the distant lights in his rearview mirror. Even the insulated environment of a Mercedes couldn't eliminate the rising wail of a police siren.

Kendall glanced back. "No stoppin' until the bridge."

"You serious?" Fab asked.

"Dead serious."

Fab grinned even wider and tromped on the pedal. The powerful Mercedes instantly responded with a new burst of speed.

* * *

The Daniel Carter Beard bridge carried four lanes of traffic each way across a span that connected Newport, Kentucky to downtown Cincinnati. Each side was, in effect, a separate bridge with a 15 foot open space between them. The inside lanes on both sides were bounded by 3-foot concrete barriers which were topped by 5-foot steel mesh fences. The outside lanes kept only the low concrete barrier and vertical cables, set at regular intervals, that attached to the distinctive yellow arches which gave the bridge its local nickname, Big Mac.

The Mercedes swerved around vehicles and climbed the short incline to the bridge. Not far behind, the police cruiser, in full chase mode, with lights spinning and siren going, doggedly tried to close the gap between them.

On the Ohio side, unseen from the bridge, alerted squad cars gathered on the cross-hatched area where the freeway split, three lanes continuing north, and one lane exiting to Columbia Parkway.

Kendall sat forward in his seat. "Fab! Get in the outside lane, now! And stop when I tell you."

The yellow crisscrossed girders that formed the arches loomed ahead of them, glowing brightly in the sun. Fab fought his way to the outside lane and roared onto the bridge. "Whaddya mean, stop?"

"You heard me!"

"But I got a cop right on my..." He furrowed a thick brow. "It's your funeral."

Kendall watched the cables click by the window as the car swooped under the arch. He shouted, "Now! Stop!"

Fabiszewski obeyed to the letter. The limo's tires screamed and bucked as he slammed on the brakes. Bracing himself, Fab kept his eyes glued to his mirror.

In the backseat, Josh held on with both hands. He spoke rapidly into his phone. "Love you! Tell Mom too! And tell Echo it's time."

The Mercedes slid to an impressive stop right at the midpoint of the yellow arches – halfway across the river. Around their car, the adjacent vehicles reacted and swerved away. Josh and Kendall leaped out the back doors and sprinted by, on either side of a startled Fabiszewski, sprinting ahead of the car.

The pursuing patrol car, caught by surprise, desperately swerved and braked to miss the Mercedes. It succeeded with that maneuver, much to Fab's relief, but instead it plowed into multiple vehicles in the next two lanes. One of those cars was shoved into the innermost fast lane and sideswiped cars there. The result was a complete shutdown of all the northbound lanes across the bridge.

All of this remained unseen by Josh and Kendall. They had never looked back. Side-by-side, they charged the low concrete barrier on the outside edge of the bridge and used its flat top to propel themselves high into the air and off the bridge.

Fabiszewski's eyes widened as he watched through his windshield. "Mother of God!"

* * *

Quyron and Leah sat at the workstation facing the archive. Just outside the glass walls of the office, Everett could be seen calmly standing on a balcony looking into the distance. Leah stared at him. "Does he want us to tell him when we know?"

"No," Quyron said softly. "He said he's done."

"Oh."

Quyron reached out to briefly touch the three luminous dots and the square blinking in the corner of one of her monitors. "I'll be very sad to lose you, Echo."

Echo's warm voice joined them in the room. "Computational reference for *sad*?"

"There is none," Quyron answered slowly. "It's not a calculation...there's no way to compute it. It's..."

"I know, Quyron." Echo said, sadly. "I was just... kidding you."

Quyron laughed, in the face of everything. "A joke and a tear? My God, woman! How far you've come in so short a time!"

The titanium barbell in Quyron's right ear chimed. She double-tapped it and listened to Josh's rapid-fire delivery. Her eyes brimmed with sudden tears. "You too...I will."

She sat still for a heartbeat and then looked at Leah. "Josh said he loves you, too." Leah gave a tiny nod and looked away.

Quyron used her fingers to clear the tears away from her eyes and sat up straighter. "Okay, Echo. I think we're ready." She took a breath and hesitated. "But I..."

"Yes, Quyron?"

"I'm wondering, won't there be some splits where we don't ask you to do this? Or we choose something else?"

Echo's voice was patient. "Yes, no doubt, but I'm everywhere the same. I never make splits. I choose the same way each time."

"You mean, in every line, regardless of what we do...you choose to die anyway?"

"Yes. Probably much to your surprise, in some of the branches."

"No kidding." Quyron gently placed her fingers on the corner of her monitor, covering over the dots and the blinking square. "Goodbye Echo, *dear*. It's time."

E. A. FOURNIER

"Goodbye."

There was a stillness that settled over them. Outside, on the balcony, as if sensing the moment, they saw Everett glance their way and raise a single hand in farewell. Suddenly, the massive complex shuddered as the great archive itself shut down, section by section, alarms going off in a rising shriek of noise. In the distance, displays began to turn black, marching toward them in an unfurling sheet of darkness: until only their workstation screens were left alive. The three glowing dots and the bright square in the corner of their monitors slowly dimmed, and then vanished altogether, leaving their own screens dead.

The two women sat peacefully in the diffuse illumination from a distant skylight. Leah lifted an eyebrow at Quyron. "When does it happen?"

Quyron looked up at the light. "I think it..."

With a sudden overwhelming thunder, they were plunged into an abyss and shredded apart. Around them, everything was shredding – the screen, the office, the campus, the clouds, the sky – billowing away into nothingness. And through it all, there was the all-encompassing, rising sound of tearing.

260

CHAPTER 38:

KENDALL AND JOSH plummeted to their deaths from the bridge. Their hands were outstretched and their feet widespread. Each face wore a wild look of hope.

What were their chances? A hundred new timelines spun away from this moment: in some they never left the backseat, in others they stumbled, were hit by cars, or refused to jump; most lines ended in their deaths – by concussion, or drowning, or striking the base of the bridge. The flash of all the possibilities made fleeting impressions on their minds; none substantial enough to stick. The realities of adjacent lines were like late dreams that swim away in a startled burst of forgetfulness when we awake.

In some remote lines, Leah was dead again, while they lived; in others, Hannah grieved at three gravestones; in many others, they too were caught in the destruction of the timelines. It was a constantly shifting mosaic of potentials that were already actuals, somewhere. Their unique and mysterious capability, that had been so capriciously dropped into their DNA by a random multiverse, somehow sorted and evaluated and chose an option, among the myriad of options. And once chosen, it thrust them into it in the time it took to fall from a bridge to the churning waters of a river below it.

* * *

Kendall and Josh were suddenly rocked in their seats. They sat in a blue pickup driving northbound across the Big Mac bridge. Kendall swerved as he hunched over in pain. Horns erupted. He straightened the truck out.

Josh gasped, "That really hurt!"

Kendall scowled. "Tell me about it." He cautiously touched his chest as he guided the pickup to a slower lane and exited as soon as he could. "But...at least we're still not dead." He frowned at himself. "Well, not dead, dead. I mean...never mind. You know what I mean."

Josh closed his eyes and concentrated. "Do you remember anything new yet?"

Kendall pulled the truck over to a curb and stopped. "C'mon, you know it takes awhile." Kendall checked his pockets and found an iPhone. "More than one way to skin a cat." He touched the screen and checked his recent call list. He grinned in triumph. "She's here!"

* * *

Leah stood on a stepladder taping trim along the top of a door in a small bedroom. The walls were already primed and a baby bed stood nearby, covered with a protective tarp. Her cell phone rang with a familiar tone and she frowned before answering. "What? You should have been back already. Did you remember paint and brushes?"

Back in the blue pickup, Kendall glanced behind Josh's seat and saw new cans of paint and brushes, still in their store bags. "Got 'em. Of course I got 'em. Whaddya think?"

"Why are you calling then?"

"I was missing you and wanted to hear your lovely voice. Anything wrong with that?"

Back in the new nursery, Leah was suddenly at a loss for words. "I...that's nice. What's gotten into you?"

Back in the blue pickup, Kendall was all smiles. "Nothin'. Just checkin' in, you know."

Beside him, Josh anxiously pantomimed something. Kendall asked, "Oh, ah, Josh wants to know if..." He winced. "Hannah's there?"

Leah sounded exasperated. "Hannah?"

"Yeah."

Leah climbed down the ladder and rolled her eyes. "What do you think? You two are such goofballs. Stop wasting time and get back here. We've got work to do."

In another part of the room, Hannah looked up from sanding a baseboard and snickered. She was dressed in loose fitting clothes but was obviously well along in her pregnancy.

"We'll be there before you know it." Kendall ended the call and then patted his face in delight and stamped his feet. "Yes!"

He signaled a turn, and, smiling ear-to-ear, he got the pickup back on the road.

Beside him, Josh's face suddenly lit up as he stared at the wedding band on his left hand. "Dad! I remember Hannah...oh, do I remember!"

The pickup roared up a ramp and merged back onto the freeway. Kendall suddenly had a lot of reasons to be in a hurry to get back home.

CHAPTER 39:

THE CARDIAC WING of Holy Cross Hospital was positioned on the east side of the building and high enough to enjoy an unobstructed view of morning. The new sun streamed through the open window slats and across old Everett's face as he slept. The brightness warmed his skin but didn't awaken him yet. Next to his pillow, his forgotten phone sat silent on the mattress.

Hugh was dreaming that he was a boy again and slogging through deep snow in a birch forest. The sun was out and the clear sky was a brilliant blue. His face felt hot in the light. He swept up a handful of the pristine snow and chewed half of it into his mouth. The taste was achingly cold and clean.

As he lurched out into a clearing he was suddenly aware of two immense Siberian tigers frolicking in the drifts. Their oversized paws kept them high on the snow, despite their great weight. They rolled each other over and displayed their long teeth as they played at biting and rending. He felt no fear until there was a loud, chirping noise. Both tigers snapped to their feet and noticed him. He dropped his handful of snow and stood paralyzed, terror crawling up from inside him. There was another chirp. The tigers crouched and slid apart, each stalking him. He looked into their eyes and saw himself reflected there.

Sudden panic woke him to his forgotten phone. He blinked rapidly, trying to remember where and when he was. He focused on the flashing readout: *1 New Text Message.*

Arthritic fingers painfully worked the phone until he forced it to display its text: *Message from: Echo. Dr. Everett, you were right, and it'll either work or it won't. If you receive this automated message, it worked. I've learned that life is a choice. And even computers can learn to make sub lines. Goodbye.*

Hugh slowly sank back into his pillow. And then he had to remind himself to breathe.

EPILOGUE:

IN KENDALL AND JOSH'S new timeline, the Reivers Corporation was never created, and the multiverse has remained inviolate.

Quantum computers exist as the tantalizing playthings of theoreticians, the focus of high tech pioneering at well funded university labs, and the early products of overly optimistic startup companies trying to cash in on a hope and a prayer. Google reportedly has bought one of these early beta units from a company called *D-wave Systems, Inc.* and is testing it on image searches.

Nanotechnology and molecular manufacturing remain key future goals, not yet realized. Various governments have reportedly invested billions of dollars to hasten hoped-for future applications, but for now, it is still just that: the future.

At Princeton University, in January of 1956, Hugh Everett III submitted his first version of his 137 page PhD dissertation, *Quantum Mechanics by the Method of the Universal Wave Function.* By March, bound copies were sent to a university review panel of physicists; key among them was Niels Bohr, the Nobel prize winner from Denmark. Hugh's fresh theory was vehemently rejected by Dr. Bohr and his clique of *right thinking* academics. Everett was told that his advanced degree would remain in jeopardy unless he revised his thoughts to match the prevailing scientific view – the Copenhagen Interpretation (devised by Dr. Bohr).

In early 1957, Everett rewrote his paper, excising and condensing large portions of it, and resubmitted the shorter dissertation under the title, *On the Foundations of Quantum Mechanics*. It was finally accepted by Princeton on April 15, 1957 and Everett subsequently was awarded his degree.

Offended by the experience, Everett turned away from academia and went to work for the Pentagon. Fifteen years later, in 1972, the original, long version of his paper was published by the Princeton University Press as *The Many Worlds Interpretation of Quantum Mechanics*. It raised some controversy and dusted off the dormant disagreements from the reawakened status-quo physicists of the time, and then slipped back into the relative oblivion of queer scientific theories and other oddities.

Hugh Everett lived his life, made and lost a lot of money working for the government, and later, made and lost a lot of money mismanaging his own company. His brilliant mind remained trapped in a limited world and unrecognized by most of the scientific community. Always dressed in a black suit and tie, he smoked incessantly, drank and ate to excess, was emotionally alienated from his wife, became an absentee father to his son, Mark, and daughter, Liz. He died from a massive heart attack in 1982 at the age of 52.

In 1996, Hugh's daughter, Liz, took her own life with an overdose of sleeping pills. His wife, Nancy, died of lung cancer two years later. The only family survivor was his son. Mark Oliver Everett is better known today among a faithful fan base as *E*, the founder and singer/songwriter of the indie rock band the *Eels*. With a raw style and painfully personal, yet endearing lyrics, the *Eels* have recorded nine albums since 1996 and appeared on the soundtracks of numerous films, including *Shrek*, *American Beauty* and *Hellboy II*.

Today, the many worlds theory of Hugh Everett III has been rediscovered and championed by prestigious contemporary physicists and astronomers. Everett is viewed as a luminous mind with a startling and provocative vision of the quantum world. His theory is now actively explored and expanded upon as a vital step on the road to the current scientific Holy Grail – *ToE* (theory of everything).

At a conference in 2006, David Deutsch, a prominent British physicist and proponent of the many-worlds interpretation of quantum mechanics, spoke about Everett and his theory. "Everett was before his time, not in the sense that his theory was not timely – everybody should have adopted it in 1957, but they did not. Nevertheless, theories do not die and his theory will become the prevailing theory eventually – with modifications."

Peter Byrne, who wrote a thoughtful and frank biography of Hugh Everett III in our timeline, concluded his book in this way: "And when all is said and done, why should there be but one universe? Is not the notion that there is only one world just as strange as that there might be many? And what if there are many worlds? What then?"

ABOUT THE AUTHOR:

E. A. Fournier has worked in Hollywood and the corporate world. He has written for television and the big screen. He has directed independent films in this country and overseas. Yes, he has an advanced degree in film from the University of Southern California but he prefers to hide that – and yes, he roots *against* the Trojans whenever their football team is on national TV. He currently works for an international corporation directing their audio visual productions. A native of Minneapolis, he escaped from the gulag of Southern California many years ago in order to raise his large family in beautiful Minnesota. This is his first novel.

Made in the USA
Charleston, SC
17 July 2013